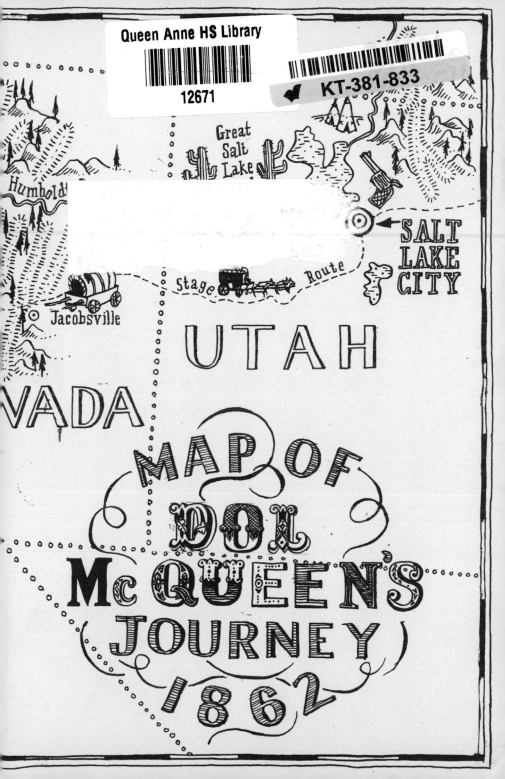

Great
Salt
Lake

← SALT
LAKE
CITY

Humboldt

Stage ··· Route

Jacobsville

UTAH

VADA

MAP OF
McQUEEN'S
JOURNEY
1862

MISSY

MISSY

Chris Hannan

Chatto & Windus
LONDON

Published by Chatto & Windus 2008

2 4 6 8 10 9 7 5 3 1

Copyright © Chris Hannan

First published in Great Britain in 2008 by
Chatto & Windus
Random House, 20 Vauxhall Bridge Road,
London SW1V 2SA

www.rbooks.co.uk

Addresses for companies within The Random House Group Limited
can be found at: www.randomhouse.co.uk/offices.htm

The Random House Group Limited Reg. No. 954009

A CIP catalogue record for this book is available from the British Library

ISBN 9780701180430

The Random House Group Limited supports The Forest Stewardship
Council (FSC), the leading international forest certification organisation.
All our titles that are printed on Greenpeace approved FSC certified
paper carry the FSC logo. Our paper procurement policy can be found at
www.rbooks.co.uk/environment

Mixed Sources
Product group from well-managed
forests and other controlled sources
www.fsc.org   Cert no. TT-COC-2139
© 1996 Forest Stewardship Council
FSC

Printed and bound in Great Britain by
CPI Mackays, Chatham, ME5 8TD

For you, Sarah

No writer was ever luckier in the editors he found. Rebecca Carter of Chatto & Windus and Courtney Hodell of Farrar, Straus & Giroux were hellish hard to please, but then so am I; and I always felt that the sharpness, persistence, and sheer volume of the criticism they offered me was born out of a generosity to the heroine and her story. In quite a deep sense of the word I felt they *guided* me. It wasn't just about the intelligence of their notes; it was like I wasn't alone.

PART ONE

ONE

I expect you have the consolation of religion, or the guidance of a philosophy, but when me and the girls get frazzled, or blue, or rapturous, or just awfully so-so, we shin out and buy ourselves some hats.

San Francisco we lived in Mrs. Liberty's flash-house, fourth story of an apartment building at Montgomery and Broadway, looking down toward the packed wharves. There were coal carriers and fruit schooners, feluccas and Chinese crates, there was the New York liner and freight steamers from Sydney. You could walk from vessel to vessel a half-mile out into the bay. It was a big thing. Every night we would get up a jollification like the sams were pals of ours who'd happened around, then we would take them to the rooms, peel their wads, and send them on their way. For anything I knew, we were pretty happy, till Alice Lebo went and killed herself. That's when we made up our minds to shove out for the silver mines in Nevada Territory and start fresh.

We put all our things aboard the *Samuel F. Doak* and rode up the river to Sacramento. There we hired two wagons, stowed our plunder in them, and headed into the mountains. It was sore on your legs if you walked, and if you lay in back of the wagon on a mattress and got boozy you couldn't get peace. That road shook you up worse than frozen mud. Three days of it stretched everyone's temper pretty far, so when we struck Placerville, the fourth morning out, in the foothills of the Sierra Nevada, and ran across a hatter's, all hands waded in and bought out the store. It was madness but we couldn't help ourselves.

Afterward we popped into an ice cream saloon to cool off.

"Why don't we lay by a day?" I said. "We could cruise around town, take in the sights."

"We could do that in a quarter-hour," Ness said. She had finished her ice cream, but she picked up the spoon and put it in her mouth. It came out clean. "This place is all played out. Let's bang ahead."

"There's a hotel across the road."

Ness put the spoon back in its bowl, making as little noise as she could. She likes food so much it makes her blush if you notice it. "I don't have the mun to put up at hotels."

"Ness, it wouldn't surprise me if you had enough dough to buy the hotel. You're stubborn as dirt, that's all."

"I wouldn't like to be a guest if Ness was running it." Sadie Marx talks out of the side of her mouth like a bookmaker or something. "Mean? She'd be all the time shaking people awake to tell them, 'Sleep faster, we need the pillows.'"

Ness couldn't hold out against me and Sadie Marx, so we put up at the Cary House Hotel and coasted about the streets.

It so happened Ness was dead right. Five years ago there was gold hereabouts and miners swarming all over the hills, picking and drilling and heading back to Placerville to buy their tools and blasting powder. It was a bonanza. The hotel clerk told us the miners would throw liquor down their necks like they were trying to put out a fire, and blow up a saloon every once in a while. Then the gold pinched out and the miners passed on. Placerville still has some lumber operations and a dance saloon where you can have your pick of three back-number girls, but after a tour of ten minutes we concluded the town was a lemon, hired a light pleasure wagon and a town Indian by the name of Julie Ann, and drove out to the river on a frolic.

Julie Ann fixed up an old Indian sweat-house by the river and heated some stones. We stripped and crawled in, all bar Cordelia; Cordelia doesn't get naked when she has a bath. She stayed outside with a gun and kept guard.

Through the sweating mist I tried to sneak a look at Sadie Marx's deformed foot. If she caught me I would right away look at Nessie's feet as though it was feet in general I was interested in. Ness has enormous ones. She's heavy around the thighs and her breasts are too small for the width of her back, but if you could see her scrunch up her neck (she scrunches up her neck the whole time. She's tall. She's tall as a clothes pole). If you could see her scrunch up her neck to listen, you'd wish it was you she was listening to. She's the opposite of me. She is as solid and dense as fog; not stupid but slow; all around you, somehow, and watchful. Me, I'm small, quick, and a funny color. The boys say you could turn me loose in any port from Kingston to Bombay or the Cape to New Orleans, I'd fit right in. There are people who think I'm some Chinese, and I have been mistaken for white.

We gassed about the people we'd left behind in San Francisco, then fell silent. It's hard to talk in a sweat-house but when you don't say anything at all it gets to be gloomy, so it was a relief when Julie Ann poked in. On the buggy trip she had told us that she'd spent the winter in Virginia City, Nevada. That's where we were headed, so I said:

"Virginia City, hey? Is it crazy like they say it is?"

"Big silver excitement. They got thirty mines, about." She had a loud, monotonous voice. You couldn't tell if she was excited or annoyed or what. "They got the Mexican. Ophir. Gould and Curry. Mines go two hundred feet underground. Hot like this sweat-house. Thousands of miners down them." She splashed water on the stones. When she could talk again, she said, "They got mines right below the streets. Road caves, stores drop right down."

The steam was tough. It ironed your throat. I said, "Don't that make people nervous?"

She shrugged. "Saloonkeeper name of Billy Best, own Gotham Saloon, C Street. Been lushing it pretty good, morning till night, who know how long. He took a header out a third-story hotel window one Sunday. They ask him why he done it. He say 'cause I was feeling tiptop."

"I know the feeling," I said. "When you lush it every minute of every day there's no telling what you might do, but you certainly see things whiz."

Ness was holding her ankle. "You just do if you jump out a third-story window."

Virginia City seemed to promise us everything we could wish for. After Julie Ann left us in darkness again, I wanted to talk about our hopes for the future and the life we had had together back in Mrs. Liberty's flash-house.

"I'm trying to remember what I thought about you both when I first met you," I began. Ness peered at me from behind her hair. "I was too busy worrying what you made of me, I suppose. What did you make of me?"

"You won't admire to hear it," Sadie said.

"I was very green, I suppose. I thought you knew everything."

"We could see you were pretty smart," Ness said, keeping something back.

"Did you think so?"

"You had a tongue so sharp it could cut a lie out a politician's heart," Sadie said.

It was a mistake to laugh in that steam. Ness said, "Dol, honey, are you all right?"

"Say," Sadie Marx said, "I heard a saw just like that," and she made like a saw cutting through wood.

It hurt so much I had to stop myself. "You can be pretty lippy yourself," I said to Sadie Marx.

That's when Cordelia crawled into the sweat-house. She had on a gorgeous purple dress and wide-brim lavender hat with feathers à la musketeer. It was a lot of fashion in the circumstances; the feathers wilted right down. She waved the steam away with one hand and clutched her neck with the other and said she didn't know how we could stand it. Finally she ordered us all to go outside. She said there was something important she wanted we should discuss. I'm telling you; if you ever happen to run across Cordelia, look out. That gal can no more scare up fun than die, and how she came to live with us, three months back, is a cautionary tale.

She got married at fifteen, only to quarrel with her husband on their wedding night; Ness found her up an alley one night, picking food off of a garbage heap, and brought her back to Mrs. Liberty's. Next morning she took her to an asylum the nuns run for deserted women and naïve young girls, but before the day was out Cordelia came back in tears, saying the nuns had beat her. We explained the business of the flash-house and told her she was too young to hang around but she had nowhere else to go and we could not get shut of her. When Ness called the cops, she locked herself in one of our rooms; so then we had to pay the cops to haul her away and mess her up a little. That didn't work either; she just came back and sat in the stairwell. She boo-hoo'd all night long. It was hard to explain the situation to the sams and look pretty at the same time; you can't help feeling hard-hearted when you have an abandoned fifteen-year-old outside your door, if she is an annoying one. She was still there in the morning; we got no peace until Sadie Marx sent her to Gabriela Higuera's stand for some cigars and gave her a half-dollar for going. The quiet was wonderful but it came at a terrible price, for there would be no peace from that moment on except we paid for it.

Sadie Marx paid the most. Cordelia was too young to enter the profession and anyway had objections to it on the grounds that it made girls lazy, so Sadie forked out for her board and sometimes bought her little treats. All Cordelia would do to earn her keep was run errands, and she crabbed from morning till night. Sometimes Sadie would say she had a nervous headache and go to bed to hide from her. Then when you thought her patience was at an end, she'd shell out for something extravagant like that gorgeous purple dress. Sometimes she would ask the other girls to chip in but Ness never would; she was saving for her retirement.

Sadie would say, "You got no pity for a girl a fifteen that sucks her thumb when she sleeps?"

"She can go wash dishes, can't she?" Ness would say. "Some of us don't have money to throw around."

Sadie Marx buys things for herself she doesn't want even when she buys them.

Anyway, Cordelia ordered us outside the Indian sweat-lodge, where we dried ourselves and clambered into our skirts.

"What's this all about anyhow?" I said.

"It's about Alice Lebo," Cordelia announced.

"Well, don't keep us in suspense. What about her?"

"She must be awful lonely on the other side, don't you think? Nobody knows she's dead barring us; her family don't. Whyn't we go to a spiritual circle and keep her company this evening?"

The girls are great on spiritualism. When any of their friends die they generally visit a spirit medium to find out if she's all right. When Pauline Healy handed in her checks, about six of us sat around a table that had a dial like the face of a clock with the letters of the alphabet written on it, whereupon a spirit crossed over from the other world and tipped the table, and the hand of the clock pointed at the letters and spelled out communications. We said, "Who are you?"—and the spirit spelled out P-a-u-l-i-n-e H-e-a-l-y. Pauline said she was dead, and told how she was killed when a runaway team bowled into her as she was crossing the street to Rijksskjaar's to buy some buns.

Well, to begin with, if the spirit was the real thing, when did she learn to read and write, I should like to know? In her earthly life she couldn't write her own name, so spelling Rijksskjaar's was coming it rather strong, you ask me. I ain't saying I'm a skeptic; I'm wondering what we learned from Pauline that we didn't already know. I mean, we knew she was dead, that's why we were there; and the runaway team was a fact; the only fresh news was Rijksskjaar's. Sadie Marx said that was Pauline all over; after a week's sojourn with the philosophers and scientists and dreamers in the spirit world, all she could talk about was buns.

"It'd certainly cheer her up," Cordelia said.

I said, "Tonight? I don't know about tonight."

Cordelia looked at the other girls in a meaning way, as if I'd pretty much given myself away. She said, "We have nothing else to do. Do we?"

"I suppose."

"Well then; don't you want to?"

I didn't want to communicate with Alice Lebo when she was *alive*. "Sure I do," I said. "But you know how solitary she was." I oftentimes found her in the bedroom crying; I would ask her what was up and she wouldn't say a thing, sit there with a face like Sunday. "I mean, you suppose she'll be more sociable now she's dead?"

Cordelia folded her arms and rolled her eyes in disgust. "She was living in circumstances that were beneath her, that's why she kept to herself. She was melancholy as a poet."

"She didn't look too poetical after she'd taken that overdose," I said. "We had to stay up all night, remember? Hitting her with hot towels to keep her from falling insensible, pitching into her with our fists and feet. We kicked the holy Christ out of her. By the time we were through I felt like we'd kicked her to death."

Her body was black as a stove next day. The doctor we called had said it was too late to use a stomach pump. Turned out he only said that because he didn't happen to have one.

Ness was buttoning up the back of my dress. "I don't think we should argue over it, Dol."

"I don't think we should argue over it either," I said. "Why don't we leave her in peace?"

"What's up?" Cordelia said. "Scared she'll tell everyone why she done it?"

Two days before Alice Lebo finished herself, I borrowed her firefly hairpin. I was in a hurry and didn't ask her for it, I hooked it from the top of her dresser. We bunked in the same room, me and Alice, so I didn't think anything of it. But I lost it and she squealed on me to the other girls. She also said I made her life a misery and she couldn't stand my company another night. When she ate her dose, nobody said anything. I mean nobody blamed me out loud.

"If you three suppose she took her life all along of a hairpin you're dumber than you look," I said.

Their faces fastened over and suddenly they were all looking at me the same way, like a three-headed monster.

"Jesus," I said. "I'll come back when you're human again."

And I put on my shoes and set off into the wilderness.

TWO

Soon as I was around the bend from the sweat-house I slowed up. I had no company barring that mountain river, and there was something miserable about the wood. Acres of it were nothing but stumps, on account of the lumber mills; it looked like an old comb with the most of its teeth missing. I stopped to take a breath and to wish I could start back to the girls, but I was too sore at them. I didn't want to go on, either, I didn't know what to do, so I sipped some wine touched up with a couple drops of medicine, out of a pretty silver flask I have.

Now, here's a piece of advice for nothing. No, first off, which brand of opium do you like? If you're a married lady I expect you ask for McMunn's Elixir or Aitken's Family Comforter; you can let the clerk suppose it's for your medicine cupboard if you go to a different drug store every week. Me, I used to favor Braithwaite's Lancashire Black Drop until one day I was broke and had to ask Ness for the lend of some cash to buy some. I said I had a terrible pain in my stomach. Ness said the missy was rotting my teeth and that it *gave* me the pain in my stomach, she didn't wonder, and made me say how much I used per day. Well, I estimated the amount I used and told her a half of it.

She turned away from her looking-glass to gape at me and covered her mouth with her hand. She didn't do it the way

Cordelia would a done, like a terrible actress, but she covered her mouth with her hand. Then she showed me this advertisement in a lady's magazine for something by the name of Dr. Golly's Painless Medical Cure. It's for all you opiomaniacs. You write Dr. Golly at Vandalia, Illinois, and tell him the number of bottles you use per week, and he concocts the cure that's just right for you. I figured out the price for the mixture I would need. What a swindle. For thirty-three dollars I could get enough missy for an entire month; why would I pay that to Dr. Golly for a miserable cure?

I told Ness I didn't need a cure seeing as there was nothing the matter with me anyway, and thirty-three scads is more than most men make in a month. Ness turned as pale as an aristocrat and said she would buy it for me. She was brought up German in St. Charles, Missouri; her pa was a freight handler for the North Missouri when he could get work. It's her character to save, so it was awful when she offered to fool away her hard-earned ducats on a potion. It was like she'd turned into a mug. I told her she was being had, but like all mugs she believed what she wanted to believe and nothing would shake her.

The day the concoction arrived I went to my room to be alone. I supposed most cures would be the strength of opiate you give to babies to quiet them, and *my* cure would be even worse because I'd lied to Ness about the amount I used. When I thought about how miserable my life was going to be from then on, I wished I'd never been born. I was nineteen years of age and I never again would have the feeling all the way down to my toes that I was something rare and good. I took my first dose watching myself in a looking-glass, like I was committing suicide. A half-hour later I was gonged out of my mind. Painless?

Dr. Golly takes all the opium you would use in a month and distills it into one bottle. Try it. You'll never use anything else.

After a sip of my medicine I braved up, left the mountain river, and went poking about in the wood. Pretty soon the noise of the river hushed; all I could hear was a bird going *quag quag, quag quag quag*, pretty flat, like something had taken all the song out of it. From a piece away I saw a flash of cream coat. He was more still than was natural, possible. I picked my way around the trees. Always there was a branch or something to keep me from seeing him whole, but I could tell the bird was guiding me toward something dismal. When I stepped out in front of him he didn't budge, not any part of him. He had a small fat face inside a large fat face, and seemed pretty stuck-up considering he was probably dead. He was standing on the very tipmost of his toes rather than truly hanging, like he'd strung himself up but hadn't taken account of the pliant character of pine or his weight. I knew what his profession was right away from the rings he was wearing on all his fingers, and the buttons on his vest. They were jet-black and ringed around the outside with tiny diamonds. I couldn't tell if they were real or false, but only a pimp would have the nerve to wear them, either way.

He was a little off his beat in this wilderness.

"You need some help?"

I blushed after I spoke and looked around in embarrassment. I mean, I knew he couldn't talk back, I was talking because I was out of my mind.

"You alive?"

A bird flashed in front of him so sudden I thought he'd moved. But he hadn't. He was perfectly still.

"Don't seem quite natural somebody as selfish and mean as a pimp would take his own life."

That's when his arm raised itself a little as though it wanted to loosen the tie around his neck. It's a frightening thing to hear yourself squeaking with terror and not know what to do next. Behind him I saw a small squareish wood crate; it looked like he'd stood on that to jump off. On top of it was a rifle, the modernest thing you ever saw. Before I knew exactly what I meant to do with it, I picked it up.

"I got a gun now, mister. I got you covered."

Silence.

"I don't know why I should save the life of a fat young pimp that wants to die. Howsoever, I'm going to knock the tar out of that branch. Hear? I'm going to shoot you down off a that branch. I just pray I don't regret it."

After I was through, a silence descended, tall and loud and scared; then there was nothing else for it, I gritted my teeth and fired. The very first bullet slapped the branch, and that sunk me. The branch bounced but it didn't turn a hair, and I reckoned the chances were awfully slim I would hit it twice. With a sick feeling I closed my eyes and banged away.

I don't know what I did right, maybe I shot the necktie. The suicide fell toward me and touched my hair. His clothes did, or his hand; it was like being brushed by a pox blanket. I screamed and jumped out of the way and heard him hit the ground with the satisfying sound of a forehead smacking a rock. While he was out the birds piped up. One asked, Are you still there? and another one said she thought so, she wouldn't swear to it though. I ought to left him there and sloped, I know that, but I couldn't. When I run across something that terrifies the wits out of me, I can't tear myself away. I can't let the thing beat me. With the rifle in my hand I walked all around him, like he was a giant or something. His nose was a little loose after his fall and his head had a dazzling wound from temple to ear, but he had the lips of a cherub. I got interested in the crate after that. It said it was a liquor crate; Perilloux's Finest New Orleans Rum; and it was made of first-rate wood, all smoothed down. But it wasn't bottles, else the bottom would have been heavier than the top. It had been repacked with something different: the weight was even all the way down, every inch of it was full. Just then the pimp stirred, dragged himself a couple of yards, and propped himself up against a tree. I think he saw me put the crate down, but I couldn't be sure.

He plumped himself up, flicked the dirt off his coat, and gave me his flossiest smile. "I don't know what got into me," he said. "Ordinarily I ain't the brave type." His voice had been scraped by a grater.

"That's why you picked the lowest branch, I guess."

He didn't like that but he kept smiling and frisking me with his eyes. "You can see what I am, I suppose. Back in Dabu I was a first-rate pimp." *Dabu* is Chinese for San Francisco. It's what the crooks call it. "I had a string a four girls sugaring me."

"Pretty?"

"Two of 'em. The other two was double-barreled." He grinned. He was hoping I wouldn't understand him and then he'd be obliged to explain it to me.

"Their assholes pretty?"

"You're a gal, huh?"

I guess I'd given it away. "Not the kind you run."

16

He had one of those smiles. He imagined you were enjoying his company as much as he was. "You're a nice piece a hair." He looked me over like I might just fill the bill.

That made me so mad I started in shaking. "And you're quite a character," I said. "I always supposed a suicide would be a little down on himself."

"Guess what they called me back in the Bay."

He paused so I'd ask him what.

"Pontius," he said. "When I give a girl her last chance and she bitches it, I get a basin and wash my hands of her. Then I nail her hands to the floor. Catch on?"

He told me that like I'd be impressed. I was shaking so bad I wanted to show him who was boss. "What's in the crate?"

"Then I got tired of girls and run some kids for a while. Kids are an art. You got to study their character."

I pointed the rifle at him, shaking. "Go open the crate, mister."

"A kid in San Francisco can slip away on a ship any day of the week. You want them to stick, they got to admire you. You have to flash them your sparks." He stopped to appreciate himself, like he was a high-priced cigar. "Your geology collection, get me?"

"Stand up, I said."

A piece away I heard Ness calling for me. "Dol! Can you hear me?"

"I hear you," I called.

"Dol!" Ness seemed farther away that time.

"I'm here," I hollered.

I was beginning to feel all at sea. For one thing, the rifle might be out of bullets; I didn't know how many cartridges it held or how many times I'd already fired it. And what would I do anyway if he did open the crate? I hadn't thought the thing out.

Ness arrived pushing past branches, bamboozled with tears and terrible forebodings. "My, you scared me most to death. I like to cried when I heard the skirmish and smelled the gunpowder." All the while her eyes were running over Pontius, looking to see how he was fixed, a six-shooter or a bowie or what.

"She saved my life," Pontius told Ness. "I hope I can pay her back one day."

He smiled but he didn't have anything pleasant in mind. "Let's go," I said to Ness. "Pontius, I'm going to leave you your rifle." I pointed. "I'll drop it over there."

I didn't want to leave him a rifle with anything in it; after we'd backed away twenty yards or so through the wood, I aimed over his head and pulled the trigger. The noise left no room for anything else in the world. The trees were fine but everything else made itself as small as it could. The birds disappeared for a while. Then I dropped the empty rifle and cut out, fast, following Ness through the trees.

When we got back to the sweat-house Sadie Marx was standing mid-river, smoking one of her small cigars. The shooting hadn't shook her at all; she was looking in the other direction, lost in her own world, as if she was calculating the value of the timber. Then she seemed to conclude it might be worth a piece of money but it was still too much scenery for her liking. After I gave them all an account of my adventure nobody mentioned so small a matter as Alice Lebo, and next day we drove on, up into the Sierra.

THREE

You never saw a wilderness like it for crowds. The wagons were nose to tail, crawling up the steep grade with eighteen-carat pianos and scrumptious billiard tables, high-grade plumbing fixtures and chests of oysters packed in ice, all bound like us for the silver excitement across the mountains in Nevada. Teamsters said the mines of Virginia City laid over anything the Aztecs had in that line. Some of the wagons were freighting heavy machinery for the works and iron castings for the stamp mills; they staggered uphill with loads as high as the roof of a barn. There were six-mule teams and eight-mule teams struggling up that narrow road; to the right there were falls of a thousand feet. You could look down on the tops of gigantic pines and firs. Along about noon we heard some whooping ahead that passed from wagon to wagon and got closer by the second. It was three wagons rollicking down the mountain, packed with bars of silver bullion and guards. When the freighters saw all that plunder they let their voices loose with a perfect freedom; I didn't make a sound but my heart kicked like a conquistador's.

I said to Ness, "Looks like there's going to be plenty excitement where we're going."

"I wonder how your mother's getting along there."

"I worry about her in a helter-skelter town like that." My mother had lit out for Virginia City a couple weeks before the rest of us girls. "Everyone says it's hell with the lid off."

"Might suit her to a fraction."

"That's what bothers me."

My mother's a drunkard. One night in San Francisco I found her asleep on Pacific Street about two o'clock in the morning. She'd lain down on the road because she was tired and it was the nearest thing to a bed she could see. You never know what will happen next; one minute she's swelling around like a duchess, the next her skirt is up in flames. And it's worse when she's *not* around; you start to imagine all kinds of accidents and catastrophes; it eats you up. I'm willing to bet the most difficult problem in mathematics is not as complicated as she is. I think about her all the time; I grind my teeth in my sleep.

Her bringing-up was in Edinburgh, Scotland, where they have the finest philosophers and the most advanced surgeons. The females are just as smart; they discuss metaphysics with their dance partners and pursue their interest in the human body in the carriage home. Mama was Isobel Murray then. Her father was an important advocate; she used to always say he spoiled her dreadfully after her mother died, but in spite of eating nothing but novels and candy, she turned into a fine-looking young woman and met her Fate in the shape of Captain McQueen of the Royals. He used to come a-calling in a showy gig and whisk her off, her in the seat and him standing behind, whipping his horses and giving it jesus like a goddamned charioteer. After they married, he was posted overseas to Fort St. Andrew's in British Guiana. The young bride didn't like to be separated from her captain and crossed the pond, only to discover on her arrival he had died of disease. And so began her adventures as a widow.

Recife, Rio, Montevideo; she neglected me in some fascinating places. I would run errands for ship chandlers, or sit by a wall somewhere and read *The Pirate's Daughter*. I liked being abandoned; it gave me the idea I was a character in a story, Moses in the bulrushes or something. It was how I got my education too. Men who were interested in my mother would take me up and lend me *The Repository of Facts* or *The Phantom Ship*; it didn't occur to them she rarely said good night to me. The first time I remember being alone with her was the night we left Rio on the *City of Pekin*. She got stinking with a boy in his teens and didn't come back to the cabin. I went looking for her in the wee small hours and found her asleep on the lower deck. I was only nine, I couldn't carry her, so I propped her up against the doors of the ash pit, pulled her arm around my shoulder, and swore to look after her, always. It's comforting, self-pity, it swells up your chest and your face, tight and full. By the time dawn knocked along, there was enough of it ballooning me up to refloat Ophelia.

She generally left her husbands on account of a ruckus over the maids. She'd complain they were too young, or too religious; there was always something. Before she bounced out of Buenos Aires, leaving me behind, she picked a fight with Mr. Sarti over one who was too tall to her way of thinking. Mr. Sarti wasn't an unpleasant man, but he was an economizing one and—after Mama deserted him—he didn't see why he should have the up-keep of a child he had known only a matter of weeks. It was no pleasure eating his food, not when he was watching. I used to leave the table before I'd finished chewing. Weeks passed; I couldn't make up my mind if she'd forgotten about me or she was dead, but on the whole it was nicest to imagine she was dead. Then, after fifty-three days, we got a telegram from Chile. That evening at supper I found a banknote beside my place: my boat fare, Mr. Sarti said; and next day I set off alone to double the Horn.

You know what I loved about her most? She was a joy to watch. She could wear an eye patch or use a cigarette holder, know she was posing and enjoy it twice as much as someone who didn't. It was the same way she enjoyed flirting. She didn't make a secret of it; she wanted the fellow to *see* she was seducing him and not be able to help himself. But she drank more the older I got. She was greedy about it and sneaky. One time when I was fourteen I helped myself to a glass of gin from one of the bottles she kept on the sideboard and almost choked when I found it was water. I suppose she diluted them to hide from her husbands how fast she drank, but nobody was fooled much.

She lost the desire to charm. Then, on the occasions she decided to *employ* it, her face didn't always rise to the occasion. She would tip a man a teasing smile and all he'd notice were the bags under her eyes, hanging like lead. I wrote a story about it— a woman who would wander off nights to look for her face, then lie down wherever she happened to be. My heroine would sleep in the orchard; Mama slept with the dog or the linen. Sometimes I found her in the maid's room, under the bed. She couldn't be trusted to look out for herself, that's for sure, so when she left Ernesto Márquez and scattered for San Francisco I got after her, traced her to Mrs. Liberty's flash-house. She wasn't pleased to see me. She said I'd been trailing her since I was seven and she was sick of it, so I left her to rot in prostitution and got myself a job at St. Mary's Hospital. After three weeks of boiling bandages stained with pus, I moved into Mrs. Liberty's at the earliest opportunity.

It was quite a revelation—for the first time in my life I belonged. I liked the company of the girls and they didn't seem to mind Mama at all. They enjoyed the stories she told, the monocle she sometimes wore, even the airs she gave herself. Everyone got along just swell till Mama flung a pot of coffee over big Mary Moose. When Mary refused to apologize for causing her to lose her temper, Mama packed her traps and headed for Virginia City and I was sick with worry from the moment she boarded the stage. By that time she couldn't cross a road; if she was sober it spooked her, and when she was screwed she didn't notice how often she was almost run over. I kept boosting Nevada to Ness but she didn't take to the idea, so it was a great stroke of luck that Alice Lebo killed herself. To smile and laugh the evening of Alice Lebo's funeral, while the sams in Mrs. Liberty's parlor sang the ever-humorous "Nelly in Her Nightie," was possible, but it roughed everyone's nerves, and next day we bought our steamboat tickets for Sacramento.

After the wagon with the silver bullion had passed us on the Sierra road and roared down the mountain, everyone's mood perked up plenty. Suddenly it was no hardship to climb that steep grade, behind those big wagons; I began to notice the size of my surroundings. In my chest I could feel the altitude I was at. The huge pines all around were still refrigerated after winter; they gave off the smallest amount of perfume, enough just to touch the edge of the mountain air. And the wind pushed you sideways now and then just to show what it *could* do if it roused itself. I wanted to take in the scene so I sat on a rock at the side of the road that overlooked the hills beneath, had a sip of missy on the sly, and thought about the times we would have in Virginia City.

When I stood to go catch up to our wagons, I happened to look back at the traffic on the road below. Pontius was less than fifty yards away, pushing a hand-cart with that wood crate in it. I supposed it was the crate, anyway; it was covered over by his coat. His shirt was soaked with sweat in spite of the wind. It was as wet as the sails of a clipper ship in fog, and he fired me a look like I had saved his life and I owed him for it. Afterward, whenever I looked back, he was never more than a hundred yards behind. Seemed he'd attached himself to me. The other girls didn't like it they were being followed by a suicide, but what could I do about it? I said look on the bright side, there might be something valuable in that crate. "Then why'd he try and hang himself?" Cordelia said.

After climbing all day it was a relief, toward sun-down, to hit a flat stretch of road where the American River runs about a mile on a good solid floor, its clear bed dotted with pink and gray boulders. There was a camping place there. It was busy but we liked it amazingly until night shut down, mean and cold. We built a big fire that spat at us and nipped our faces—and we were still frozen. The rims of our ears hurt, tits ached. Champagne wasn't ideal in the circumstances but it was all the liquor we had, so we drank the chilly stuff and shivered like crazy around the camp-fire.

Pontius arrived, pushing his hand-cart, just when supper was being cooked. He joined us around the camp-fire and asked for some rations. He had that rifle in the crook of his arm; we didn't like to argue, so we gave him some bacon and beans. He smiled when he was done, tossed the plate to one side, got aboard our wagon and didn't come out again, like he'd bedded down for the night. We couldn't let him get away with that but we weren't sure what to do exactly. We crawled into our tent, all four of us, and had a powwow. We had our clothes on and blankets over us.

"I used to run across that munk in Dabu." Sadie likes to hang out in low dives; she knows every crook and every cheap alley queen.

"Well, what was he like?"

"He was a very numerous person. He was all over Aherne's bar like a candidate. I hope he don't freeze to us, that's all. I wouldn't like to meet the fellas he's running from."

"What makes you suppose he's running from anyone?"

"He tried to hang himself, Dol. You think his conscience drove him to it?"

We were shaking like steamboats.

"Well," I said, "how do we get shut of him?"

There was a big silence. Nobody said it was my fault, why didn't I go and get rid of him. Maybe they weren't even thinking it. It was mortal cold, maybe they weren't thinking anything, but after ten minutes I got out of the tent.

I stopped outside the wagon and said, "It's me. I'm coming aboard. Light a lantern, would you?"

I waited till I saw the flash of a match, then I loosed the tailgate. It dropped with a trap-door thud and ringing rattle. When he held the lantern up, I could see he was sitting on the rum crate with the rifle on his lap. Bacon grease slicked his face, like some of his own fat had melted. I hauled myself aboard, climbed onto the lid of a piano I'd bought in San Francisco on an installment plan. Good plan; I paid two installments and skipped. My intention was to say nothing. Be patient. Let him talk. But the piano was cold as the lid of an ice chest. Even my shoulders trembled.

"I just came to tell you we don't want you along. You better cut out tomorrow morning first thing." Then I said, "We got guns."

"You got a strong will. I like that."

"I'm stubborn as rust. I will wear away iron."

"That's the sort I can use."

"Don't imagine I'm anything like the girls you ran back in San Francisco. Why would I give some strange man all the dough I make? I wouldn't get that confused if you talked to me for a week."

"You suppose a hard-scrabble whore has a weak will? I never ran any girls that didn't kick and back-talk, I wouldn't know how. What I like to do is pick a fight with them before they go out on the beat. That way they come back sore as a toothache, gunning for you. They got to get the better of you, see? The more stubborn they are, the longer they stick."

In the darkness you could practically hear him accept the applause that was his due.

Then he said, "You put me in mind of them."

"I do, huh?"

"When something pursues you, you pursue it right back."

My neck was stiff and sore from my shoulders being hunched against the cold, and my hands were beginning to hurt. I knew I should go but I couldn't. I sat there, frozen to the piano lid with fury.

Outside Ness called out, "Dol? Are you all right?"

"I'm fine."

"You just holler," she said, after a little. "I'll hear you in the tent."

After she went, he didn't say anything. I had stayed to get the better of him like one of his whores.

"You look like you didn't sleep in weeks," I said. "You must be awfully afraid of something."

"Not you."

"You're still a little hoarse from the hanging," I said. "What's in the rum crate?"

"What makes you think it's not rum?"

"Well, I can tell the lid has been opened."

"Did you look inside?"

I let him wonder about that. "Why'd you hang yourself, you cross someone up and scamper with the booty?"

I was afraid he might fly at me. He considered his answer for a couple minutes. Then he got to his feet, placed his rifle on a dresser, and opened the crate. He removed a tray that was sitting on top of the contents, held up the light for me. "Well, take a look."

I slid off the piano and bent over the crate so low I put my hand down to lean on the side of it. It was packed with tin boxes, as neat and nice as bars of silver bullion, only standing up. There were hundreds of them.

"Go ahead," he said. "Open one."

The tin had a rich smoothness, like there might be expensive candy inside, and it was closed pretty snug. It opened with a *dff* and the tiniest rustle of paper inside. I caught a scent I recognized and put it to my nose. I got a stirring right down in my melter. Opium is so wonderful it's hard to believe it's allowed, and this was first-rate *chan du*, about as fresh as it comes. Sometimes it's hard and tight, like vulcanized rubber, this stuff you could squeeze between your fingers. I put the tin back with the others. It slid into the vacancy and filled it to perfection. Silver bars? Each of those tins was better than bullion. When I tried to figure up what it was worth, well, I lost my guess, that's all. I started fogging up the wagon; I couldn't breathe right.

He said, "You want a taste?"

"How much opium is that?"

"You want to hit the pipe?"

"I never saw that much *gow* in an opium joint."

"You want a taste or not?"

I was trying to hold my breath, else it might run away from me. "Sure," I said. I laughed. "I need some after seeing that. I need to tranquilize myself a little or I won't be able to sleep."

He took the tray he'd put on the dresser and sat down. He had a pipe, a tiny glass lamp, the whole layout. I found somewhere to sit down and piled some clothes on top of me; by now I was shivering inside as well as out. I was so excited I bit at my nails for something to do. I knew it would be difficult to explain to Ness why I was hitting the pipe with someone I didn't know too well and didn't like and we all wanted rid of, but about the best part of opium is the closeness with strangers. In an opium joint you lie there, gonged out of your mind, so near to some old man with yellow in his white beard that you can smell his dreams. After a pipe it's like you're all in the same bed. The covers are warm and heavy and smell a bit, but nobody bothers you up. You can lie there with your legs open and nothing will happen. You're all dead. That's why you know so much.

It was dirtier with Pontius because we were in bed on our own. He was sitting up with the tray in his lap; I was leaning on one elbow. He handed me the pipe and I leaned over the tray to put the bowl over the lamp. I couldn't keep my hair from trailing all over the tray. He finished cooking the pill, scraped it into my pipe bowl with the needle, and I inhaled. Right away I almost threw up all over his lap. It's common, the first whiff you take, but it fairly makes you look like a mug when you white like that, so I took another whiff, when I'd recovered, and filled myself up down to my toes. You know what the smell puts me in mind of? A dirty slum girl with a mouth full of colored candy. I always wish she'd come under the covers with me but she never does.

Pontius cooked another pill and gave me the pipe again.

I said, "Don't you want any?"

"No," he said.

"Don't you like it?"

"I have to keep a clear head if I'm going to wipe you out."

It was so still it was like being in a photograph. He won't do that, I thought. I could scream. He wouldn't want the trouble.

I said, "What would you want to go and do that for?"

He pushed out his lips. "You might blab."

I wondered if he was being humorous. "But you showed me it yourself."

"You already knew too much. You knew it wasn't liquor."

"You heard my friend. She's waiting for me. I could holler."

His hand was around my neck almost before I'd finished. "Try it."

Oh, the desires that drowned in those eyes. It was a close thing what he wanted most: he would love to watch me expire—to feel me cease to be and relax in his hand—but if he killed me he wouldn't be able to kill me again, and that would be a disappointment. It annoyed him he couldn't do both, and he squeezed me harder in frustration. Right when I had reconciled myself to dying, he let go. He decided to keep this rarest of wines for some other occasion.

"I can't hurt you if you're dead," he said. "Go ahead. Lie down and take it easy."

I turned away and closed my eyes. After I was chased by some thugs through a strangely built city, I was thrown aboard a ship, more dead than alive. I could smell the sweet stinking crew in their bunks all round me, and hear their drowned voices. They called out the names of sweethearts and fancy-girls in every jolly port from Madagascar to Marseilles, and Jamaica to the Sea of Japan.

By and by the ship was sailing toward a harbor. But the bay was blood-crimson and we didn't put ashore there. Instead we rode upriver into the hinterland. It was night. Deer grazed in the woods and we passed pretty Chinese temples. I saw Ness waving from the shore like a lost soul, but it was only an evil spirit that had stolen her appearance and wished to win me to my harm.

Some birds appeared and asked me would I like to meet the Queen of Heaven, and I said yes. They led me to a palace and the help came out to see who I was. She was as plain as can be; she was ugly, in fact. I said I wished to see the Queen of Heaven and the help said that was her. I split out laughing; I said the Queen of Heaven has thirteen stars around her head and stands upon the moon. The maid got sore; she said she was sorry she wasn't as pretty as I would like her to be, but she was the Queen of Heaven all right and I better be satisfied.

FOUR

Next day there were places where the road hung to the mountain by the fingertips of one hand. Farther on it cut through banks of snow that had slackened some and thawed, till the ice looked like the dry inside of a meringue. The road streamed with melted snow, and we trudged uphill with cold wet feet, jealous of the teamsters who were sitting high and dry on their wagon boxes, enjoying the sun in their shirt sleeves.

There was no sign of the pimp. I was relieved to be rid of him, sure; just the same, I was a little shadowy all day, like something was missing, and it wasn't till we reached the summit that the scene opened out and you could see snow-topped mountains on all sides. Then we headed down to an immense lake that was a cold jewel blue, where we camped. Ness and Cordelia went to a nearby hotel to buy brandy and fruit, came back saying there was a wedding party that night and we'd been invited.

The Lake Hotel was a resort in the mountains for the wealth and swank of Virginia City. The groom owned a sliver of one of the mines there; the guests were mining engineers and lawyers and go-ahead young men who ran freight companies. None of them seemed to care they were sweating; they were having the largest time you can imagine. The water tanks of the hotel had been filled with gin sling and, almost for the fun of the thing, the guests kept running off to fill their glasses from the faucets. We made our way to the dance room, and stopped on the edges of the thing.

The din was something like a ship being made, but instead of a conglomeration of hammers and iron the noise was built out of laughter and gin. There were too many gents for the ladies and some of the extra ones were playing a form of baseball where glasses were pitched and the batter laid into them in classy style with the leg of a chair. The broken glass went over the dancers, some of it, and some sprinkled the table where the wedding cake was. It was looking rather forlorn, and a young lady—whose hair had been undone by liquor and her emotions—made a heartfelt plea on its behalf. The baseball players were unmoved, though.

The pandemonium was more than I could stand, so I dug out for the ladies' room and took a right good dose. Then I examined my face in a mirror. When you take missy you spread out like a peacock's tail, and it feels like that's the number of eyes you have. I wanted to see if I actually *looked* that way. Ness might wonder about the cure she'd bought me, if I did. But when you have that quantity of eyes it's rather peculiar when you look in a glass. You can't know what anything looks like for certain. I had turned my head to one side and was studying my face when Ness appeared in the mirror and gave me a start.

"Dol, can I talk to you confidential?"

I hoped I didn't seem suspiciously happy. "Sure. Let's find somewhere. What is it you want to talk about? You look awful solemn."

"We can't talk here?"

"Let's find somewhere we got room."

The closer we were, the quicker she might notice the sudden improvement in my mood. On the stairs our path was cut off by a wall of architects; I suspected Ness was going to jump me for spending the night with the pimp and I reckoned I would get all twisted up trying to give an account of myself, so it suited me fine to flirt with them. I let on to be an invalid with a fatal but pretty disease and clung to Ness for support. To embellish the thing I took out my silver flask and sipped some of my "medicine," dropping a hint to the gents that the wonder of creation was much more truly cherished by those about to fall lifeless into the arms of death's bright angel. I was looking (I hoped) enchantingly pale, when suddenly every last particle of my body and soul exploded. I was experiencing more bliss than a dying girl ought to, and I lost the use of my face, and my fan. The fan flew off and had to be retrieved, and I don't know *what* happened to my face exactly. Thankfully someone suggested I wasn't well, and I was taken to a hotel bedroom to recover my strength. I complained the light was hurting my eyes, so they closed the curtains and left me there with Ness.

"Did I look hideous?" I said. "I have this idea my tongue was lolling about in my head."

"How do you feel now?"

"Weak."

"That's a sign the cure is working, I reckon. You are bound to be tolerable weak sometimes, Dol."

"I suppose so."

"I can't expect you to be grateful. But you don't hate me, do you?"

"No."

"Your eyes are just as skied as they used to be but you don't nod off as much."

"What is it you want to tell me?"

You could hear the hop downstairs. "I made up my mind," Ness said. "I'm tired of the flash-house life. I'm going to square it."

The entire hotel gave the tiniest sort of bounce, like a billiard ball dropped onto heavy old wood.

"When?" I said. "Next year?"

"Soon as I make the silver town."

"Soon as you hit the richest place on earth?"

Ness was leaning against the wash basin. She put on her spectacles to look at me better. "It's a short life being a flash-girl. You have to make your pile fast and quit. It's hard to live with three other girls, and the house is liable to fire you when you turn mean. It's a hard life on the loose. Those street fairies been chawed up pretty good."

"I don't intend to set up as a cheap pick-up."

She frowned a little. "It don't bother you what happened to Alice Lebo?"

After Alice died Mrs. Liberty stripped her bed naked. Two nights I shared a room with that bad-stained mattress.

"Won't happen to me," I said.

"Never a week goes by without one of the girls eats her dose."

"That's their lookout."

"I'm right down sorry to hear you talk this way. I hoped you'd come in partners with me. I want to start a dry-goods store."

You know you're going to die but you don't know the day and the month and the year, and that way you can put it off. It was like Ness had named the day. In the dance room below, someone was making a speech, holding that dizzy crowd of drunks in a perfectly wonderful silence until the snap line. Then they laughed and stamped their feet so loud the scrub women in the kitchen stopped scraping the crockery for a few moments.

I said, "Ever run a dry-goods store?"

"I bought a book on single-entry bookkeeping. I been studying it in snatches." She wasn't any louder than a rustle. She got a fright when she heard herself sound so feeble, and petered out.

"I don't mean to be cruel, Ness, but we wouldn't know where to begin."

"We have capital, don't we? We don't need to persuade a bank we can do it."

"Why don't you ask Sadie Marx?"

"She wouldn't be the least bit interested. Can't you see what's happened to her?"

"She don't seem any different to how she's always been."

"She makes my blood run cold."

I suddenly realized they hadn't liked to be alone with each other lately. "Ness Boschert, it's not like you to talk so wild."

"It's a fact. She's turned into a ghoul."

Ness was wearing her hair in a new way that night, a sort of braided crown that made her look foreign. I began to wonder if she was touched in the head. "What do you mean she's a ghoul?"

"Watch her the next time you see her," she said, and left the room.

I was devastated. Didn't she know me any better than to propose I spend the rest of my life selling curtains? You can say what you like about the trials of the flash-life but nobody asks you to

36

tone down your personality. Would you ask an actress to serve behind a counter? She'd be a nothing. I turned on the faucet, but I was so mad at Ness I let the gin run through my fingers. It was like I was treating it with the same contempt Ness had for me. I mean, I'd fondly imagined she *liked* my personality.

I wanted to tell her exactly what I thought of her, but where would that get me? I had to convince her she was wrong. I turned off the faucet, went to the door of the hotel room, and peeped out. She was outside sitting on the stairs.

I went and sat beside her. "Don't you think it's lovely to be one of the gals?" I said. "The fun we have."

She kept her face turned away from me, toward the wall.

"It's not utopian," I joked. "The number of suicides tells you that. But it suits me to a dot. I don't want to live alone with Mama. This way I can live in the same house as her and still have some company."

That softened her some, but she wasn't going to give up. "I was counting on you," she said. "I can't cross the river on my own."

When you give up the life, the girls say you've crossed the river. "I don't know anyone over there," I said. "I don't know a soul. Do you?"

"No."

"Might be awful, just the two of us."

There was an ovation downstairs and three cheers. Pretty soon the entire wedding party, which had gathered for the speech, would jar loose again, and men would start getting in our hair. Ness ran her finger down from the top of her nose straight down to her chin, and considered her next move. "Well, you can think it over, anyway."

Already the wedding guests were filling the lobby below us. They didn't care how noisy they were. I stood up. "Let's get the others and slope."

We found Cordelia playing billiards. She was lit by a chandelier suspended low over the table and had left the door open so any passing gent might look in and discover her there, in the glamour of that light and the interesting circumstance of being alone.

"You see Sadie Marx anywhere?" I asked.

"She's in the kitchen." She sneered at us in her fifteen-year-old way. "Seems you flash-girls got no idea how to behave at a wedding. You fly off here and there like the kids."

Sadie Marx was having a tiny party with a few of the scrub women and a cook. The dishes were washed and the kitchen had cooled some, now that everyone had knocked off. Our ball dresses couldn't hardly maneuver down there without being soiled, or nearly set alight when the stove door was opened and the fire was shaken down. The scrub women looked at us with secret smiles of criticism like we wouldn't last very long in those clothes if we were scrubbers.

But Sadie Marx they had taken to their hearts. She was wearing a deep red riding dress, with black gloves, and was teaching the cook how to fry steak and onions the right way. She was smoking one of her little cigars with one hand and prodding the onions with the other, and the cook (who had her own ideas of how to fry steak and onions, I guess) listened to her and let on to be memorizing her directions. As she cooked and smoked and drank, Sadie Marx taught the scrubbers the essentials in life: how to pick a winning horse and leave their husbands. They watched her as if they were enchanted until suddenly one of them started to leak. She was fifty or thereabouts. She had a small face with pretty bones and skin that sagged; it turned out she was crying because her man had flung boiling water over her and cleared out. She didn't reckon any other man would have her. No man ever had wanted her, she said, except he was looking for someone he could lam. Everybody tried to cheer her up, barring Sadie Marx, who told her she was better off without a man anyway. Maybe it was a little hard how she said it but it was probably the truth, and nothing in the way she spoke to the old scrubber, or the swank of frying onions with her kid gloves on, seemed the least bit ghoulish.

It was pitch dark when we got outside. A lake that is six thousand feet high has a sort of loneliness that makes you want to listen to it, but Cordelia was jabbering about the wedding and Sadie Marx was humoring her with a question or two. Underneath that, I could hear the deadly silence between Ness and Sadie Marx.

FIVE

Ness is timid in some ways but she's left two husbands. All next day, from the moment we rolled out, the thought that she would strike out on her own when we got to our destination made me sick with suspense.

After we shook the lake, we made one last Sierra summit then descended thousands of feet to the Nevada desert and crawled across the plain. I walked behind the wagon, eating dust and filling up with dread. Night fell before we made our destination, but Ness said we were so close we might as well push on. Those last few miles Cordelia was quiet as an injured rabbit hiding in the grass. What if we gave her the mitten, she must have been thinking, and made a fresh start without her? Presently we began to pull uphill. Ahead I could see a necklace of lights around the throat of a mountain, hanging there all serene. It disappeared and reappeared, and after a little we came to the town. I ought to of known better; I'd been picturing a hell-fire mining town with gaudy women and gambling-tents, miners in red shirts with pouches of gold dust like something out of an old-timer's tale. Instead it was too badly lit to make out anything very well, and what you could see was pretty ordinary—a brick hotel, a bank, a few stores. A mother was pulling a child along the sidewalk just like anywhere. They both wore headscarves and slight frowns. The way they hurried past, the little girl seemed as disapproving as her ma of the saloons they passed and the men that stood outside them.

All we could see was this one street. Ness asked a man leading a mule if this was Virginia City.

"Gold Hill. Carry on a quarter-mile, up and over a divide. That's Virginia right there."

Inside fifteen minutes I stood on the summit of the divide and looked down. Even in the black of night you could tell it was a factory town. There was the sickish smell of used-up steam and chemicals, the silhouettes of smokestacks, the vibrations of large engines, and eight or nine long streets, one below the other. The lights from the houses made you imagine the town had slid down the mountain, and all my hopes slid off into the night. I'd imagined Ness would get carried away by the wildness and romance of a frontier town and fling herself into the life again, but a town as drab as this might make a dry-goods store look like a good idea. We drove down to the business street and got held up by traffic awhile. The road was choked with delivery wagons, even at this late hour, and I began to perk up. It wasn't romantic but it was pandemonium. The sidewalks were jammed with people, hundreds of them, and the saloons were going full blast. I spotted hairdressers, three-story hotels, a store that sold guitars and banjos, and two jewelers; by the time we had unloaded our plunder at the freight company's depot and put up at a hotel, we certainly wanted to see the rest of the town.

The sidewalks were an awful scrimmage. Every now and then one of the girls would lose a bonnet or get separated, and the others would have to wait till she caught up. I kept my eye on Ness. I didn't want to lose her for two seconds in case she vanished.

All four of us knew, though nobody said as much, that we might go our separate ways tomorrow. It ragged your nerves. We got to talking with a fellow who'd arrived two years back, he said, day after Lincoln won the Republican nomination from Seward. He entertained us with stories of the town's beginnings; we laughed but quieted down soon as were alone again, as if we were only letting on to be friends when required to do so. It was the owliest feeling. We were on our way back to the hotel, weary of the strain, when a saloon fired out its load of customers and we got pushed onto the road. They were all drunk as miners on a Saturday night, only these miners had Navy revolvers in their belts. They said it was wild and lawless here; you had to protect yourself. You bet it was wild. They were three months' travel from their loved ones and marooned on a geological-looking chunk of the planet. Even when they were drunk and *happy* it was frightening; they emptied themselves all over you. Some lads, more crazed with liquor than the rest, offered us their protection, and we were escorted to our lodgings, quiet as a squad of prisoners.

I was sharing a room with Ness that night. She lay down on top of the bed with a wet cloth over her eyes. She said she was wore out after all the noise and excitement. But it made me uneasy she could shut me out that way.

"Ness," I went, "I been thinking about what you said. It's a short life, sure enough, being a flash-girl. I suppose I didn't think of that before, seeing as I'm only nineteen, but I been wondering if I didn't ought to start giving some consideration to the future. Maybe a dry-goods store wouldn't be so bad after all."

She didn't move. She lay there with the folded cloth hiding her eyes. "You don't sound too convinced."

"I don't know that I can throw in with you right now, that's all."

"I see."

"How long can you wait?"

She was still as a corpse. "I can wait a little."

"I appreciate I can't be a flash-girl forever, but I got to make my pile first, don't I? I don't want to go into business with you except I can chip in my share. And I got to get used to the idea of a dry-goods store. I never imagined I would be dead so young."

She took the cloth from her eyes and sat up. "You want to be dead in a dry-goods store or dead in a box?"

"Oh, Ness." I laughed. "You sound like a preacher or something. I know we've had some scaly times but least we let our back hair down sometimes. I don't know how the girls across the river amuse themselves. They don't drink if they're nice. They have to hide their bottles of missy and get them out in secret."

"They do other things besides lush, Dol."

"If life is a choir practice for heaven I don't want either of them."

I thought she'd laugh but she didn't; her face got icy and thin-looking and she lay back down. "I don't mind waiting for you but don't leave it too late." She put the cloth over her face. "Don't take a genius to run a dry-goods store. We'll do just fine."

I went to bed wishing I hadn't promised to quit. It was like I'd borrowed a large sum of money I couldn't afford, and all I could do from now on was put off the day I paid it back. But for the time being I had kept us all together; and next day the four of us got fixed up inside an hour, a saloon on D Street called the Empress.

Now, look here, it's none of my funeral if you stay where you are, what are you making, two dollars a day? The Ohio coal region, I hear you miners make two chips a day. You'll take home a little more supposing you're a carpenter or you sharpen tools in the blacksmith's shop, three dollars if you're a big bug like a foreman or an engineer. Well, you'll earn twice that here. The poorest miner in Virginia City won't strip off for less than four scads. Us girls *might* take off our shirts for six but only after we've squawked about it; we generally earn more per diem than a senator, and our reputations are less spotted in the eyes of the public.

The Empress was kept by a Mrs. Bird; she wanted for us to work the saloon for free, receiving no money and bestowing no favors but just, you know, being square company for the boys, writing their letters to sweethearts and mothers, sympathizing with their tragedies and falling in with their moods and humors. We were by way of an attraction; saloons are plentiful here, the company of females scarce; and Mrs. Bird had drink to sell. Before the bar closed we were to pull a sam in the bar and get up a jollification in the parlor. Then it was seven dollars a single jump, twelve to spend the night. Mrs. Bird took three dollars a day board. She had fired her whole crew of girls the night before, after one of them got sore and set fire to another girl's bed while she was asleep. She held the reference we showed her from Mrs. Liberty at arm's length, as she read it; it could just as easily be a fraud, she said, but unfortunately she was a trusting fool who got bitten every time.

The saloon opened onto D Street, but the backside of it (seeing the town is built on a mountain slope) was nearer to E; that was where the parlor and our rooms were, down some stairs at the back of the saloon. Ness and me bunked in one room, Sadie Marx and Cordelia took the other; and all hands declared themselves happy. But five days after we started at the Empress I ran out of Dr. Golly's Painless Medical Cure and was obliged to hide the bottle of Black Drop I bought, in case Ness found it and was disappointed in me. I snuck into my bedroom to have a sip of it, about a quarter after eleven, got back to the parlor to find Sadie Marx entertaining the boys in fine style.

Sadie Marx is a genius in a parlor full of gents. She talks about Tweed and the machine as though he used to boss New York City from her apartment; and if the boys like anything better than to talk corruption it's to talk corruption with a wicked-looking girl in a bodice while her breasts peep out like sleek-headed seals. When we gathered around the piano later, one of the mugs sang a song about a man that has lost his path in life and hopes the memory of his dear dead silver-haired mama will help him mend his ways. After he finished the lads wiped their eyes and the chump who had sung the song said, when he thought of his sins on the one hand and his dear departed ma on t'other, why, his soul shrank with shame like paper thrown on a fire.

"Thanks be," he said, spreading himself, "I do have shame. I'm not like some fellows that don't appear to know any different; maybe I was raised better, but I suffer the stings of remorse plenty, I can tell you. When I think of my mother waiting for me on the echoless shore" (he shook his head in dismay), "well, I expect I'll catch it, that's all."

Most of the time I'd sooner fuck a sam than listen to him.

"You know," I said, "that song makes me think of my own mother. I've been asking for her all over. Seems she's disappeared off the face of the earth."

"Well, what's her name?"

"Isobel McQueen."

"You don't say. There's an Isobel McQueen who's a waiter girl in the Last Chance, corner of E Street and Washington. I heard her sing once. You could have knocked me down. She had a voice as pure as a lark."

That sounded like Mama, all right. Soon as we got through, Ness and me skipped out for Washington Street.

"I didn't like it here at first," I said, "but now I think it's amazing. Don't you?"

"It's a mining town. I don't see anything to get enthusiastic about."

The atmosphere, that's what. The mines and the stamp mills are on the go day and night. When you're varnished, the pounding of the engines gets into your blood; it's like you're in the engine room of a big liner. It even smells good, even though it doesn't, if you know what I mean. "I wish you were a *little* happier," I said. "I suppose it's too much to hope you'd *abandon* yourself or anything."

"I'm happy enough."

"Didn't Sadie Marx look delicious tonight? I don't know what on earth you can mean when you call her a ghoul. She's the same as she always was, far as I can see."

"She's the most awful example I ever saw. I've seen it happen to other girls but not to someone I liked. Don't *you* get that way."

"What way?"

"It can happen in a day. They get scared to quit."

"I can imagine *that*."

"If a girl is scared to quit, well, she knows she *has* to quit else she'll get mean and hacked; so if she's afraid, it gets so she don't like what she sees when she looks in the mirror. She starts to drink all day. She don't know what to do with her cash, so she spends it for trifles. She's got no reason to keep humping but she's scared to knock off. That girl is a ghoul."

The Last Chance was shut. As we backtracked, I said, "Well, I'll know to quit before that happens. I'll see the signs."

"I hope you do."

"I will." I wanted to know how long I had left to enjoy myself so I said, "I'll quit just as soon as I've made my pile. That shouldn't take more'n five or six months."

Ness fell as quiet as the grass in the shadow of a tombstone. "Five months?"

"You'll wait for me, won't you? I got to have my fun first before I work in a dry-goods store."

Ness didn't say another word the rest of the way home and I snuck off to my room, feeling I'd let her down.

He was large as life and twice as ugly, sitting on Nessie's bed with the rum crate at his feet. The carpet was lousy with female articles that I suddenly wanted to tidy. I picked up my hairbrush and started tugging hair out of it.

I said, "Anybody see you get in?"

He started taking his knucks off. You don't see rings like those in any stores; they are so big and ugly they look false. I hoped he was taking them off so as not to hurt my looks *too* much, but he probably just liked the effect. He was righteous-looking, like I had what was coming to me. "You saved my life," he said, pressing his double chin tight against his neck. "I promised I'd pay you back."

He came toward me with those nude fists. I said the first thing that came into my head. "Where you been?"

He took ahold of my hair. "I been holed up in the Savage mine. One of the worked-out levels where the timbers are all over fungus and nobody goes. I been paying a boy to bring me some chuck. But they've about tracked me down."

"Who has?"

After he cracked my face on his knee I could feel the blood in my mouth, as thick as cream. "Last night they searched one of the other mines. The boy told me."

He banged my ear with his fist. When I dropped to my knees, he kicked the tar out of me. After he was through I lay on the floor, still holding my hairbrush. The back is glazed, white with blue flowers, and the rim is edged with gold. I studied it awhile. I had the serenity you get when it hurts to move and you can't do anything anyway.

"I'm going to leave the boodle here," he said. "Blab to anyone and I will stick a knife up your jam. The same if you hit the pipe. I will slice your titties off. It won't take more than two minutes. It won't take less either. Girls don't keep still no matter what you tell 'em. Catch on?"

He went away and I lay there till Ness found me. It was all she could do to keep from blubbering over me. Then she went and woke up Mrs. Bird, came back with a key, and locked the door behind her. Ordinarily, Mrs. Bird kept the keys to the rooms.

"He left the rum crate," she said in a cotton-wool hush.

I heard her open it, then two of the tins, quiet as anything. Then she pushed the crate under my bed, popped out to a pill shop, and came back with a bottle of Black Drop. I couldn't hardly open my mouth; when she offered me a spoonful, I made as though I wanted to push it away.

"Please," she said. "For me."

Her eyes were dark inkwells right at that moment you dip your pen in. When I took the spoonful, my mouth didn't work; I dribbled it down my chin. So she dipped her finger in it and put it in my mouth. As I sucked, I half remembered a poem I once read all about sherbets and concubines and heavenly pleasures, which had finished with the words "Paradise only sleeps."

SIX

Now, hats. Our first morning in Virginia City, who did we bump into in Phil Escobar's ice cream saloon but Rose Bulger—and Rosie's word was: Mrs. Jaffa. Well, if you're the turban kind, her store's at B Street near Taylor. If you're after something tonier, look up Niven's on C Street, opposite the Plata Hotel. Don't be smashed if the hats in the window are sickly-looking specimens and Niven's stewed to the eyeballs—take the fashion magazine you like and show him an illustration; he'll give it to Mrs. Johns and Mrs. Church and pretty soon you'll have yourself a whole parade of bang-up hats, built to order.

Five days after Pontius gave me that lacing, when I was presentable enough to leave my bed, Ness said why don't we go to Niven's as a treat. I was in rather slim spirits; all the way there I clung to Nessie's arm and felt rather bullied by people's elbows and dwarfed by the height of the quartz wagons. I didn't even order a hat, not until a girl we knew saw us through Niven's window and dropped in to give us tickets for a ball. The married ladies here certainly try their best, but they can only have so many affairs or even dance partners, so when three Missionary Fathers who were here to convert the heathen decided to get up a ball in aid of their funds and wished to boom the tickets, they put the fancy-girls on the free list—though all business was to be suspended for the duration of the ball by mutual agreement.

Some of the girls still have dreams about husbands but most have been married all they want. They still like to get dressed up for a ball, though, and have a knock-down-drag-out fight with their lovers in front of all the other girls; and *we* were keen because we were newcomers and wanted to see who all was in town we might know from San Francisco. Only Ness had no appetite for the thing. When we were in our room getting ragged out, she sat there in her silver dress and studied her reflection in the looking-glass. "I don't know why I'm going to this ball," she said. "I'm tired of men and I can't dance any." In the carriage she seemed in a trance. When we stopped, I touched her hand and told her we'd arrived. She fiddled with her necklace and said, "To think I been married twice already." Then she despaired of herself, nipped her cheeks into bloom, and dived into the hall.

There were too many men and they were all on the marry. They pinched your dance card, scored out some names and wrote in their own, then dragged you onto the floor and flung you about till you looked like biled laundry. Soon as one dance was over they swarmed all over you; there was no relief from them except you holed up in the ladies' lavatory, where I tore up my dance card and condoled with the other wore-out gals.

"Guess who's here?" Sadie Marx said. "The chief of police."

"You're gassing me."

"He's here with some dame he's having an affair with."

"An affair, your granny," another gal cut in. "That's Mrs. Messenger. The chief's wife runs the Episcopal Ladies' Mite Society, and they're having a mass meeting tonight. He brought Mrs. Messenger 'cause she's a widow."

Sadie Marx said, "*She's* keen on *him* anyway. Anyone can see that much."

"I don't care how cops conduct themselves on their nights off," I said, "but the amount of grease they collect off us gals is scandalous. I'd like to get him in a corner and give him jesus."

"I'll introduce you if you want," one of the girls said.

And right away somebody pulled me and somebody else pushed me and before I knew it we were piling into the supper room, all in a tangle, excited that something was going to happen we could talk about tomorrow. My hair got afoul of some girl's bracelet, and while we were being untied the gals pointed out the chief of police and Mrs. Messenger. She was a small woman in her forties with a face that was not much older than it had been twenty years ago, you could imagine, and no prettier.

"Dol McQueen," I said, and offered my hand.

"Pleased to make your acquaintance, Miss McQueen. Chief Duffield." He'd lost his right arm; after he gave me his left hand to shake, he threw his shoulders back and presented that missing arm like a soldier standing to attention. "This is Mrs. Messenger."

"I'm here in behalf of the flash-girls," I said. "We have a beef about the cops."

Mrs. Messenger had thin skin that revealed everything. She had been disappointed in her hopes tonight and was trying not to show it. The effort was tiring her out. "If you want to give him a piece of your mind, you go right ahead," she said, trying to be humorous. "I won't rush to his defense. He hasn't danced with me once tonight."

"I don't mind paying taxes," I said, "but what do I get for it, is what I want to know. Cops who call around to choke more money out of me. You know what eats me the most? The way they smile when they call to collect their boodle. They're exactly like ladies on the goody-goody racket."

"Well, what have you got to say for yourself, hey?" Mrs. Messenger stood right beside me. She practically took my arm. "Seems the whole town is disappointed in you; the female part, anyway. We don't ask much. All we want in a man is a thorough integrity; a police chief, especially."

Duffield gave himself a little room. "I'm afraid I can only assure you of my own integrity."

Mrs. Messenger had the softest, brightest cheeks and a hard mouth. She had squirreled away a hoard of disappointments in her time. "If we could be certain of that it would be something."

"As for the men I command, they have no principles of their own and I can't seem to make them adopt mine. They're not necessarily *bad* in a moral sense; but if they were a better grade of man they would get better jobs, that's the simple truth of the thing. And on the whole they can't control their appetites."

"Can't you do anything about them?"

"I don't know if either of you two ladies ever had lice in your shirts," he said, keeping a solemn, god-almighty face, "but believe me, there's not a thing to be done about it except you burn your shirt, or fling it to a nest of red ants. Now, Miss McQueen, if you'll excuse us," he finished, and took Mrs. Messenger off to the dance room.

But before he went he winked at me, as if we might have a more satisfactory and better-informed discussion on the subject if we were alone.

53

I was making my way back to the girls when I spotted Ness sitting with a young black man. He was good-looking, broad around the shoulders but dainty in his movements; and right then the two of them put their feet together to compare sizes, like young persons flirting at a church sociable. He looked the sort that might compliment middle-aged ladies on their go-to-meeting hats; when he couldn't find something handsome to say about Nessie's monstrous feet, he stroked his chin. It was strange to see a young man stroke his chin. Then he stood up, told her he'd be back (I guessed), and left the supper room. Ness stretched her neck to follow his progress but, after he'd gone, a solid body of men almost crushed her against the wall. She was hard pushed to keep his seat, and placed a hand on it that showed off her evening sleeves (short, to the elbow) and her long, elegant arm. Some lad grabbed her other hand, got down on his knees, and proposed to her. He was still hard at it when her young colored man returned. Ness listened to the proposal with one arm on the rack, and touched the velvet nap of the free chair with the tips of two long fingers till her fella took the hint and sat down. Then she flatted the marriage proposal and gave the young black man all her attention. Her face was like a cake that was all lit up with candles. I couldn't tell if she was playing him or not; either way it was sickening, so I went outside.

A wind was getting up; the rattling of stovepipes was a bigger racket than the dance. Two gals I knew from San Francisco, Willy Crowe and her small fat pal Desdemona Ball, came scooting out and headed for the hack stand, holding on to their hats in the wind.

"Where you going?"

"Nan Connolly's birthday party."

The girls have pretty loose morals in regard to their birthdays. "What was wrong with the birthday she had two months back; didn't she break enough windows?"

"Say!" Desi Ball said, pointing at a hack that was pulling up outside the hall. "Ain't that your ma? She looks pretty good considering."

I said, "Considering what?"

"Didn't you hear? She was waiting in a saloon till she got fired two days ago. Now look at her. That gal won't be licked."

Mama was drunk but dignified. She had on a night-blue ball dress and wore her hair up at the back, pinned by a comb six inches high, in the fashion of aristocratic Mexican women who are married. She had come in an open carriage with two men I knew from the Empress, the drunken law firm of McNattan & Mudd, who were proving to be a disappointment to her. McNattan fell out first. Mr. Mudd propped him against a lamppost then went to attend Mama. McNattan straightaway dropped to his knees, arms by his sides. For a few moments it seemed he would remain upright, but unluckily for him he has a colossal brain; soon as he leaned forward from the perpendicular just one inch, the weight of it overbalanced him. He fell, arms fixed by his sides, and smacked the sidewalk with the full of his face. Mama, as she was handed out of her carriage, gave him the smallest glance and swept royally past. She didn't appear to see me, either.

"Mama!"

"Are you addressing me, dear?" Sometimes she makes out she doesn't know me.

"It's Dol," I said. "Your daughter."

She has a long neck and a commanding manner. "I don't think so, dear. I believe I would remember a mulatto love child.

Well, these gents are my legal agents and executors, if you wish to make a claim on my estate, but don't waste *my* time." And she sailed into the Freemasons Hall, leaving me in the hands of her lawyers. Mudd was busy hauling McNattan up the steps, backward, while letting me know by the dirty look he gave me that he did not tolerate fools or charlatans.

It's hard to explain what it's like when your mother pretends not to know you. I don't know why she does it. I mean, when she gets off a good one at my expense and then plumps herself up, I can see the enjoyment in that, but where's the fun in acting like I don't exist? It's just peculiar. On this occasion I decided to be calm and humorous about it and laugh out loud. But that made me feel stupid. Why was I laughing? Nobody had said anything funny. I took a turn up and down the street and let the wind play with me. There was no way for me to even things, that's what riled me; I could pretend *she* didn't exist, but she probably wouldn't notice.

When I went back into the dance hall she was in conversation with Chief Duffield; he was laughing so loud he was obliged to lift his head back and let it out to the ceiling. They made a good couple. My mother has the kind of shoulders and bust a ball dress likes to display, and he put you in mind of a man who likes to pitch into his food with his sleeves rolled up. He was stocky and energetic.

I sashayed up, took Mama's arm, and smiled at Duffield. "Can I introduce you to my mama?"

That set him back; he gunned our faces for a resemblance. I smiled and looked as dainty and creole as I could. "Didn't she tell you about her mulatto love child?"

"She was born at sea," Mama said, trying to make a humorous anecdote of me.

"In a ship called the *Josephine*," I said.

"And what sort of vessel was she?" he asked.

"She was a double-masted brig in the guano trade," Mama said drily.

"That was the start of our adventures," I said. "If nothing else, I learned to be independent. Mama says, when we were on board the *Infanta* bound for Rio, I was two years of age or along there and liked to box the sailors' ears, make them take me way up into the rigging. Ain't that pretty?"

"And how was your mother entertaining herself while the life of her only infant was hanging by a sailor's pigtail?"

"She would wave to me," I said bouncingly.

"She always picked the most obliging sailors," Mama said. "She had an instinct for it."

I said, "I suppose you know what a bigamist is? Mama's a pentagamist. Listen!" I exclaimed. "A Scotch reel. You could ask me to dance if you like."

As he offered me his arm, Mama said: "I'd be glad to teach you some Scottish songs. Which ones do you already know?"

This was something they'd been discussing before I interrupted them. He said Mrs. Messenger—who had a passion for all things Scottish—had taught him two, but he didn't doubt Mama would know the ones with the sweetest airs and the most romantic lyrics; and he would be sure to call on her. He was often asked to sing at suppers got up by the local Scottish society, he said, and it would be a good joke to surprise them. I supposed he was being polite and that when he turned away from her to take me to the dance floor he would tip me a wink. But he didn't. He'd been serious about it. He was quite stiff, as a matter of fact.

Well, now; I daresay you never danced a reel with a one-armed man before. Say I was supposed to take his arm; I mean, suppose I was supposed to take his missing arm, he would look at me as much as to say, "Don't tell me you never had the pleasure with a one-armed chap before. Or perhaps you're dazzled, perhaps you're thinking that's the handsomest stump you ever saw." He made a feature of it. He flirted with it. He did more with that stump than most men can do with a whole arm. With his good arm, he didn't fling me around as some men are apt to, but kept me within the compass of his strength, and for so long as we kept her up it seemed to me all hands were looking on and applauding, bar Mama.

Duffield and I had four dances in all and faded the other couples. Even his face seemed attractive. He had red cheeks and a thick face that had been flattened in a round pan—but there was nobody else you wanted to look at. Then "Ladies' choice!" was called and there was a terrible commotion. In the thundering stampede one of the girls got a bloody nose, but in the end the ladies got lined up along one wall, the gents along the opposite one. They outnumbered us three to one but Mama led the charge handsomely and the ladies were as pretty and dashing as anything. I loitered in the rear to see what she would do. I mean, I wasn't going to fight with her. She chose Duffield, and I walked off the floor and stood at the side with Mrs. Messenger, who had been to the cloakroom to get her things and was putting them on.

She had little blond curls that seemed a bit girlish now she was in her forties, and her ball dress and cloak were prettier than she was. At the close of a ball there's always a few miserable females who look like they can't wait to get home and shuck the gorgeous clothes they had such high hopes of, but Mrs. Messenger knew people were watching her and for the life of her she wasn't going to appear mean or sour; so she stood there and clapped her gloved hands in time to the waltz—tiny miniature claps—and smiled, the way old women do when they want to join in.

Duffield waltzed Mama first-rate, and she shot me as many triumphant looks as she could get off. All hands gave a good account of themselves, even Ness. Generally men maneuver her around a dance floor like she's a rolled-up carpet that's taller than they are, but the handsome young black fellow made light of her. In his arms she only seemed a trifle behind. Then came the last dance and, after all the spurious excitement, the ball fizzled out without any consequences to anyone.

Outside the hall the wind had gotten stronger and wilder and the whole crowd was blown away in ten minutes. The young black fellow said goodbye to Ness at the hack stand without kissing her; Mrs. Messenger could barely hold up to the wind and Duffield was obliged to see her home. He said goodbye to both Mama and me without favoring either of us over the other, except perhaps that his last look was for me. Mama had disappeared into the depths of the ladies' cloakroom after the last dance and reappeared a good deal drunker than before. Soon as Duffield made his exit her face collapsed like a marquee when they take the main pole out. She could barely work her tongue. Since she had no address that she could remember we took her back to the Empress and let her bunk in with me and Ness.

The wind grew and grew and I didn't sleep very well. I was glad to have found Mama at last and wanted to lie awake and enjoy the feeling she was in the same room as me. It was quite a storm got up. I was varnished, and it seemed to me it was a shoulder-hitting bully who had come to town on the fight, fixed with chains and steel hooks. He threshed canvas awnings and banged on stovepipes and tore at roofs, but he wanted more than that. He didn't know *what* he wanted, and that got his mad up; he started in worse than before, wrecking the streets. I even thought I could hear someone outside yelling and banging on a door, begging to be let in. I woke up about six in the morning to find the storm had slackened off and my mother had gone.

SEVEN

"Why does she act this way?" I complained. "I take her home and give her a bed and she disappears in the night like she woke up and found she was in a room with strangers. She's supposed to be my mother."

Ness was having buttered biscuits and eggs for breakfast but she couldn't enjoy it much because she had to listen to me and be sympathetic. She has a sick mother in Missouri that she left to die. She only told me about it once, sitting on the side of her bed bent over like a half-shut penknife. She said her ma knew she was planning to skip out; she had a suspicion anyway. "Ness, don't sneak away and leave me like cat shit under the stairs," her ma had told her. "You'll know what you done."

But Ness shabbed out. She's had a bad conscience ever since, that's why I can depend on her to listen to me. She suggested we could go see Paul Rikehart, who keeps the Last Chance, and find out what he knew of Mama, the last accounts.

After the damage done by the tempest, all sorts of repairs were going ahead that morning; people in the streets had an unsure look about them, like they'd been blown here from some-where else. When we made E Street and Washington, Rikehart showed us into the tiny room he used for an office. We stood with our backs to the walls, with hardly more room than we would have had in an elevator. Rikehart was huge. He wore a suit with a fob watch and had to stoop to fit in the office. He said it was true, he'd given my mother the sack; somebody had been stealing whiskey and fronting up the bar with bottles that were mostly tea, and some of the barkeeps had come under suspicion, the dumb ones anyway. After Rikehart had watched the saloon like a detective for two full days, he warned Mama he'd about traced the whole thing home. Everything seemed to be fine after that, he said, he thought she'd hollered on the racket, until the day young Brad Ireson got plugged by Rod Korns.

I'd heard about that. Mrs. Korns had gone crying to her husband when Ireson gave her the bounce and Korns shot the unfeeling bastard as he was buying steaks in the butcher shop.

Rikehart said that Ireson tried to walk home from the butcher's, but dropped to the ground right outside his saloon. The dying man got carried in and laid out on the counter of the bar, and Rikehart didn't know what else to do with him, he said, except take off his boots so he would die decent. The whole of the saloon was watching the tender scene when Mama went back of the bar, past three barkeeps, the doc, and the dying man, swiped a bottle of whiskey, replaced it with a more teetotal bottle, and slid. Paul said it was just supernatural the way she done it. He said she didn't appear to know she was a human being in the midst of other human beings (with her weird white skin and hair that was almost orange she was more visible than most), and next day she arrived at work as if nothing had happened. She didn't recollect nipping the whiskey or being fired or anything.

After Ness and I left Rikehart's, we didn't say much. We stopped at some D Street bars and flash-houses where I tried to find a berth for Mama. No go. Seems she'd tried to shove coun- terfeit whiskey at two bars before Rikehart's, and people talk to one another. Even Jerry Klopstock turned his nose up at her and his nose has been broken twice.

Nobody knew where she was anyway. In the Empress the next day I asked McNattan if he'd seen her anywhere. He was standing at the bar not talking to anyone, alone in that vast brain of his. The more he drank, the more it expanded, and he'd been at it for days. He gave me a withering look like the information I was looking for would take an hour to find and did I really want to put him to all that trouble. "I wish I'd never seen her at all," he said, and turned his back on me.

That night me and Ness were in our room, getting changed for the parlor, when I got such an ache in my stomach I could barely move. I didn't know what to take for it seeing I was pretty gonged already. "I don't think I can screw anyone tonight," I said. "I got a lump of lead in here that won't shift."

There was a small silence. "You take too much of that missy. Can I get you some medicine?"

"Some bad whiskey might help."

"What will that do?"

"Burn it?" I was in agony. "Make it the worst whiskey you can find."

She brought me back some alcohol that Mrs. Bird used to clean her tub, and I necked it. It burned right down to my toes. It was horrible at first but then I bust out and laughed. It's a wonderful feeling when you know how you work.

"That's fixed me," I hooted. "Just don't come too near. I'm inflammable." I leaned forward to look at myself in the dressing-table mirror. "Seems other people know more about her than she does herself," I said. "How do you help someone like that?"

Ness was using the mirror too; she had hairpins between her teeth and a fixed expression in her eyes. "Someone like who?"

"Mama."

Ness took the pins out of her mouth. "Nothing anyone can do if the person is oblivious to her situation." She peered deep into the mirror and started in fussing up her hair.

"I don't agree with that," I said. "I'll make her listen if I can find her."

Things were a little strange in the parlor that particular evening. Almost since the first night we started here Ness had been working one particular sam like a mine. His name was Ed Stainback; he was a locksmith. He was shortish—five feet five or so—but that was the only thing small about him. He had a huge head, big lips, long arms, and a nose that was wide and thick and fleshy. He wore a robe and lounged around the parlor in a loose, open-legged kind of way that made you imagine he had an enormous dick. He was a strange customer. He would arrive like Papa, with some sheet music for Cordelia and candy for Ness. In the parlor he would step on the other boys if he didn't like their manners or their jokes, and generally he treated them with the ill-concealed contempt and bad grace that a father might show to his daughter's suitors. At other times, in humorous vein, he'd feel your tits, passing-like.

It's difficult to be too strict about a person like that—a flash-house only works if people allow each other their freedom of belief. The boys, for instance, like to suppose that all hands gather in the parlor of a flash-house for a sociable evening of fun and fucking; and even the dumbest and worst-tempered of the girls is apt to believe she's good company. Both parties can keep their illusions if everyone hands each other some Santa Claus for a couple of hours and there's plenty booze. But what do you do when someone actually believes in it?

Ness has a birthmark on her backside that looks like a daguerreotype of someone's grandfather, and sometimes she displays the phenomenon for the fun of the thing. People have a different character naked; Ness is easier and more humorous, and everybody agreed she played her part with great wit and was no way outshone by her ass. We were calling for an encore when Ed Stainback ordered her out of the room. He was mad at her.

"Those two are so peculiar they could be married," Sadie Marx joked.

Mrs. Bird smoothed down the boys by pouring them drinks and making nothing of it, but in an undervoice I heard her say to Sadie, "She's seeing too much of him."

That was the first I knew it wasn't just me who was concerned, and right then I made a decision to straighten Ness out. She slept with him too often. She humored him too much. When he ordered her out of the room, she went. I lit a hasheesh cigarette, handed it to my mug to keep him occupied while I was away, and slipped out of the parlor. I had nothing on that rustled. I stood outside our room and stretched my ears. He was telling her how hard he worked. There was the slow drag of self-pity in his voice. He was talking about freight prices, due bills, a combination lock with four tumblers he'd made for Sydenham's safe that Sydenham reneged on when it came time to pay. After all that, didn't he deserve better when he came home? All he wanted was to see his girl happy. I kept waiting for

Ness to tell him he was loony but she didn't, even when he began to talk more slowly and with intervals between.

"Are you happy?" he kept asking. "Are you happy?" It was disgusting enough when I heard *him* making moans of appreciation and pleasure but I lost my mad when she joined in. I didn't like to imagine what she was doing—was she kneeling at his feet?—I reached for the door handle and broke in on them.

He was sitting on the bed with Ness standing in front of him, wearing nothing but her evening sleeves and riding boots. Her dressing gown was at her feet where she'd let it drop and she was touching herself. It was a few seconds before they saw me; they were in another world. Ness almost smiled, and I told Stainback to go take a walk. The house doesn't like you to talk that way to the sams and neither do they, naturally, but it was like I'd fired a shot; he didn't argue. After he went I looked Ness up and down, then at her robe on the floor.

"I'm beginning to think I don't know you. I don't know if you're blinding yourself out of greed or there's some other reason, but this one's a little loose in the head. I don't think you ought to see him again. I say that for your own good."

She made out she wasn't ashamed. She left her dressing gown on the floor, went and sat on the edge of her bed, practically naked.

"Do you *enjoy* fucking him?" I said. "You've gone to bed with him every night lately."

"Not every night."

"Five nights out of seven."

"I don't know. I didn't count," she said, twisting her silver evening sleeve.

"Can't you see he's jealous?"

It was as if I heard an echo saying, "*He's* jealous?"

"You're playing him for a mug," I said. "Don't complain if he gets annoyed about it."

"I don't see why you're throwing such a fit. What do you care about Ed Stainback?"

"I care about people," I spat at her.

That was so ludicrous the wallpaper cringed and curled up. Ness blushed for me, all the way down to her tits. Suddenly I could hardly look at her and she was trying not to look at me.

"Ness, will you for heaven's sake put on your robe?"

She was resting her head against the tobacco-colored wallpaper, her legs a little apart. She got to her feet and picked up her robe. Her arms seemed slim in those evening sleeves but her shoulders looked wider and farther apart. "My," I said, "your shoulders are as broad as that young black fella you met at the ball. Did you tell him what you did for a living?"

"He didn't ask."

"You were talking all night. Why not?"

"He wasn't interested, I suppose," she said after a pause.

"Maybe he guessed. Maybe he didn't like to ask."

"Anyway, he didn't," she said. "Look here, I better go find Ed, but I been meaning to say to you, he heard where your mother's been staying."

"Where?"

"McNattan and Mudd's." She pulled her robe closed with her fist. "They asked him to change the lock to their door today. They want shut of her, I suppose."

Why couldn't McNattan have told me that?

That night I took more missy than usual, had waking night-mares, and only slept a couple of hours; my head was still full of bats when Ness and I set out next morning for the legal office of McNattan & Mudd on B Street. The pair of them lived off an inheritance, people said. They knocked about the bars till four in the morning, shooting off their mouths about harmony and social evolution before crawling home to sleep under their desks. They had bedrooms upstairs but they seldom made it there, according to the help. We found the place without any difficulty, a smart two-story frame house, painted a ghostly blue. In the hall a very slim clerk was squeezed between a desk and a wall. He held his head high and to the side, as if his purpose was to see as little as possible. He gave the impression he would be very strict if he made an inventory and found a pencil was miss-ing; he was only able to relax a little when there was utter pan-demonium, as now.

At first I supposed the ruckus behind the door to the left was Mama bawling at someone who was threatening her person with violence or eviction, but after a couple of minutes I still hadn't heard a peep out of the other person. Slowly it dawned on me there was nobody else in the room with her; she was cre-ating the shindy all by herself. It was eerie. Everyone else in the house had stopped what they were doing to listen to her. The door to Mr. Mudd's office was open; he was sitting across the desk from a client, a large woman with a small pretty face, but they had suspended their business to listen stary-eyed to the din Mama was making.

Suddenly she bust out of the room to the left, swept past without seeing us or noticing the clerk, and headed for Mudd's office to lay into him. She had cuts near her ear and at the back of her head that she didn't appear to know about, judging by the regal way she held herself.

"It's enough to upset a person's reason. Of course, that's exactly what he wants," she said to Mr. Mudd's client. She pointed at Mudd with a shaky hand and yelled, "He's trying to unhinge my mind." Her nerves were raw and so was her voice, and there was something raggedy about her movements, the way there is when she's had a little liquor but not enough. "Only a legal brain would have the—I was going to say the cunning—the convolutedness to hire someone to break into his own house and place of work. Don't deny it," she shouted when Mr. Mudd protested, "you wanted to terrorize me. He hoped to frighten me out of my senses, dear, so he paid someone to break in through the window while I was sleeping, take money from my purse, and pick his way through my possessions. Can you imagine the derangement of my thoughts when I woke up and saw a scene of such squalor?" Mudd's client was a big, cushion-hearted woman who, out of habit, I suppose, had leaned forward to sympathize with Mama. Now she was stuck. She smiled, but watched Mama the way a small dog watches someone who's slapped it.

Mama said, "I see what you're thinking, dear: Can't he keep her better chained?" She gave a short loud laugh, but then she saw that she had struck the large woman's thought exactly. "That *is* what she thinks. She doesn't believe me. You don't think Mr. Mudd would stoop that low, is that it? I'm afraid a few short weeks ago I was as naïve as you, dear, but I've learned a dreadful lesson about the character of lawyers," she said. "And I can show you the evidence." She took the ample woman by her wrist and dragged her out of the office, back past us. Well, Chaos draws everything in its train. Mudd pushed back his chair and started after them, followed by me and Ness. The slim clerk, whose neck seemed strained from keeping his head in the air, was obliged to watch us from a very obtuse angle. His lips were pouted like he was about to whistle a pleasant tune.

Mama was evidently using the half-furnished room as a bedroom.

"Look!" she said, and covered her mouth with a handkerchief. "Look at the uproar."

There were clothes all over the wash stand, the folding bed had been tipped up on its side, there were drops of blood just everywhere: the carpet, her clothes, the wash basin. In some places it was still the original red; on the wood floor it had turned brown or black. Almost the whole window was gone except for a large jaggedy near-triangle of glass that was still attached to the upper part of the window frame. It hung there like a guillotine waiting to drop. There was blood on the bottom of the frame. She bent down to look more closely at it, then drew herself back as if she was going to faint. "There's pieces of material caught in that glass. How on earth did he get through that without bleeding to death?"

I wondered how long it would take her to notice the cuts on her head and the blood on her dress and see a connection between the window and herself.

"Does this not give you the shivers?" she said. She was still holding the large lady by the wrist but suddenly she saw there was no need. Her face was a pillow of sympathy. Mama grew more confident, and sarcastic. "Seems strange he didn't tamper with anything in Mr. Mudd's office," she observed to her new ally. "If a burglar breaks into a lawyer's office, you might suppose he'd ransack the room where he'd most likely find money and consols and other documents of value."

"What did he take?" her friend asked with hushed concern.

"Take?" Mama dropped down in a chair. "I'll tell you what he's taken. He has broken in here" (tapping her head) "and stolen my peace of mind. Who can I trust now?"

"You have some bad cuts on your head, Mama."

She felt of it with her hand. "As if I didn't have enough troubles."

"You're probably cut all over if you broke in through that window," I said.

Her hand came down and rested on top of her knees. She noticed the front of her shirt-waist and skirt were scarred, and I could tell by the way she smoothed her dress that her knees were scraped and her hands torn. "Why would I break in to my own place of abode?" She straightened her back. "I never heard anything so ludicrous."

But part of her suspected the truth. "Mr. Mudd here got a new lock," I said. "You couldn't get in any other way."

In the space of half a minute all the snap went out of her. She stared at the window, bewildered. She didn't notice anyone leave the room. And when Ness and I told her Mrs. Bird had a situation at the Empress she was looking to fill, she followed us there without a murmur.

EIGHT

Before she started work in the saloon that first night I told her a few home truths. I said the other saloons and flash-houses in town had closed her out and this was her last chance. I said I didn't expect her to swear off liquor altogether so long as she toned it down. It was about six in the evening and she was drunk in a very quiet way but she didn't want to hear any sermons from me, so she handed me one of her invisible sneers. Often when she's polluted she's too superior to sneer with her nose and mouth like an ordinary mortal, but back of those eyes she's looking down on you from a great height. After I got through lecturing her, she drank all she liked in the saloon and was a great hit with the boys. It was among the girls she caused ructions.

The day we had all got fixed up at the Empress, Cordelia said she was seventeen and gave Mrs. Bird the impression she was on the game like the rest of us. Mrs. B used to be a flash-girl herself; she's a slim thing with breasts so large they strain her back; she hazes around in a world of her own, full of plots and suspicions. If you take a rest break from the saloon she'll follow you anywhere you go. She'll open your bedroom door and catch you taking some drops and she won't say anything, she just looks at you. She keeps a tab on the whole operation like that, ghosting into rooms to pick up tidbits of information and spying in the most obvious way you can imagine. Anyhow, that first day Mrs. Bird looked at Cordelia and said seventeen was younger than she liked her girls but she was willing to make an exception since we were all friends.

But soon as Cordelia unpacked she went on the sick list and never looked like recovering. Mrs. B crabbed about her from morning to night.

You ever tried to wash a greasy frying pan in cold water? Mrs. Bird has a voice like that; it makes you want to give up. "She told me she was seventeen. You didn't contradict her. None a you did. What's the matter with her anyway? I don't reckon she knows the business end of a gal from a cupcake. She won't hump. She can't cook. She don't lift a finger, she can help it."

But she didn't make any moves; she was trying to figure out what would happen if she booted Cordelia out. Would the rest of us bolt? When me and Ness brought Mama to the Empress and asked if she could have the free berth, that was all Mrs. Bird needed to know—Cordelia was Sadie Marx's pet and nothing much to the rest of us. An hour after she started Mama, Mrs. Bird told Cordelia she could pack her things, and Cordelia forted up inside her room.

I told Mama she could have my bed for the night; I wanted her to be comfortable so she would stay. I slept on the floor. That way I could make sure she didn't go rooting under my bed in the middle of the night. The rum crate was hidden behind bandboxes and a small hill of shoes; nobody was liable to poke their noses into such a mess, except a drunkard on the prospect for some booze she thinks she's hidden there. While she snored in the bed above me, I got varnished and thought about the swag. All that pandemonium in a box excited me; it was as good as a cocktail whizzing through my blood. I knew it was dangerous—the kicking I'd got was still fresh in my mind, and back of this was something that scared Pontius—but sometimes when I'm gonged I have an immense feeling inside me that I can govern Chaos. I didn't have a plan just yet, just the first distant flashes of one.

Next day the war between Mama and Cordelia began. One of them would ambush the other and there would be yells and screams at intervals like they'd turned Indian. I made out to avoid Sadie Marx till the following afternoon in the saloon, when she walked over to my table. She drags her bad foot, but from the waist up she carries herself like she is being watched by an admiring public. I thought she was going to roast me about Cordelia; instead she said, "There ain't going to be a split-up, I hope."

"Me too," I said.

"She seems dead set on it."

"Who?"

"The soul saver she met at the ball, he cut you out. He turns out to be a teamster. No kid. He hauls flowers, would you believe. The two a them's going to open a florist's." She saw my face. "You didn't know?"

"When did this happen? She never mentioned anything to me."

Sadie put her weight all on one foot. "Ness don't take the interest in you she used to?" she said, like the same thing had happened to her. "That's what happens when you ain't in the chips."

Ness was out meeting a lawyer about something, so I couldn't find out the truth of the matter. To stun myself I bought a rum, threw it back, bought another, downed it. Then I went to my bedroom and stood with my forehead against the wallpaper. The tobacco-colored flowers have lovely leaves, and I picked one. Back in the saloon I got stuck with a young miner who was getting corned on his own. His buddy had fallen out of the elevator cage that day while being lifted to the surface. They had brought him back up in candle boxes, he told me. It didn't have the same effect when he told me for the seventeenth time but I couldn't bring myself to walk away. I was too miserable. It was almost nine o'clock before Ness came into the bar, and right away she got ambushed by Charlie Cooke and the B Street Baths crowd, who wanted her to shoot craps. Ness doesn't see too good, she's always looking about her as though she's been kidnapped and has no idea where she is; she wasn't any different this particular night, so I had no way of knowing if her conscience was bad.

When you believe you've been betrayed you want to know for sure and you don't want to know the least little bit. You examine the evidence from as far away as you can get. Anyway, I couldn't think of anything to say that would upset her as much as I wanted to upset her.

In the parlor after shutting-up time she sat beside me on the sofa and said, "I'm going on the German picnic tomorrow. Can you come? Something amazing has happened."

I was tempted to lie and say I was busy but I didn't have the strength.

The fellow I hooked that night was Gedney, the druggist. I wanted to rush him through express so I could sit by myself and figure out what to say to Ness next day, but it was no go.

After the failure of his first attempt, he asked if he might place a pillow o'er my head. He had a bad-tempered face so I said a pillow was fine by me. He went at it another twenty minutes but he still couldn't get his gun off. He said it was generally easier when he was on his own and he wondered how I would feel if he put a smutty picture on the pillow that was o'er my head. I said go right ahead and he got one out of his jacket pocket that he'd evidently brought for the purpose. He went at it again fifteen minutes more, in total silence, till I started in chunking the mattress with my fists, I was that mad. I don't know if that's what did the trick but he came at last.

Maybe a thousand Germans paraded out of town next morning to a spot in the hills and listened to a German manufacturer make a speech about the war in the States. He said he didn't reckon the newspapers of this great nation would have the audacity to call his countrymen "Dutch cowards" now, not after the boys of south St. Louis and Chicago had gone down to Tennessee three short weeks ago and gotten in that mix at Pittsburg Landing and Shiloh (*a frisky cheer from the crowd, which the sober half straightaway regrets, remembering so many had died*). And it wasn't just the St. Louis Germans who perished (*the roar fades out entirely*). The Louisville boys of the 6th Kentucky and the lads of the 32nd Indiana also had laid down their lives on that dreadful battlefield (*silence*), for the cause of freedom. And if any young man present was to be mustered into the California Volunteers now being raised to protect the Union from the secessionists, that man would have the deep and abiding gratitude of all his countrymen, German and American both (*deep-throated approval and applause*).

It seemed to me the manufacturer was getting all stirred up about something awfully far away but Ness listened like it was her solemn duty to understand the meaning and import of every word, and by the time the band started up I already had a headache. The boss German river is the Rhine, and we listened to the band playing drinking songs in its memory. I can only suppose the music hadn't acclimated to these hot and dusty hills, because it wasn't harmonious.

"You thought I'd be happy for you?" I said. "Sure, I am. I thought we'd agreed to set up in business with each other, that's all."

"You didn't seem in any hurry about it."

"I don't even know this party's name."

"Dig Squiers. We hooked up for a morning chocolate and talked about the eternal things in life, *Pilgrim's Progress* and money and that. Before I knew it we were business partners."

"You suppose he's on the level? I mean, I appreciate you only banged into him about two days ago, but do you know *anything* about him?"

"Well, he was just a boy when he came west."

"Ship?"

"Wagon train. They was cholera in the States that year. It tracked them into the wilderness; they were burying the dead in floods. He says you can't get lost on that road. Two thousand miles cross prairie and desert from St. Joe, Missouri, to right about here, graves marking the road every step of the way. Mr. Squiers promised Dig freedom when they got to California but it was cholera redeemed him. He planted Mr. and Mrs. Squiers and three kids by the road. He was twelve years old. Then he drove a wagon over the graves so the wolves and the Indians wouldn't find them, else they would rob 'em."

"I can't hardly hear you, the racket that band's making."

"He was twelve years old and all alone when he got to California. He tried his luck in the gold-diggins, then cashed in his pile to buy a wagon and mule. He says in them days they was more dust to be made in teaming than digging the gold. Miner camps sprung up any old place they struck pay dirt. The miners needed sheaves of shovels and stacks of drills, and wearied to get tobacco, and billiard tables, and papers written in all the languages under the sun. Prices? He says prices were self-raising."

"He's a go-ahead buccaneering business man, huh?"

"He just is. He's a self-made man."

"What's he worth?"

"Same as me. Together we have about a thousand dollars in bank."

I had twenty-two dollars at the last accounts. "That's a lot of dirt. Did he show you his savings book?"

She gave me a sideways look as much as to say there was nothing doubtful about *his* pile. "We'll make an agreement before a notary."

She said it would be a contract between business partners and separate from any other arrangements they might happen to make in due course, such as uniting their persons in the sacrament of marriage.

I said, "A florist's? You think that's a go?"

"The hotels buy flowers. And the ice cream saloons. The theaters, they got to have bouquets for the star actress and the foyer. Then there's church sociables and Masonic dinners and sewing-bee circles. You saw the marquees here, weren't the flowers lovely? And there's funerals, of course."

"We already got a florist's."

"Didn't you ever hear people complain about him? That funeral three days back, the gals bought out the store. The florist didn't have a single bloom left by ten o'clock. I never seen a funeral procession yet that didn't have one carriage full of wreaths."

"This is hopeless." I got to my feet. "Let's go somewhere quieter."

We moved away from the cranky band, past some kids in German costumes. She bought me a lager and we sloshed about looking for a rock to sit on.

"Did you tell Dig Squiers yet you go to bed with men for money?"

She blushed. "Yes."

"The two of you don't foresee any difficulty on that account."

"There's some things he would like to talk to his minister about." She was getting redder by the second. "He's handsome as Lucifer, don't you think?"

I was too sick of her to answer, and for two days after that we hardly spoke.

On the second day there was a muss in the bar. Now maybe in your neck of the woods cues and billiard balls are used to play billiards and pool. Maybe glasses and tumblers and bottles are for the purpose of drinking refreshments. Same here sometimes.

I didn't see how the argument started but all of a sudden Frank Husband whacked Paddy Crozier with the butt of a billiard cue, and scooted. Some boys got after him, and when they couldn't find Frank they took it out of each other. There was trouble in spots all evening long after that, and the smell men give off when their blood's up and they don't wash much. The mood I was in, I was hoping the place would blow. I happened to be leaning on the piano when two miners went for each other's throat and the long-faced sodomite of a piano player decided to make a humorous comment by playing some tune Franz Schubert composed in his coffin to while away the trip to the boneyard. When the boys chucked tumblers at him and the broken glass splashed onto the keys, he pulled out some salmon-pink gloves, put them on real solemn and showy, and started over playing the identical same tune. One of the glasses ricocheted and I felt a nippy sensation all over my cheek. Before I knew it, I was being hustled away to the parlor.

When Ness poked in and saw my face, she wanted to send for the doctor. I gave it to her dead. I said much she cared. I told her the sooner she crossed the river the better it would be for everyone else. I said she was going to be hideous lonesome over there. I said it was a desert. I said it was a rocky waste with pillars of rock by the name of Death and Destruction, and other pillars of stone worse than that named Home Knitting and Ladies' Temperance Meetings; I said German bands would sit on top a them pillars and play Rhinish tunes to their hearts' content and she'd have a headache all the livelong day and no one to chat with, barring ladies with baby buggies. I said I'd be pretty blue this side of the river, but least I'd have company. I'd have Sadie Marx and Cordelia (Lord help her), and Mrs. Bird would start another girl, Willy Crowe, maybe, and pretty soon we'd be scaring up fun, going to balls and bickering and making up. We'd be drinking till breakfast.

I said she'd be all alone in the world. She'd be all alone in the world *with a husband.*

NINE

That's when Ness said she'd had a bust-up with Dig. She was the palest you can be. She was so angry her skin hardly seemed to be there at all, and to make matters worse the bedroom stank of dying flowers. Duffield, the police chief, had been sending me bouquets for some reason. I'd run out of vases and saucepans, so the carpet was ankle-deep in cold dead lilies and blackened poppies that were soft and moist underfoot, like satiny river weed. It was as if I'd put them there on purpose to upset Ness now that her dream of a florist's was wrecked. She sat on the bed, straight and tall, as though she didn't intend to notice them.

"What was the hitch?" I said.

"He's been talking to his friends in the colored Methodist church. He leans on them considerable, I suppose, being alone in life. Mrs. Johns, Niven's maker, she's one of them."

"What did she say?"

"I have more money than she likes."

"She said that?"

"She squints at it."

"She doesn't like money?"

"Don't like how I made it," Ness said. "She believes the wages of sin are death."

"Even when you put 'em in a bank?"

"They're the wages of sin with interest, I suppose."

The atmosphere in the saloon didn't improve any as the evening went on. There was one mill after another. The boys had no room in their thoughts for girls, so we backed out downstairs to our rooms, all bar Ness; she said she could be just as miserable in the saloon as anywhere else. Meanwhile Mrs. Bird chose this particular evening to tell Cordelia that if she wasn't gone by the morning all her things would be thrown out on the street. But it's like I said, sometimes I can govern Chaos, and in the midst of all that pandemonium I settled down to write a poem for Ness.

The pressure per square foot was tremendous. From time to time there would be more trouble upstairs, and I'd hear a stampede of hooves on the floor above, but it didn't disturb my concentration in the least. It was the furnace I needed. I wrote lines and scored them out and wrote some more. Rhyme by rhyme I hammered it together, then beat out each line to the perfect length. The poem was all about me and Ness and our friendship, and how we would help and comfort each other until our tragic deaths. Only nobodies write happy poems.

Alas, sir knight, bewail thee!—alack!—and waleyday!

How's that for genuine antique? I had *shoon* for shoes and *affray* for fight, and just as I could feel the end, Cordelia dropped in.

She was quiet something fearful, had her arm in a sling. I felt sorry for her, but only for a moment. She was hogging a bed; what if Mama stormed out in a black humor and didn't come back?

I said, "You all right?"

She rolled her eyes and snapped shut my jewelry box. "I'm dying, seeing as you're interested."

"What's up?"

"Oh, nothing. Least, you'll say it's nothing. I have cancer of the breast."

"Again?" The last time she had cancer I whacked up three dollars to fee some smart-aleck doctor in a forty-dollar fur coat. He felt her diddies and diagnosed a nervous exhaustion, for which he prescribed high-grade opium and complete rest. "That's too bad," I said. "Does the sling help?"

"The sling's for my sprained wrist, funny." She kicked a vase of flowers over. The dirty water and dead leaves made a puddle. "I don't reckon that last doctor knew what he was looking for. Would you feel my breasts?"

"I don't know what it would accomplish."

"It would set my mind at rest."

"I'm writing a poem." She has tits like cold semolina. "Why don't you ask one of the boys to feel them?"

She slammed the door so hard it shivered behind her. Almost right away I had a premonition something bad was going to happen, and went after her.

Before she banged out the door, she'd nabbed some of Mama's clothes that were lying around. She went upstairs, blazed through the saloon, and dumped the clothes on D Street. Of course, that only relieved her feelings a small amount; she had to repeat the same thing again and again, and soon as Mama heard what Cordelia was doing, she went into Cordelia's room, took her things up to the saloon, and threw them all over the tables, the men, and the floor. The childishness of their behavior scared me; when people get that way there's no telling what they'll do next. There's nothing to hinder them—embarrassment, shame, nothing.

And of course, the boys in the saloon didn't need anything to touch them off. When Cordelia passed through the saloon with my mother's capes, Ralph Brand stood in front of her and said, "Never seen you before. Where've you been hived up?"

"I've been sick," she yelled. "Want to feel a cancer? I got a first-rate cancer right here if you do," she said, flinging him off. "How much'd you give to see a novelty like that? I need the money. Mrs. Bird wants rid of me 'cause I don't pay my way."

Ralph Brand was about twenty. He had a white cravat and a thin black beard interrupted by ugly red boils. "What age are you anyway?" he said. "You're a little young to have cancer of the breast, ain't you?"

She would have slit his throat if she'd had a knife; instead she stole his beer from under his nose and started downing it. Most of the boys thought this was funny, but Ralph Brand had too many boils to have a sense of humor. He drew his gun and said, "Hands up!" The boys sniggered when he said that, and Cordelia backed away from him, drinking from his glass and spilling beer down her chin and front, enjoying the appreciation of the crowd. Well, Ralph Brand is a wheelwright. He has broad shoulders that are stiff with muscle; he doesn't carry himself lightly. Slowly but surely he cornered Cordelia, and it got to where he would have to shoot her, just to save face. "Hands up or I shoot!" he said.

Cordelia belched. While the saloon roared with laughter, Ralph considered the problem, his forehead bulging like his muscles. He wanted to shoot her, bad, but somehow he knew he had to find a humorous way to beat her, and by a lucky chance something occurred to him at last. He went back of the bar, came back with a slops pail, and emptied it over her. The boys in the saloon banged the tables with their fists and punched each other on the shoulder; three of them took out their guns and got off some joyful shots at the ceiling. Cordelia stood at the bar, her hair soaked, and her clothes. The incident was over as far as the lads were concerned; but she still had the glass she'd taken from Ralph Brand and she smashed it on the bar rail.

She didn't *intend* to finish herself. She considered where to cut herself and put the broken edge of the glass to her arm carefully. Then she held it there a moment before she dug in. Nothing brighter than blood, it's dazzling. The boys gasped and silence dropped; Cordelia smiled at them with hatred and wanted a little more of their attention, so she gouged the glass into her arm just a little longer and a little deeper—the exact amount she thought she had to cut herself before people would take her seriously.

She liked the sight of all that blood. It was only when it kept pouring out that she got afraid and fainted dead away. We carried her downstairs, damming the blood and yelling instructions at one another that none of us heard. By the time the doctor arrived and starting in sewing her arm, we were all used up. Ness sat at the piano, playing a single note, her eyes full of Alice Lebo, and I noticed my jaw was sore. I'd been grinding my teeth to keep them from chittering. I couldn't get it out of my head, the way Cordelia had calculated the effect she would have, before she dug the glass into her arm. I couldn't put my finger on it but it seemed to me I'd done the exact same thing sometime in the past. There was something familiar about it, any rate.

After the doctor left, I wandered back to my room in a daze and tried to finish my poem. I had barely gotten used to the silence when Sadie Marx came in, scraping her foot behind her. She leaned back against the wall at the doorway.

"Mrs. Bird says Cordelia can bunk on the folding bed in the parlor from here on out. She wants two dollars a night for her." She waited. "I'm good for a dollar."

This way Mama could have a bed and there would be universal peace. I said, "Will Ness kick in?"

"No. She says a fifteen-year-old girl copies what she sees. She don't want her around."

After a few moments I heard myself say, "I'll go a dollar a day. I don't like her much but you got to admire her. She wouldn't die if you killed her."

Right away I knew we were friends again even though Sadie barely smiled. She pushed off the wall, said "Good," and sloped.

Well, now; I wonder if Tennyson gets through writing poems and says to himself, "Alf, old chap, you're some pumpkins!" After I finished my poem, I couldn't wait to read it out loud and hear Ness say it was lightning and wish it published in a ladies' magazine, but first I waltzed into the saloon and pulled a young'n. I was in a hurry to get through, but alas! The chump came before I got naked. The quicker the better, ordinarily, seeing as the sam's a stranger and Christ knows what. Howsoever, there's a Latin saying, *post coitum homo tristis est*, it means "after a fuck a man is too sad for anything." Well, here's a piece of advice in my experience: *post coitum homo wants his money back.* You have to be careful. As soon as By Grooter spent his load, I opened my eyes as big as big can be and told him what a pretty compliment he'd paid me. I was a long time consoling him. After a while he went as quiet as a stone, then said it wasn't fair and asked for a discount. He wouldn't leave till I went up to the saloon and fetched Giz. Giz is our bouncer; he had a shotgun and a bad earache.

I stayed in the saloon while Giz did the business; I wakened up about three in the morning. The silence rang with the after-echo of the roaring boys and there was a small lonesome pool of blood under one of the tables. I went downstairs and found Ness was awake with a bad pain in her gut. Ed Stainback had ponied up another twelve dollars for a night with her, and every time his snores stopped it sounded like he'd died. It was a dreadful disappointment each time he came to life again, and it wasn't the right atmosphere for verse, so I asked Ness to come upstairs to the saloon. We took some blankets; and there, by the tall light of a lamp, I read her the poem I'd written.

THE FLASK

In the secret of a forest underneath a milk-white moon
Danced a lady and her handmaid to some otherworldly tune;
Never did my lady think who might pass, what man or beast,
Or how his lips would hunger for her, how his eyes would feast
Unsatisfied, until she slept, and he could gaze at leisure.
From her dress he cut the buttons and from her breast a treasure,
The shyest curl of all her hair; then home and spread the tale.
    Years passed
—no secret forest now!—many a hellish squall and blast
Did strip it bare, and moan, and howl, and wreck, ere he came
    back.
Says he, "Ye wretched ghost or apparition, what evil here,
    alack?

What wicked sin or battle fought, what hideous affray?
And what of the lady I spied yon night in silver dress and shoon
  of gray
Who danced with the stars and made them dizzy, and smiled
  askew
Till morn did come and she had spun a lace of cobwebbed dew?"

"Alas, sir knight, bewail thee!—alack!—and waleyday!
My lady's dead."—"I saw," he said, "the stars last night in
  dreadful disarray
Hurl themselves about the skies with all their hair let down
Then throw themselves into the sea as though they meant to
  drown."
"After you came many; whose minds were fire, whose thoughts
  were ashen.
They kissed and bit and pinched her till she was mad with
  passion.
Her breast was overrun with eyes, her tongue swole up with all
  the lies;
Black and blue she went to them and said, 'Here is your prize.'
Twenty knights and none did recognize her, they took her for a
  twin
And called her name throughout the wood till silence made its
  din.
Here is where I found her dying, this the bower in which she
  lay;
These the hands that cooled her brow and this the heart that
  begged her stay.
From a silver flask I bade her sip precious drops of cobweb dew;

And when she asked me if I danced, if I danced still,
I answered, 'Yes, with you.'"

Soon as I finished the last line of my poem something tugged at my insides and it all came out. I split up and foundered. Ness put her hand on my back and said, "Hush, now. Hush," like she didn't know what to make of me. Neither did I at first. But halfway through the crying jag it struck me that this was the happiest I'd ever been, living with Ness and the other girls, and I didn't want it to end, and I was bawling like this because I suspected that pretty soon it would. When I was through, the saloon seemed colder than before and bigger.

"Do you like it? It's all about you," I said, drying my eyes. "You're the lady, I'm the handmaid."

Ness had both arms folded and clasped around her middle like she had a pain in the belly nothing could kill. "It's lovely," she pressed out. "I don't like the ending, that's all. It's too sad for anything."

"It's supposed to be sad."

"It's beautiful," she said, trying to make up.

"It's hard to believe in happy endings when you have a mother like mine. I'm surprised you still do. Did Dig Squiers make you happy in the end?" I sounded a little more venomous than I meant to.

After a little she said, "You know what he wanted me to do?" She took one arm away from her belly and pushed her hair back. But then the pain got worse than before and she doubled up. She talked like she was wearing a corset that was far too tight. "He said whyn't I move in with Mrs. Johns, his Methodist friend, she's a widow, and see how I liked it. See how I liked what, I said. It'd be a three-month trial, he said. I could quit *doing what I do* and see how I got along. He said Mrs. Johns could sew, cook, draw up a trial balance. She could learn me all them things."

It sounded like he wanted to put her in quarantine, and that hushed us for a minute. A drunk, who was maybe a street away, made a noise like a cow that's been separated from the rest of the herd. I said, "It's worse than I imagined over there. It's worse than heaven."

She leaned back as if the ache in her gut had toned down and she could move freer. "I still want to square it," Ness said. "I haven't hollered on that. I won't superintend another funeral."

"I had a good view of that. Cordelia didn't mean to cut herself as bad as she did. She got carried away."

"What if it was you?"

I laughed. "Why would I finish myself?"

"You seemed awfully sad about something, the way you were crying."

Mrs. Bird had come into the saloon while I was bawling my eyes out to see what all the racket was about and gone away without saying a word, that's how big the crying had been. It seemed remote already, though. You know when you see a volcano? You're impressed, curious, but that night in the hotel it's almost forgotten. It doesn't have much to do with anything. "I don't think I'm sad deep down," I said.

Ness was staring at me the way you do when you're in pain. "Well, I don't want to die young." She stood up. "I'd as leave have you for a partner as anyone. But you don't seem too struck on the idea. I suppose I'll just have to bunk in with Mrs. Johns, after all."

She started for the door.

"How'd you like to run a saloon?" I said.

"A saloon?"

I was surprised myself; I don't know why I'd never thought of it before. "I'll be glad to straighten up if we can go on a bat once in a while," I said. "We could all stick together in a saloon. There would be a berth for Mama. We could hire Sadie Marx if she liked. We know the bar-tenders that are bad and the girls that cut up. We know all the tricks. I mean, you're right, there's only one reason to enter the profession and that's to get ahead, and when you've made your pile you have to square it. But we can hardly start in talking dress patterns and joining glee clubs. How much you got in the jug, five hundred scads?"

"Around that."

"We could call it the No Rest saloon."

Ness tried to stay cautious. "Well, how much do you intend to throw in?"

"The same as you."

"How much you got now?"

I wasn't sure about the size of the lie I should tell. "I don't know *exactly*. Around two hundred and thirty-two dollars or thereabouts. I can find the rest inside a couple months, I guess."

Ness let her long hair fall over her face so she could hide behind it and look at me at the same time. Then she pulled it aside. "I've had two disappointments already. You better not let me down, Dol."

"I won't. I promise."

TEN

The following evening Jim Duffield strolled into the saloon, in a dark steel suit, and asked if I wanted to go to a show that was about to start. If we didn't entertain the boys in the saloon, evenings, Mrs. Bird docked us a dollar, so I said I'd better square it with her and she said she'd look the other way this once. The whole saloon was in a stir; the boys cheered when he handed me a bouquet of flowers and the pianist played "Hail to the Chief."

Mama behaved like a jealous fifteen-year-old. First she let on she didn't care a snap—took her hair down and put it up again. Then she decided to introduce herself to Duffield again. She left the table she was at and walked across the room with an alarming smoothness; because she was drunk she was thinking about where she put her feet and trying to avoid any hitchiness. Arrived, she took my arm like we were sisters or girlfriends and started in flirting with Duffield.

"Isn't she pretty?" she said about me. She straightened his waistcoat. "Don't you lead her astray. *You* know what you're doing but she's just a green thing"—she examined his buttons—"sour and hard!" she quipped, presenting a lot of front.

I didn't like how long Duffield lingered over the items on display—it struck me he had a humorous look about his eyes but a greedy mouth. She looked up at him from under her eyes and begged him not to break my heart, the villain, and he listened to her for a good deal longer than was necessary. But in the end he left with me, and by the time we took our box at the theater, I'd forgiven him. Ever had a standing ovation from four hundred lads? I was wearing a sassy little white beaver hat and got more applause on my appearance than the poor heroine, and Duffield sat down with a complete contempt for the acclaim of the audience and a vast amount of style. It was almost like taking a bow.

The boys liked Duffield because he was straight and hated crooked cops same as they did; I suppose it tickled them he wasn't simon-pure in his private affairs. I was beginning to feel a little different to them. I didn't want him to be corrupt all the way through, but I had to find five hundred dollars to make good my promise to Ness, and a police chief who was willing to relax his principles for a weekend might be the making of a gal with swag under her bed. I didn't underrate the difficulty of seducing him from his customary rectitude in public affairs; I took it as a test of my powers. Who could say what he might be tempted to do for a girl he was dippy about?

I got enough of the play after ten minutes. Did you see *The Maid of Kildare? The Sewing-Girl Seduced? Beulah the Abandoned?* It had the same plot as them. The villain wears a black cloak with a crimson lining and the heroine dies, only in a different costume. I suspected Duffield wasn't enjoying it either but I couldn't be certain, so we both sat there like a pair of stiffs. Then something sort of naked happened. It was a little like *Mazeppa*, did you see that yet? I saw it in San Francisco. The actress Adah Mencken takes the role of Ivan Mazeppa the Russian nobleman and the audience dozes through a big lot of speeches until the Russian nobleman is stripped of his clothes, and the boys perk up. Now, I don't want to raise your hopes, there was nothing as exciting as Adah Mencken's naked-costume; but the villain in the black cloak was having a secret affair with the heroine—in the wings. Whenever she had the chance, she scooted off and ran into his arms, and wept (foreseeing, I suppose, some tragic end), and he clasped her face. It was a whole show in itself, howbeit the acting was no better. She was a finger wringer.

I leaned toward Duffield and he bent his head so I could whisper into his ear. "Look at the canoodling in the wings."

Sitting in that box we watched our private show awhile. While the villain (played by Mr. Terence W. Quinn) was comforting the heroine (Miss April Delancey) in the wings, the heroine's mama (Mrs. Terence W. Quinn) was on the stage bewailing her daughter's fate, saying she'd sooner die than see the girl seduced and betrayed.

I said, "Who does the mother remind you of?"

The interval was difficult. Duffield had been cavalier about the public while looking down on them from the box, but in the bar he was more conscious. These were people he knew; brother Masons, no doubt, and women who worshipped in the same church as Mrs. Duffield. He gave himself less room than he generally did, though still more than most. He bustled through the jam, keeping his eyes on the backs of people's necks. At the bar he bought drinks for everyone without looking them in the eye. "Jerry! Livvy!—My treat, what'll you take?" Glasses of refreshments got passed over my head or spilled, and I stood there, unintroduced, about as happy as a girl with liquor in her hair *can* be. I knew he was ashamed of himself rather than ashamed of me, but it was just as unpleasant.

After the interval we watched the play another ten minutes, then I leaned toward him and said, "Let's go. You can take me to Pelosi's."

The entrance lobby of a theater has a particular silence when there's a show on and the theater is packed, and we didn't disturb it. He didn't like the scene I'd made and I was mad at the way he'd neglected me in the bar. The expression on his face was very faraway. That riled me even more but I wanted we should at least get a little acquainted before the night was over, so on the way to the coffee house I asked him if he read much.

"Some," he said.

"Well, what sort of thing do you like?"

Already he'd forgotten what we were talking about. "Pardon me?"

I gave him an example of book conversation so he would know what to do. "I'm partial to melancholy and melodrama, myself. Have you read Mrs. Stanley's *Cora the Captive*?"

He said no, he hadn't. And fell into a silence.

"Well," I said, stepping on every word with a great deal of contempt, "what was the last book you picked up?"

"I guess recently I looked into *The Voyage of the Beagle*."

"I like the title," I said. "Is it thrilling?"

He stirred a little at last and walked along with more of his usual ginger. "I'm an atheist," he said, "but to me it's a work of such wonder it ought to be classified as a work of religion."

I said religion was very well but I liked pirates, and did the author oblige? He did not, and we consigned Mr. Darwin to the district of hell reserved for authors who make up titles that hold out the promise of adventure, and dish up turtles.

After that he began to roll up his sleeves and enjoy himself, as if he'd remembered why he liked me. In Pelosi's we ordered two chocolates and I told him all about Chile and the port of Valparaiso, how the people in the poor quarter made knitting needles out of thorns; and how the old women would wear a piece of cloth over their shoulders that they got for a receipt, to show they had paid for a plot of ground in the cemetery. Then we talked about his travels. He had left the States when he was thirty, got to California with the gold excitement of forty-nine, thirteen years back. He'd been here right from the beginning.

"My!" I said. "Did you dig for gold?"

"A short while."

"How'd you lose your arm?"

"In installments." He put his good arm over the back of his chair and spread himself out a little. "Then I went back to the Bay and bought a schooner."

"Why?"

"I got her at a discount. The harbor that first year was jammed with vessels. Scows, junks, brigs. There was even an abandoned prison hulk. No ship that reached San Francisco could keep a crew when they imagined there were lumps of gold the size of a swollen fist lying about loose in the hills a hundred miles away. Some boats were run aground, some half-sunk. I turned the *Minnie Fantom* into a boarding-house. I had accommodations for twenty-three boarders below decks and fed them of a morning, at twenty-five dollars a week. I was mining the fat of the vein."

"What did you do to get poor?"

"A bank failed."

He told everything that had happened to him, good and bad, with the same relish. Both could make him grin from ear to ear. He'd certainly had his share of adversity. The one arm he had remaining, it had a bad skin disease. Under a thin fretting of papery flakes the flesh shone red and polished like a precious stone. It was irritated as hell, that arm, and couldn't be pacified, and he couldn't scratch it either, not having another arm. To get relief, he put a fork in his mouth and scraped with that. Naturally he couldn't do that and talk at the same time, so he asked me all sorts of questions about my mother and did it while I was talking. When his arm started to bead with blood, I ripped the fork out of his mouth and refused to give it back.

I said, "Isn't there an ointment you can use?"

He grinned. "The best ointment for pain is pain."

After that we discussed pleasure and suffering. He might not have been handsome, but after an hour or two of his company I wished I could talk to him every day. He listened to you with an enormous appetite.

As he was taking me home he said, "Can I see you again?"

We stepped aside to let a couple of older ladies past. When they saw who Duffield was with, their faces lit up with excitement like paper lanterns, before they remembered to be shocked.

After they passed on, I said, "Look here, I'm a flash-girl. I won't marry you and I won't fall in love. The girls I know don't recommend marriage and neither would your wife if she saw you now. I probably won't hump you much either. I have a good rule in life," I said: "I only screw one man a night. Leastways I only screw one type of man a night, a sam or a sweetheart, otherwise it's like wrestling a two-headed monster. I'm willing to go on frolics and benders and have number-one conversations, and that's about it. If that don't suit you, don't call on me."

He stood there kind of stunned.

You have to tell the truth or it gets too complicated. "I mean I think you're charming," I said.

In the middle of the road was a man on his hands and knees, throwing up in front of a wagon that wanted to get past. Duffield looked right through him. "I'm all at sea," he said.

It was an observation. He didn't mind if I overheard him but he didn't look at me when he said it. Afterward he glanced at me sideways with his liver-colored eyes, said goodbye, and crossed the road.

When I got back to the Empress I had to hook a sam fast before the bar closed. After I did the business, I sat about the parlor in a sort of dreamy exhaustion while the girls told me what had happened in the saloon and I let on to be interested. It was like reports of events in another country. I thought about the round of applause I'd received when I took my seat at the theater, and whether Duffield would send me flowers tomorrow. It dawned on me he wouldn't; I'd damped his enthusiasm too much. I never would hear how this town was run, or get my dirty mitts on the boodle under my bed. It would just sit there tormenting me.

"Poor Dol," Mama said when she saw my mood. "I daresay you look pretty enough in a saloon, dear, but not in a foyer full of ladies. Did he regret it soon as you made the theater?"

The other girls were perfectly pleasant but they started to rile me too, even Sadie Marx, and she was in full possession of her genius that night.

She was wearing the wide round fur hat that makes her look like a grand Russian lady or a Jewish man on Sabbath. When the spirit is upon her she takes something you've said or some little incident you've forgotten and embellishes the thing with such killing touches that before you know it you are one of the greatest characters that ever breathed. People clap their hands and laugh till they are sore. When the tale is told and they are drying their eyes, you almost feel obliged to explain to everyone how you have gotten to be so dull nowadays. Of course your moment passes and then she's telling about another of her pals, and when she's through, she goes to bed. You know when a lightning storm has passed over and you feel a little gloomy and a little giddy inside? That's what it's like when she's finished. You carry on drinking but there's no purpose to it.

I saw the mood she was in and didn't want to be one of her characters, so I took myself off and sat in the hall. Later when I went to bed I couldn't sleep. The stuff under the bed made me toss and turn; it was the idea there was a fortune right underneath me and I couldn't touch it. Ed Stainback couldn't sleep either. He was in bed with Ness, five feet away, in a sweat over the money he needed to sleep with her five nights a week. Mrs. Delano, the pawnbroker's clerk, said he'd hocked items every day for a week, his own valuables as a starter, then his wife's. When he moved, I could hear his hair grease the pillow. Later he got up and pissed in a pot for about a minute; that was in the first thin light of day.

Something, maybe condoms, made me think about Charlie Ching—he keeps an apothecary shop in Chinatown. He has a stock of potions and cures: stag antlers and queer-looking funguses, long-haired black grasses and ma-hwang, as well as a variety of articles we girls need in order to conduct our business. And it struck me all of a sudden—what if Charlie took the *gow* and cooked us a bang-up concoction? There was enough raw opium in that rum crate to buy D Street, and when I tried to figure up what it would be worth as a medicine, well, I lost my guess, that's all. We would double our money, more. If Charlie advertised it as a POWERFUL CURE for opiomaniacs we would clean up, I reckoned. He could do it all by mail like Dr. Golly. I wouldn't need Duffield; I'd make so much out of the drug that Pontius would give me the small share of the dibs that I needed.

I slept for about an hour. When I woke up I spent an hour arranging my hair to put off going to Charlie Ching's as long as I could, and even at that I got there too fast. I couldn't tell Charlie my idea without letting him know I was in possession of the opium. That made me uneasy. In Live Fox Street I shied about the Chinese market. There was all the large panic of poultry getting loose; there was fish so fresh they were still swimming, and boxes of desperate little quail; but food isn't the kind of thing I buy, and Charlie Ching's was right around the corner. It leans against the neighboring building like a man with his arms folded, leaning against a wall. Charlie was serving a stout Chinese lady. I think maybe they spoke different sorts of Chinese or something: he would speak and then she would speak and then they would stare at each other until their eyes dried. When she shoved out I told him the racket I had in mind. I told him in Portuguese as a precaution, and he looked at me for a long, long time. He looked at me for so long I began to think he didn't recognize me, or he didn't speak Portuguese, and nothing that used to be true was true. Then he said:

"Are you fuck Our Lady crazy? Holy Mary Mother of God is an ugly fat pig of a whore if I listen to you. When you leave my store, keep right on walking till you come to the crack of doom, and when you get there be my guest and jump in. Thank you," he said, bowing me out, "thank you, thank you, thank you, thank you, thank you."

I was outside on the sidewalk before I knew what was happening. I walked up one alley and along another, terrified, as if I was trying to shake somebody. Charlie Ching knew something I didn't—that much was obvious—if nothing else, he knew how hot the opium was. No wonder Pontius hadn't been able to fence it. H Street near Union (if you want your pots and pans mended) there's a row of Chinese metal workers that sit on low stools, hammering and soldering and all that sort of thing. I caught the smell of burning black metals in passing and stopped to throw up. I suppose it was a malgamation of different things. It was the smell of hot chemicals, and Charlie Ching throwing a scare into me, and not having had any missy that morning to tighten my stomach.

ELEVEN

In the saloon that night I got a message from Duffield, saying he accepted my terms. I smiled to myself all evening and disappeared a couple of times to reread his note in private. After the fright I'd gotten that morning, it was comforting to feel I had the interest and protection of the most powerful man in town; I wrote him acknowledging his surrender, and next day we started in.

We would drive out to the desert in a carriage and smoke some bang, or go to Chinatown and drink till ten in the morning. He would be cold at first, and distant, as if he hated me for not loving him the way he wanted; but later he would give way to a wild strain of humor. We never managed to fuck, but we did have the most wonderful conversations about despair. The human mind is too small, he would say. It thinks the same thoughts over and over and seems smaller with every passing year. It was obvious he was going through some crisis that had unbalanced his mind a little, and that just suited me. There was more chance his principles would come unfixed.

I was pretty unsteady myself. One night I'd be swanking around town with Duffield, the next I'd have to listen to some mug tell me his opinion about things before he laid me. Pretty soon I was in hock to Mrs. Bird for my rent—the sams riled me the moment they touched me, so I took nights off. It was a strange existence I was leading. When you do nothing all day except liquor up, you get blown along like a balloon in a fast current of wind. The only thing I had for ballast was the worries I had about my debts; then I would remember how rich I'd be if I could sell the boodle under my bed, and I'd get so giddy I would have to dose myself. At Essie McCutchin's birthday party someone said something funny and I fell to the ground and rollicked about with laughter for five minutes, then lay there like I had banged-up ribs. By the time I was done the entire company was watching me in silence.

I wasn't sure what my circumstances were, exactly; I suppose I believed Duffield would help me fence the swag if I could persuade him it was for a good purpose. As a matter of fact I had just made up my mind to try him, when I heard the rumors he was having an affair.

At first it didn't bother me. "I know he's having an affair," I thought. "With me." When gossip suggested the female in question was an older woman, I wondered if people had spotted him in company with his wife. That was the only explanation I could think of. Next thing I heard was that Mrs. Messenger, the widow he took to the ball, had collapsed in the street and summoned him to her deathbed, heartbroken over his dissipations with me. It turned out, when I asked him about it, that he'd dropped around with some bought scones and found her recovered enough to eat three of them right there in front of him. Her maid was scandalized. She told Mrs. Messenger that real ladies don't have the appetite of a sawmill, or, if they do, they hide it. They don't drop their crumbs all over the carpet.

The rumors kept coming around. I was sitting in a bar with

Willy Crowe and Desi Ball one afternoon, and Desi Ball, who's small and fat and glistens with sweat when she drinks, she leaned across me to say to Willy: "You know the alley runs up alongside Murray's Melodeon? Three in the morning two nights back a street fairy I know was working a job there, and who do you suppose walked out the stage door but Jim Duffield." Then she looked right at me, as if I had the measles and didn't know it. "I mean, who was he meeting there at that hour?"

Ten minutes later I stood up and walked out of the bar. It was going on for four on a bright windy day. I wanted to go home and look in a glass to see if I was all over spots. In the saloon that evening I was too embarrassed to enter into conversation with anyone, but I didn't like to be alone either, so I sat with a table of miners who were getting drunk in Welsh. Mama bought me a drink and leaned over me as she put it down. "You want to know who she is?" she said, putting a drop of poison in my ear. "I could tell you if you like."

"How would I know whether to believe you or not?"

She put a rum down in front of me. "Might be better you never find out, I suppose."

Then she walked away in that high-headed way of hers, as if everyone in the saloon knew the truth of the thing except me.

After work that night I dug out for Murray's Melodeon on B Street. I walked up one side of the street, crossed the road, and came back. The building was dark as the inside of a cow. The doorkeeper had a tiny room by the stage door; that was all the light there was. I tramped the street for almost two hours. It was hard to do that and look natural, and I was wearing high-heeled boots that rang out on the plank sidewalk at that hour of night and would not let up. Every so often some fellow would mistake me for a hooker and pester me.

I had stopped to look up the side of Murray's toward the doorkeeper's cubbyhole when out of nowhere came the sound of a girl's heels. Someone who looked like Willy Crowe was heading in my direction. I didn't want to explain to anyone why I was hanging around Murray's at that hour, so I dodged up the stage-door alley. It was a narrow passage between two tall buildings and there was no light to guide me except the leakage from the doorkeeper's window. I felt my way to the back of the alley, ten yards beyond the stage door, and hid myself in the pitch blackness back of the theater until the French heels had passed by.

In such a lonely spot I suddenly felt all my misery. There had been rain earlier that day that had laid the dust; the smell reminded me of a damp library in a large house that nobody went into now. I pressed myself against the wall and rubbed my cheeks against the brick, first one cheek and then the other. The bricks were smooth but the edges scraped. It was comforting. I told myself I'd had enough for one night and was about to start home when I heard a lock being drawn with a hard *chock*. The stage door opened with a rattle of small chains and a burst of air, like it had been shoved open with a shoulder, and I heard the voices of a man and a woman as they hurried out and away. My first impulse was to cringe against the wall, but eventually I poked my head around the corner of the building. I was just in time to see Duffield put on his hat, and the female disappear. I didn't even see her figure, I caught the tail of her skirt. Duffield kept looking after her. She must have faced around, because he smiled and gave her a wave, then turned on his heel and hustled away.

On the way home from Murray's I felt so humiliated it was like I'd taken my skin off. I wasn't in love with Duffield in the least but right away I was furious to know who she was and in what ways she was better than me. By this time I knew that Duffield had womanized his whole marriage and liked them all shapes and sizes. He once told me about a female with a nose the length of her pretty little hand, that he had banged for a night and a day. He'd never been prejudiced against good-looking women, he said, he just didn't see any particular advantage in them. Maybe he'd been taking a shy at me. When I recalled how innocent our liaison had been, I could have cried.

It took five minutes of rapping at the window to waken Giz. He let me in without a word; he didn't take any notice of you if it was possible. As I crept down the stairs to my bed, the door to Mama's room closed, like she'd been waiting for me to come home. It was suspicious enough that she was awake. And the more I thought about it, the more it seemed to me that she'd waited till she heard me on the stairs and *then* snapped the door shut—like she was trying to rouse my suspicions on purpose. Does that sound too childish to be true? I'm afraid that's Mama all over. She's like a girl in the school yard who's stolen your sweetheart and can't wait to see you sick with jealousy. That's the only reason she wants anything—because you've got it.

Before I'd made my bedroom I remembered how she and Duffield had been drawn to each other at the ball and how fine a couple they had made. I recollected the time he came to squire me to the theater and the ten minutes it took to get him out of the saloon. And earlier this evening, when she let drop in my ear that she knew something I didn't, she had done it with the kind of hatred that is luxurious. The kind that has confidence in itself. Now here she was, home just ahead of me, it seemed, with her door ajar, so she could hear when I got back, and then close it—to let me know she'd only just gotten home herself. She must have seen me sloshing up and down the street outside Murray's, and had a good laugh. Perhaps they both had. "Well," I thought as I got ready for bed, "if she wants a fight she can have it." And next day I watched her plenty.

I'd say she's more attractive than I am. She's not especially handsome but she carries herself as if she is, and you don't tend to look any closer. If I was a man, I'd pass the night in philosophical debate with me but I would go to bed with her. She probably enjoys it more than I do.

I knew he was going to call for me about ten that night. That was all I could think about, so I didn't go into the saloon, I let Mrs. Bird dock me a dollar for the evening, stayed in my room, and got shellacked. At some point I put my head under the bed and dragged out the rum crate; it had been lying among shoes and bandboxes and grown a dust carpet. I got out one of the tins of opium, opened it, and smelled the *chan du*. I knew better than to smoke any. Only two nights before I'd heard Pontius crashing around outside, fixing himself a place to hide between the back of the Empress and the hay yard on E Street.

When Ness came in, I was sitting on the carpet surrounded by the silver boxes, like a boy king who's been given silver bars to play with. "Don't you have any sense?" she said. She went over to the washbasin, washed blood from the insides of her legs. "What if Mrs. Bird walked in and saw that?"

For a moment I imagined she'd asked me what I was playing at. I said, "Nothing."

She stared at me hard. "Are you gonged again?"

"What makes you say that?" I started packing the tins into the rum crate.

"You been having too many nights off lately. There's more money in sams than opium," she said.

"I know," I said. "I will."

"You will what?"

I'd lost the run of the conversation. "I'll work harder."

"You think you'll have enough dimes saved up in a month or so?"

"Sure."

"More than a month or less?"

"About a month."

After she went, I made up my mind tonight was the night I would find out how much pull I had with Duffield. Would he make me rich or not? I napped a little and woke up pretty sober—ready for the task ahead.

"Where will we go tonight?" he said when I met him outside the Empress.

"Somewhere private," I said, and squeezed his arm.

"Sure," he said, taking my meaning. "I know somewhere. It's not pretty or anything, but it's all sorts of a place at this hour."

As we started up the steps to C Street, we were jumped by three bankers up from San Francisco, said their specialty was investment. They'd boughten a share in a silver mine that afternoon, and three brand-new shooters, and they'd been drinking till you can't rest. Did they want to get their guns off. You can say that again. Seeing as this was a lawless frontier town, they were all whooped up and just desperate to sin. Almost at the top of the steps, when the five of us were out of breath and weak-legged from the climb, the noise of C Street reached down and pulled us up by the ears. Drunk men yelled at the tops of their voices and stepped out in front of wagons that could have crushed them, the drum of the crowded sidewalks was like continual volleys of small shot, and some fellow with a Navy six-shooter was blazing away at an old white dog.

The dog was drugged and all serene. He didn't move a scant hair all the while the fellow cracked away. Back of him some men jeered and waited in a line. This was a business operation: the dog belonged to a gang of kids; they'd found it and dosed it, anyway. They advertised a four-dollar prize if you shot the dog clean dead, charged the men a dollar a pop.

The boss kid had no face. I mean he had a nose and two eyes and a mouth, but there was nothing written on it—no ma, no pa, no nothing. He looked you over like he was deciding when he would rape you. Then there was a Chinese boy in huge boots that made his legs look as thin as poles, a fat girl, an ugly kid with camel lips who kept fiddling with his pants, and one that walked like he was toiling with the clap. He took money off the boys and kept his eyes skinned. It was a rattling good business. The kids made sure the men formed an orderly line, and not more than twice in all that roaring cannonade did the dog catch a bullet; whereupon he yelped, raised himself onto his legs, and took a few steps, before he forgot who he was sore at and settled down again, snarling in a dozy sort of a way.

The drunkest of the bankers had pure white hair and a ruby face. Almost before he caught his breath after the climb, he was taking in the smell of gunpowder. It ain't a particularly pleasant smell but it promotes itself, and the sweet-faced banker had no notion of waiting his turn—he got his gun out and banged away at the poor hound. It was a shame.

The dog was just fine, but next thing you know the banker was on all fours spitting blood and it was a mercy he couldn't see what was coming to him next, because the kid with no face was about to bat his mug with a used-up bottle of lager he'd picked up on the street. *We* could see what was coming to him. One of the other bankers said, "For pity's sake." He said it pretty quiet, though; he didn't want the kid with no face to look at him: he scared the filling out of you, that kid. He whacked the white-haired banker on the top lip. It curled up in a bad imitation of a sneer and showed his bleeding animal teeth. The lip couldn't help itself, it just wanted to avoid any more pain, but the kid took offense. He pounded the banker's ear with a meat-softening thud. Welcome to the wild west. The banker wrenched away from the next blow and I stepped back too late, after the blood flying off his face spit my white shoes. The fat girl—who had those fat-girl tits—she pointed at my shoes and laughed, and they went back to their operation having made their point.

I stayed with the bankers while Duffield walked to the middle of the road and had a few quiet words with the kids, then we continued on our way.

"Where we going anyway?"

"Murray's Melodeon."

My heart doubled in size. "Won't it be all shut up?"

"Closed to the public."

Up the pitch-black alley there was the same light from the doorkeeper's room there always was, but this time I walked up to the door with Duffield. This was the place to try my strength, I reckoned. When the doorkeeper answered the door, he stared at us like he was our father and he was sick of us coming home at this hour. Duffield hazed the old so-and-so into giving us a spirit lamp, and a little later we stood in the very wing where Miss April Delancey had flung herself into the arms of the villain and acted so badly. Everything was a little ghostly in the light of that lamp. I was wondering where he took Mama when she came here.

I was tense and cold. I said, "You went pretty easy on those kids."

"They didn't use their guns. I'd say they were pretty handsome about the whole thing. The banker could of put them out of business."

"What did you say to them?"

"They just blew in from Dabu. Some opium got lifted in the Bay and they've been sent to get it back. I let 'em know we're keeping an eye on them."

I walked out onto the stage, glad to hear the solid ring of my shoes upon the boards. Standing in the darkness, I said, "Do they know who pinched it?"

"Yes."

"Who?"

"A fella name of Billy Violet."

"Violet, huh?" It rhymed with something I could half hear.

"Calls himself Pontius." He was back of a piece of machinery. "He used to pimp those kids, till they were played out. They get their mitts on him they will make an awful mess." After a minute he came looking for me with the lamp. "Say, there you are!" he said. "It was so quiet around here I thought you'd fallen through a trap-door."

"I was thinking." If they found Pontius and croaked him I'd be rich as anything. "Do *you* know where he is?"

"No."

"Don't you think you ought to find him before they do?"

"I don't have the men to search the whole town. I guess the kids are the same; they'll just bide their time. He has to eat and he has to shit. He'll leave sign sooner or later."

"Won't the kids get bored?"

"Those kids? Not those kids," he said. "Those kids will stick."

I tried to put them out of mind. "Where'll we go to fuck?"

"How about the peanut gallery?"

I almost said, Is that where you generally go? That where you take my mother? It didn't seem likely when we got there. The atmosphere was cushioned in stale smoke but nothing else was soft. He held up the lamp and showed me into it like it was a bedroom. I could see he wanted me the worst kind, but he didn't want to hurry me. He set the light on one of the chairs where it half lit a small part of three rows. "Don't worry," he said. "The doorkeeper won't leak. I know enough about him to put him in hell."

"Why would *I* worry?"

He didn't answer.

I said, "You used this place before for your affairs, huh?"

It was better not to say anything after that. It was smuttier, too. I sat him down on a chair, stood behind him, and took off his necktie and shirt. I let my nose and lips touch his ear, but as if by accident, just because it was practical to be that close for the purpose of stripping him. When I had his shirt off, I came around to the front of him. His naked torso was white and hairless. His stump was raw, and his eyes nipped when I looked at it. I almost fell in love with him for that.

It was an unusual place to be naked, the gallery of a theater—it made him nervous people might be watching, and I liked that. I knelt in front of him, took off his shoes and socks, and put them on the floor. The circumstances were so unpleasing it was almost humorous. The floor had been wiped after the tobacco-spitting crowds had left; it had a swish of cleanness. There was the faint aftersmell of a mop. I was careful where I put his feet once they were naked. But I could see his cock was keen, so I leaned my arms on his knees and started a conversation.

"I'm worried about my mother," I said. "I think she's having a liaison."

"What makes you think so?"

"I know just by looking at her how much drink she has aboard, I could tell you to a fraction. So I guess I might just notice if she's all tangled up in an affair. She's been having them since I was a girl." Then I handed him some silence.

"You must have had an interesting childhood."

"She was usually married then. Valparaiso, she was Mrs. Hector Mack. I would wake up nights as her carriage arrived home and hear a gent escort her far as the verandah. Then they would disappear awhile." They would drop into a silence louder than the night.

"And where was Mr. Hector Mack all this while?"

The empty theater seats seemed to be eavesdropping on us; I kept my voice low. "He'd pace the hall outside my bedroom or spy on the lovers from the bedroom next to mine. I was thirteen.

I would lie in bed wishing Mama would hurry up and kiss her lover good night, come to bed, and tell me all the gossip."

"She had other ideas, huh?"

"They'd kiss till I would think they'd died." I started to unbutton his pants. "I would stare at the dumb wardrobe in my bedroom till I was furious with it. Then I'd hear them whispering again, each whisper sounding like a last gentle farewell"— one of the buttons was difficult and needed a little more care and study—"except the last farewells went on for an eternity. Finally the gent would return to the carriage and Mama would have an ugly spat with Mr. Mack and come to bed with me to escape his vile accusations."

"Poor Mr. Mack." He skidded it out pretty quick. He was breathing faster than he liked.

Kneeling in front of him, I said, "Stand up."

He stood up in front of my face.

"Sometimes she'd fall asleep in her clothes," I said, taking his pants down. "Other times she'd lie on top of the bed in her evening dress. She'd gossip about the gents she'd met at the governor's ball, or the officers aboard the *Almirante Cochrane*."

"It must have been intoxicating for you."

I eased down his underpants. "I loved the scent of panatella cigars that crowded her dress."

"I guess it was the scent of her admirers," he managed to say.

"You ready? You look ready." Still kneeling, I caressed his soft cold ass.

"Don't you wish we could be more alone?"

"It's just the two of us in a dark theater," I said quietly. "We couldn't be any more alone than this."

"I can almost feel the hands on my shoulder," he said.

"On your shoulder?" I kept my hands where they were but they'd lost their sense of purpose. They were just there. "Whose hands?" I said.

"The people that sit here."

He picked up his clothes, moved a little away from me, and started to get dressed.

I felt as though he'd pushed me aside. "I've heard some feeble excuses," I said. "Is she better company than I am?" I jeered. "Or maybe you don't talk much?"

"Who?"

"My mother."

He straightened his shoulders as if he didn't have that nubbins of a stump. "I only met her twice. You were there both times."

I was lost. "Oh," I said. "Then what's the matter you don't want to screw?"

"You keep running on about another woman."

Right away he said "another woman" he regretted it. It rang out too loud. He was screwing *someone*. He combed his hair and put the chairs that had been disarranged back where they were supposed to be. He was a little too exact, like the smallest mistake would give him away. We each took a seat and sat there with one chair and the smell of dirty mop between us. I wanted him to love me more than the woman he was banging, and that made me ache. I leaned over and rested my hand on his knee. "I wish you'd hold me."

He did; and I clung to him hard. It must have seemed lunatic, me talking about my mother while I seduced him. He held me, not too close; stiff. After a long period of immobility, he said: "I guess you worshipped your mother when you were young."

"I wish you'd known her back then. She was special."

"I wish I'd known you back then."

It was a sweet thing to say; and after that we were able to stand up and go to the green room together, though it still wasn't easy to look each other in the eye. We cuddled on a sticky sofa in an atmosphere of mutual suspicion. Toward daylight we snuck out of the theater one after the other. I got home and sat on my bed and wondered about the woman he was seeing behind my back. Did he see me in public because I was more to him, or less? I couldn't decide, but it didn't matter for my purposes that he was in love with me so long as I could work him; and I was trying to figure out if he liked me enough to do what I needed of him, when a strange girl walked into the bedroom and said, "Howdy do."

TWELVE

"Who are you?" I said.

"Genevieve Butsch." She smiled like she'd answered the question pretty good.

"I didn't ask your name, Genevieve. I asked you who the Christ you are."

"I'm the new girl."

"Oh, really. Someone been fired?"

Genevieve said all she knew was she was the new girl, so I headed to Larkin's, where I found Sadie Marx having a nip with three pick-ups she knows.

Izzy Wink is around four feet and six inches, but she calls her pimp her "baby." She was telling all about a duel two fellas had fought over her. Navy six-shooters, twelve paces, fire and advance; six shots apiece they got off. Izzy said if one of her babies had died she'd of been upset pretty bad; and if *both* her babies had died she'd of been upset something dreadful. But when neither of them so much as stained his frilly shirt, my goodness, what a chump she looked! Three days she had stayed in bed, dying of shame.

Sadie Marx kept telling Izzy how brave she was being till Izzy believed her, and dabbed her tiny eyes with a tiny hankie. Sadie has that flash air about her, street hookers look up to her.

Anyhow, I had to wait a little until I could ask about the new girl, and then when I finally *did* ask, what a palaver! You probably suppose that alley queens like Annie Paddock and Olive Ptoots get used to bad news. They *are* used to it but it makes them so nerved up all the time they are apt to go off like a rocket for any reason at all. They can't even stand for anyone else to get bad news, that's how touchy they are. Soon as I asked about the new chum, they couldn't keep still. Olive Ptoots stood up— tossing her mane like an old, half-blind horse—and offered to stand the company drinks, whereupon Annie Paddock said it was her treat and threatened to belt Olly if she didn't sit down. "Look, will someone tell me who got fired!" I yelled, and Olly dropped to her seat like a lump of lead.

"It's Isobel," Sadie Marx said.

"Mama?"

Sadie Marx chinked her glass against her teeth. "Mrs. B caught her dipping someone's wallet."

Now the news was out, the three pick-ups were greedy to see how I handled it. "Now listen here," I said, "I ain't no slouch when it comes to slanging my mother, I hope, and if she *had* any redeemable qualities she'd pawn them; but she ain't sneaky and she ain't dumb."

"Takes a lot of liquor to run her," Sadie said. "She's got to get the cash somehow."

"She never smouched a pocketbook before!" I said.

"Poor soul," Annie Paddock said. "Them shantytown gals don't grow old, or pretty neither."

"What's shantytown got to do with anything?"

"That's where she's gone." Annie Paddock doesn't get an opportunity to feel superior often, she has to grab any chance that's going. "I hope she don't finish up like Licky Pudding. Licky would do the biz for a bottle of beer before they found her drowned in that puddle."

Fat Annie's a dollar a jump if you're interested. You'll find her up the alley next to Larkin's. You can tell her I sent you.

I went home and sent a message to Duffield. Nobody was going to employ Mama on her own merits, but all the hurdy houses and madams have to suck up to the cops; Duffield could find her a pleasant situation so long as he was willing to use his influence. It might be against his principles, of course, but if he made too many difficulties over this matter he wasn't liable to be of any use when it came to the larger business of the boodle under my bed, and it was as well to know at the earliest opportunity to what amount I could depend upon him for my future happiness.

He sent me a note saying he would see what he could do, and next morning we set off for shantytown to offer Mama a fresh start. All the way down Washington he was silent and solemn.

I said, "You look like you've been forced to go to church by your wife or something. I don't want you to help me out of duty."

He looked at me out of one eye, like a bird. "I'm worried about you, that's all. I know how much you care about your mother."

Past H and I Streets the town begins to pinch out; shantytown is down there in a scooped-out piece of hill. There's a dump heap around the rim, and goats graze among the garbage, looking shitty and perplexed. One goat was crowding a bigger goat, so the bigger goat rushed him. The younger goat lost his footing, leaped into a gulch full of cans and bottles, and started a sickly avalanche. He was in desperate earnest awhile but he swam out and struck firm land.

Duffield and I picked our way down. First thing we saw was a man sitting on a box. Beside him was a sign that said GROCERY and the articles for sale—two cans of fruit and one shoe, badly stoven. He yelled abuse at me in some language he was the only one that spoke it, and my nerves scattered. I mean, in some ways it was nicer here than I'd imagined, more pastoral. The pounding of the mine works was duller. There were dragonflies, and drunks sleeping in a Sabbath peace and quiet. But it was worse in other ways—the sheer reality of it. We stepped around a male and female who were fucking while she sipped a pint of liquor. The male saw us and stalled with his ass in the air; it had a bunch of black leaden spots. The female asked Duffield if he wanted to do the business after she got through.

I didn't see how Mama could survive here, not with her airs and graces. She wouldn't even like for anyone to see her here. I told Duffield he better be careful what he said to her or she might take offense. The worst thing he could do was say anything kind, I said. He mustn't say anything cruel either, but kindness she would not endure.

We found her sitting on a candle box like the Queen of Sheba. Her ankle was swollen, and some ill-looking fellow with pretty curls was nursing her. He unwound the filthy rag around her ankle, studied the swelling, then wound it up again. Such devotion made me suspect he didn't have any income of his own. He wasn't dressed like a pimp, he wasn't gaudy, but there's a trashy, weak sort of man who has one gal, and this fellow had the look. I'd nursed a hope that landing up in shantytown would bring Mama to her senses—that she would learn her lesson at long last and change her ways—but I could see right off the opposite had happened. I guess when Life gives a person a good kicking, it teaches them a painful lesson; it teaches them they don't want to learn any more lessons, and makes them harder and more fractious than ever.

When her ankle was done, she settled herself on her candle box, arranged her dress to her liking, and raised her chin. "Well?" she said. "Are the boys asking for me?"

"You know the boys," I said. "They class you first-rate."

She narrowed her eyes. After a night on the booze her peepers were like two bad-made buttons but she narrowed them anyhow. "Who? Who's been asking after me?"

Two years ago in little Los Angeles, as the wife of Señor Ernesto Márquez, Mama had led the first dance to inaugurate the new assembly rooms for the cream of Mexican and American society. Now she was in shantytown, imagining ex-customers of hers would be concerned for her well-being.

"Oh, various," I said. "One of the newspaper boys said he would get up a petition on your behalf."

She acknowledged the compliment with a queenly nod and fussed with her hair. "And did he?"

It was something he said when he was half-cut. "Not yet," I said.

Her eyes glittered with tears, then iced. "If there was a pressman in this town worth two cents he'd write this up in the paper. That woman has taken my character! Well," she said, with iron resolution, "I'm not going back. I won't go back suppose they send a deputation to ask me."

She was pretty deluded if she'd been expecting a delegation. I skinned a look at Duffield. "It must be hard here," I said to her. I was trying to soften her before he made his proposition.

"We'll get along," she said. When she said "we," she looked at the pimp fellow with her chin up, like they had won through some pretty hard times together.

Already the dirt had gotten under her skin. She was a smudged gray, like she'd been sketched in pencil, rubbed out, then sketched over. Her shanty was an amalgamation of tin and brush. "Where do you keep your dough?" I asked her. "I don't suppose there's anywhere better than shantytown if you're a footpad on the choke."

"They wouldn't dare," the fellow with the pretty curls said.

I let my eyes go dead for a little. That was all the comment he deserved. Then I continued. "You have more courage than I have, Mama. If anyone can make out a week here, it's you. What if you're unlucky, though?"

She was beginning to see how bad her circumstances might look to outsiders, but the superior sort of drunkard always rises above the appearance of a thing. She straightened her back and raised her head like she was playing a role on the stage. "I've never asked for sympathy and I won't start now. I don't even ask for respect," she said, and turned her nose up at the very idea. "Not for myself, anyhow. The female that's sat here on a candle box, that used-up female, well, the least said about her the better. But Mrs. Captain McQueen," she said, and she got taller as she said the name, "Mrs. Captain McQueen is the wife of a British officer. She can worry along without servants, or maids, or plumbing, or even good manners; she can starve with hunger or cold and keep her dignity because *she knows who she is*."

She started leaking the sort of tears a lush weeps. They're as wet as anyone else's but you see them and say to yourself, "Oh, look—tears." And if you think somebody that acts their sadness isn't as badly off as a person who is straight-out sad, then you're a way off. There's nothing worse. A chilly feeling crept up the rope of my spine to the back of my neck and I wailed out, "Oh, Mama. I love you."

She looked disgusted and waved me away like shooing flies. "Don't talk rubbish."

A fellow started to open his bar yonder. He rolled two barrels into position, set a plank on them, and stood two bottles of liquor on the plank. That was all the bar he had, besides a sign: BAD WHISKEY. Mama started to fidget when she noticed him, and her pimp put a hand on her shoulder and offered to get her a drink.

"Thanks, Lance. Seems you're the only one around here who appreciates what I have to endure."

Lance started to the bar with some coinage she gave him, and Duffield took his courage in his hands. "Mrs. McAulay has a free berth," he said. He was careful to say nothing kind. He told her the whole story; how Nan Connolly had sloped with a rich married man twice her age and left Mrs. McAulay with a situation to fill. "What do you say? It's you or an A Street maid that wants to spread her wings. Mrs. McAulay has had her fill of maids."

Mama didn't like Duffield to see her in this condition. Soon as he started in talking to her she could hardly sit still; she kept changing the angle and set of her head, up and down and to the side, the way you do when there is no position that will show you to advantage. I was almost glad when Lance came back with the whiskey and gave her something to hide behind. She took a sip while Lance stood over her like he was a waiter or something. She made a face and he said, "Is it bad?"

"Disgusting, but never mind."

"I can take it back."

Mama reared up. "Take it back and what? He only has one sort of whiskey."

"I know that, sure."

"Then what in hell are you talking about?" She was shaking, so she put the whiskey down in case she spilled some. "Your brains as rotten as your teeth?"

She enjoyed putting him down so much that right away she looked around for her next victim. She turned to Duffield like a queen with a stiff neck and said, "You can tell Mrs. McAulay where to find me if she wants to discuss terms."

I didn't want to touch her on the raw. I was careful as anything. "Mama, you're a good-looking woman and a good prospect for an employer—"

She jumped to her feet, rattling like fury. "How dare you talk to me like that? Do you want me to give you one?"

"I don't mean to tell you your business," I said, "but if you suppose Mrs. McAulay is going to come here and—"

"Did I ask any favors of that bitch? Or of you, come to that."

"Mama, won't you at least think it over? I asked Duffield to use his pull with Mrs. McAulay. You know where he stands on corruption, though. He won't do it again. This is your last chance, I reckon."

"You need someone to take the swell out of your head,

missy. You talk like you have some special influence over him. Ask him who else he's humping."

"Why don't you tell me if you know so much?"

She made out she knew but she wasn't going to tell me, like a kid, and I said if she knew why couldn't she tell me, like another kid, and the conversation petered out in more of that style. Even as I was losing my temper at her, a part of me was thinking, "In a few days she'll be used to things here. Already she's got a pimp. She's found a niche." That's why I was furious, of course, because it was hopeless. In the end I stormed off in a fury; and all the way up the steep grade to D Street, Duffield followed just a little behind. I paid him not the slightest bit of notice; I was consumed with Mama. Seems that no matter what I do to help, she's determined to destroy herself. It's like she's doing it to spite me. You know what her secret is? The reason she's practically invincible? She doesn't think there is anything wrong with her. Even when events in her life might be taken as a hint to the contrary, she continues to see things her way.

I got back to the Empress all over dust, and frazzled, but I wasn't going to let her beat me. I asked Duffield downstairs to my room, where we could speak in private. He nodded, like he was expecting me to give him jesus and he might as well face the music sooner rather than later. I was still unsure what his feelings toward me were exactly but it didn't seem that important now; all I had to know was whether he was willing to help me or not. I sat on my bed and he started walking up and down the room between the two beds in that large way he has. He talked about Mama and his concerns for her safety, and every so often his head dropped as if he was ashamed. I just sat there and bided my time. The boodle was right underneath me. I even got a slight cramp in my leg, with the excitement of knowing it was there. I stretched my leg out, bent my toes, and waited my moment to nail him. The other woman he was seeing, that was his weakness. He had such vast appetites he'd gotten confused about what things he liked and what things he needed; either he liked this other female too much or too little, but either way he had a conscience about it.

"Don't see what more you can do," he said. "She drinks like she's got a spark in her throat, that's why nobody will employ her. And she's dishonest." He ducked his head. "That doesn't help."

"Mama needs a situation that don't nip her personality too much," I said.

"I agree with you there. But where?"

"Ness and me are going to go in partners in a saloon, soon as I ante up my share. Ness has banked five hundred dollars these last two years."

"You girls are aiming to square it?"

There was a hush after he said that, like the hush after an avalanche.

"Will you help us?" I said. There was a great weight of quiet in my voice.

"I wouldn't like to see you wind up like your mother."

I got down on my knees and pulled the rum crate out from under the bed, then I opened one of the tins and showed him. There had been something scattered about his appearance since we got back from shantytown, but when he saw the *gow* every single atom of his face changed and moved its whereabouts, and when they all had settled in a new place he looked like a police chief again; solid cop all the way through. He smoothed his thick black curls with the palm of his hand. "How long've you had this?"

"Since we got here. I banged into Pontius on the Sierra road. He made me hide it for him."

"Put it away."

I pushed the crate back under the bed. He went and stood with his back to the wall.

"I was hoping you could sell a small amount," I said, "and give me the proceeds."

"You were, were you?"

"Was I wrong?"

Suddenly I had a big nothingy ache right in the middle of me and this crazy desire to panic.

"Why do you suppose I would do this for you?" he asked. "I'm a police chief."

"I suppose it depends on how much you care about this woman you're banging."

Like a tree before it topples, nothing happened for a few moments. It was only later when he was sitting on the bed staring at his shoes that I could see he had been felled by that one stroke. The pain he was in wasn't pretty to see. He'd gotten himself in a bad fix; he just didn't know what he was going to do next, or which of us he loved most. Looked like he was trying to pull the answer out of his guts. In the end he stood up and walked to the door. With his hand on the doorknob and his back to me he said, "I won't see you for a couple days. I'm going to the lake with Mrs. Duffield." He looked over his shoulder at me. "It'll take all of that time to figure this thing out."

After he left I still had no idea how much he cared for me, and now I was left with a vacancy of two days in which to dwell on it, knowing that it didn't matter what I did or thought or felt, my future was going to be decided somewhere else. I went to bed and slept like a boa constrictor. When I woke up, it was still only one o'clock in the afternoon.

THIRTEEN

It's a matter of finding a balance. If you torpedo a port with a couple drops of missy, it keeps you more sober and that means you can drink for longer. The opium sort of stuns the port. When you drink the mixture, it seems to sink right down into you and fill up all the chinks. Of course, sometimes you will take too much varnish or too much liquor and then you have to even things up. The night before Duffield came back from the lake I took too much of both; I was more screwed than the boys in the saloon and the jollification in the parlor I remember only in spots. But Og Dorff you couldn't forget. He had a bad tooth and his poisoned face had risen like a pastry. About once an hour he took Ness through to the bedroom, and that killed the pain for a few minutes.

I'd pulled Louis Tremblay—a fat dandy of a man who danced around the billiard table and cleaned all comers, in spite of his round belly and smutty eyes—and Cordelia was madly in love with him. They were affinities, according to her. This particular night she made cakes in his honor and handed them around. She waggled them in front of Og Dorff's puffed-out face, pushed her hair behind her hot pink ears, and said (sticking her tongue out at Louis so he would know she was really talking to him), "Did you ever see anything so delicious? You can have all you want, you know."

Og stared at the cakes, in dreadful pain. "O inx. Oo ay."

"You ain't going to refuse me, now, are you? Can't I tempt you at all?" She tapped Og under the chin with the plate. "You don't know what you're missing."

She was too busy making eyes at Louis to notice the expression on Og's face. He couldn't scream, so the pain jumped out of his eyes as though he'd just been guillotined.

Later Cordelia offered to sing "Mother's a Drunkard and Daddy Is Dead." It's her favorite song. I said why didn't she take Louis to my room and give him a private performance, seeing it was his birthday next week, and the balance of us piled into the room next to it, to listen. Cordelia never sings the same wrong notes twice and she plays the orphan with all her heart and tragic actions. We couldn't laugh out loud so we lay back on the beds, Sadie Marx and me, and laughed with our arms and legs, like beetles.

After that everything was a little strange and humorous. First there was an incident between me and Louis Tremblay because I fell asleep on the job. Next thing Mrs. Bird took me to her office to say I owed her twelve dollars and she would have it before the night was out or I could pack my traps. I couldn't ask Ness for the lend of it or she'd wonder what had happened to the two hundred dollars of savings that I'd lied about, and Sadie Marx wouldn't have that amount. I sat around the parlor and turned into creepy wallpaper. Andy Ballantyne, the schoolmaster, was entertaining everyone by making sarcastic remarks at Genevieve Butsch's expense. The more nobody laughed the more educated he talked, and the louder he laughed at his own jokes. Finally he got off a crack in Latin.

The silence was colossal. "Listen to that," Sadie Marx said. "That's all the dead Romans laughing their socks off."

Then she took me through to her room and showed me the pair of snow-white lovebirds she'd just bought. She said they were fourteen dollars out of Hister's that morning.

"How'd you like them babies?"

"Fourteen dollars," I exclaimed. "Jesus. Do they sing?"

"Not yet, they didn't."

"Do you think they will?"

"In this dump heap? Those dames won't sing except it's a opera house."

I said, "What was the damage for the fancy cage?"

"Thirteen dollars. No wonder they look like millionaires, huh?"

"Where'd you come by that kind of currency?"

It was all on account of some wildcat mining stock she'd bought. You see, the mines in Virginia City are solid investments, so you can't make much profit speculating in them. People know how much that silver is worth. But there's fresh claims being made a hundred miles away in Star City, and nobody knows if the mines there are the inventions of fertile imaginations or the real thing. It doesn't matter either so long as you guess when to buy and when to sell.

"I bought at six dollars," she said. "Sold out for fifty-three."

"I don't suppose you could give me fifteen, could you?"

"Sure." She went into her pillow and fetched out her wad like it was nuts. "Ness don't look too good," she said. "I guess she's sick with worry."

I prepared for a long, dull siege. Once Sadie Marx started crabbing about Ness you couldn't get away from her, lately. She harped on about her savings and her cold heart like they went together. She didn't say anything funny on the subject; I kept waiting, but she'd lost her sense of humor where Ness was concerned. She said the same thing a hundred different ways; she didn't stop supposing you agreed with her.

"What about?" I said.

"Didn't you hear about Ed Stainback?"

"No."

"He's bankrupt. There's a bill outside his shop advertising a sidewalk sale of his tools. His wife has shoved out to her sister's in Sacramento. You mean Ness don't know?"

"I haven't spoken to her much these last few days. I'm waiting till I got some money behind me. Every time she sees me take a dose it's like she's keeping a tab in her head of how much I spend." I knew Sadie would like to hear that. "You suppose Stainback will try and get even with her?"

She was wearing her Russian fur hat and a new dress. It had the sleeves cut open down the front of her pudgy white arms. "She scalped him. What would you do?" She stroked the front of her arms. "I wonder how she can live with herself. As for tonight? What kind a company do you call that anyway? His throat is all puffed up like a frog's. He can't speak. How she'll stand the sight of herself tomorrow, I don't like to think. If it was me? I'd break every mirror in the house."

I didn't see anything terrible about humping Og Dorff, if you did keep the dough. Did she want Ness to burn it? Did she imagine she was a finer human being than Ness because she flung her money away? It made no sense; but I was holding fifteen dollars of hers in my sweaty hand, so I was obliged to listen to her. Even after I'd gone she continued to crab—I was halfway to the parlor before she gave out. The silence was like a big ship at sea when its engines stop; you could hear her mind fumble around, wondering what to do next.

After I slipped Mrs. Bird her twelve dollars, I had three scads left, and I toddled off into the night, looking for a drink. Somehow I found myself up the alley where Annie Paddock works. Maybe I wanted to imagine what it would be like to be a crib whore; I get curious when I'm gonged. Anyhow, when I looked back I saw Pontius was following me. He pushed me up against the wall of Bett's livery and put a bowie to my throat. My mind slurred over the details of the scene even when it was happening.

He said it wasn't safe for a girl to wander around the way I did nights. Did I want to get myself killed?

It's surprising how seldom anyone murders you, I said.

He threatened to slice my ear off and showed me how easy it would be. He said if I crossed him up he would do it in a minute. He'd heard about me and Duffield, he said. I don't remember everything he said, but after he went I needed a drink to sober myself and went to a Chinatown bar that opens till four in the morning. I have a vague idea I was thrown out of there when it shut, and I walked along the sidewalk bent double, trying to stay on my feet. Later I stopped to lie down on the road. It was pretty fine there, I liked it; but I guess I'm always restless, always want to better my condition in life, and I decided to go prospecting for a bed. Next thing I knew I was poking into someone's house and bunking in with a Chinese girl. She didn't stir, and I fell asleep next to her.

When I woke up she was gabbing to me in Chinese. She took a handful of my hair as if it was a material she was interested in, then she yanked it. I couldn't tell if she was playing with me or didn't want me smelling up her bed, so I turned out. I didn't recognize her ma or her pa, and they looked at me like they didn't know what in the world I was doing in their house. Outside, the sun was up and the street was crowded with Chinese people going about their business. I guessed it was around nine o'clock but when I got out of Chinatown it was a lot quieter and I began to think it was after seven o'clock but before eight, seeing as there were no miners going to work yet. It was interesting, morning; it was the first I'd seen here. I didn't try much to remember what had happened the previous night. You know when you open a wardrobe of clothes and find all your lovely things have been eaten up by an infestation of moths? I was afraid my memory might be full of things that would make me cry if they flew out, and bright holes.

When I made the Empress I wasn't too surprised to find Genevieve Butsch sitting in the saloon with her coat on and her things packed. I was feeling too poorly to be taken aback about anything, even when Genevieve said the other girls were downstairs with the corpse.

FOURTEEN

After the undertaker came and took the body away, I went into the bedroom. The bed was stripped to the naked mattress, just like after Alice Lebo died. It wouldn't be out of business long. There was a slight smell of arsenic and sick but that didn't bother the lovebirds, they sang and preened and all that.

Ness came in and sat on the mattress. All Sadie's things were laid out on it so that when the girls called to offer their condolences they could choose something as a keepsake.

"Some of these dresses are brand new," Ness said. "Did you take anything yet?" She looked like she'd been crying for hours.

"No," I said.

"You ought to have something to remember her by."

Sadie's Russian hat was there. I tried to imagine someone else wearing it besides Sadie. Instead I picked up a pair of handcuffs some New York cop had pinched for her. "I don't catch on," I said. "Why did she spend a fortune on those stuck-up lovebirds if she was going to finish herself? Did she make a mistake?"

Ness tried to dry her eyes with a soaking wet handkerchief, then looked at it as if it had let her down. "No, she done it a-purpose. After she sold her mining stock, she went and bought the lovebirds, the cage, and the arsenic."

"She went in a store and bought those birds when she knew she'd be dead next morning?"

"Seems that way."

Last night, when she was crabbing about Ness, she'd already decided to kill herself. "I don't get it," I said out loud. I mean, she'd been so determined I should take her side.

Ness cleared her throat and said, "We found three dollars in her pillow."

"That's all she had left?"

"It's all we could find."

"She was in the biz three years. She ought to been lousy with coin."

"She just spent it, I guess."

"You were right about her," I said. "She didn't know what money was for. One time I saw her spend fifty-two dollars for six hats she didn't even like. Went home and burned two in the stove. She'd a burned the lot only they made a poisonous smoke."

"Mrs. B says Sadie lent you fifteen dollars." Ness picked at the mattress. "Where did all your savings go?"

The inside of my scalp squirmed. "Why'd she tell you that?"

"You had better than two hundred dollars. You said you did, anyway."

I didn't know how to tell her I'd lied to her. I mean, there isn't a nice way to tell someone that. Oftentimes Ness complains in a humorous way that I'm about as reliable as a boarding-house gas fixture. This time she listened to me explain myself till it looked like she couldn't swallow another word and keep it down.

"Some of it went for clothes," I said.

"Two hundred dollars?"

"I chipped in to keep Cordelia."

"How much did you spend for liquor and opium?"

"I don't know. Some."

She stood up. She was almost out of patience with me. She folded up a shirt-waist of Sadie's and laid it on the bed the same way you would find it in a store. "Well," she said, with her back to me, "I hope you don't become a ghoul too."

"I think I would know the signs."

"You didn't see the signs with Sadie Marx," she said, and left the room.

After she'd gone, I went over and stood right next to Sadie's bed, as if that might help me to feel how miserable and disgusted with myself I was. I almost reached out and touched it.

Later that day Ness visited Mrs. Johns, the Methodist friend of Dig Squiers, to consult her about the funeral arrangements. Ness has already buried three girls; she didn't need any advice from Mrs. Johns. It was a chance to make up with Dig Squiers, that's all. I knew then that Ness would quit the life soon as the funeral was over. She would go it alone if she had to, and all evening I was desperate for Duffield to drop around. He was my one hope. I heard later he had dropped in to Larkin's—he had gone there on business, so no doubt his mind was occupied, but it was only a block away.

Among Sadie Marx's effects was a book about Buddhism with its pages still uncut; in spite of this uncertain evidence of Sadie's religious inklings, Ness decided to bury her as a Presbyterian, seeing as Mrs. Bird was one and she would be the principal mourner for the purpose of the day. The funeral was priced at a hundred and twenty dollars. None of us wanted to pay that much but you can't give a flash-girl a cheap send-off or you'll make her look like a bum. The girls have gaudy tastes; Mrs. Bird and Ness knew a lot of style was expected, and for different reasons we were all prepared to meet the expense. Ness ponied up partly out of love and partly, I think, to have the last word in her argument with Sadie. I agreed to throw in forty dollars, same as the other two, because I'm stiff-necked and proud, and next day I went to the hock shop with a baby carriage full of my dresses and cloaks. On the way I spotted Duffield across the road. He didn't see me; he was deep in conversation with one of his officers. I didn't like to go chasing after him pushing a baby wagon. I didn't even yell. He'd been back from the lake almost two days and I hadn't heard from him yet. What if I stopped him in the street and he acted like he'd forgotten who I was?

For two days the house was closed for business. Girls called to pay their respects, and I dished out coffee and cakes while they waxed sentimental about death and angels. Hetty Hoch was just saying what a great comfort it must be to us that dear Sadie had been so sweet-natured, when suddenly all the dead Romans in the room started laughing themselves sick. I heard them. I mean, I appreciate it was a hallucination but it spooked me just the same and I went to look for Ness. She'd been gone a quarter-hour or so.

She was sitting on her bed with Dig Squiers. They had all their clothes on, and were looking at something they tried to hide from me. If you'd seen the guilty look on Nessie's face and the suspicious way *he* was stroking his chin you'd of supposed it was something smutty.

"What's that you got there?"

"My savings-bank book."

She gets her savings-bank book out from inside her pillow nights and reads the gripping account of her transactions under the sheets like a boy with a spanking story. I said, "You two going into business together?"

"If the church thinks it's all right."

"I see," I said. "Without me?"

She looked awful ashamed of herself and said, "You don't have any money, Dol."

It was one of the stupidest facts I'd ever heard, but it sat there and wouldn't go away.

Sadie Marx's body had been taken to the undertaker's on B Street, and the night before the funeral we all went to sit up with her. Through the windows you could see what looked like a waxwork figure laid out on a bed, footlights of candles raising her high. All around, folks were drinking cups of coffee and eating cake and having a good old sociable. You know when you open a book and you see an illustration and you don't get it because you haven't read the book? It was like that. Under the illustration it might say something like *Mrs. Shad was a merry old soul!* Inside the undertaker's there were some gals, a couple of the dressmakers and milliners who depend on the girls for their business, and a bee of married ladies who had little to occupy them in a small frontier town like this one and were plenty willing to shed tears over a gay-girl, she be young, and white, and dead. The smell of powder and the hiss of skirts depressed me, and the way everyone said it had been an inspiration of Nessie's to lay the corpse out on a bed, it looked as though the dear girl might wake up at any moment. It had put the under-taker to a deal of trouble but we were paying high.

I had barely been led up and introduced to the corpse when I noticed Duffield was there with a lady who looked suspiciously like she might be his wife. It was the way they stood beside each other and didn't hardly speak, barring quiet asides. He was shorter than her maybe four inches. She was got up in black from hat to toe and looked rather solitary, the way tall ladies are apt to look in company. She was beautiful. There's no other word for it. She was about forty, slender and strong, with a height and lightness that made you think of a tree, a lodge-pole pine, maybe. Duffield stared in my direction once or twice with-out rightly seeing me, but whether that was his wife's influence or the result of a change in his feeling toward me, I couldn't tell.

Then the praying commenced. Tea and cakes were laid aside and all hands took a chair around the corpse. It was hard on the nerves. When Catholics sit up with a stiff, they say the rosary; by the time they are through you've done a good shift. But those Protestants kept up a cruel silence; you had to make up your own prayers. "Oh, Sadie," I tried. "May the Queen of Heaven take thee in her arms this eve. Amen." I wished I felt sadder, but the waxwork of Sadie Marx resembled the genuine article in such a poor kind of way it was hard to believe it was her. Some rambunctious lads passed by outside and distracted me. They got spooked by the sight of us and hushed each other loudly. Duffield was sitting on a hard chair in front of the window. There was nothing about his looks to recommend him except a general thunder about his presence and violet eyes, but he sat next to his beautiful wife in the confident attitude of a hussar. It was a sensational effect. You could practically see the cavalryman's pelisse slung over one shoulder. It didn't surprise him at all that he could bowl over gorgeous women. He was used to it.

He gave no sign he knew I was there. He wasn't praying, being an atheist; he had his legs stretched and appeared to be examining the shine on his shoes. Then all of a sudden there was a great deal of stir. I didn't see what caused it, I only saw what happened afterward. Mrs. Messenger was sitting next to me, dressed in spite of her age like the youngest teacher at a female seminary; she scraped her chair back, dived into her reticule, and snuck a candy into her mouth. She was blushing and Mrs. Duffield was looking at her, scandalized. That was all; but it seemed to be too much excitement for a prayer meeting. Then Duffield turned his head toward Mrs. Duffield a little, as if she might have said something, and she turned her head toward him a little as if he might have said something, like two horses talking.

I reckoned this was my last chance to speak to him and I got to my feet. Even though he saw me coming, when I touched his shoulder it seemed to give him an electric shock. In not much more than a whisper I said I needed to talk to him in private. I could smell Mrs. Duffield's scent and feel the stir between them. In the cool of the night air I walked a hundred yards, not knowing if he had followed me or not. Then I glanced back. My rib cage tightened with excitement and satisfaction, and I steered off into the darkness of a vacant lot to wait for him.

You've seen couples having back-lot affairs, they don't care much when they're caught. They might smile a little, if they notice you at all, but they can't keep their hands and their eyes off each other. He came and stood inches away from me. His shoes were built for fine carpets; yet here we were, up to our ankles in debris and junk. It was good to know I exercised such power over him, because I couldn't stop my knees trembling.

"I don't know why we're hiding," I said. "You just left your wife and followed me."

But we didn't move, either of us. In this darkness there was only me and him.

"She's beautiful," I said. I put my hands behind my back. "More beautiful than me, anyway." He stayed exactly where he was. "Did she come to the undertaker's to have a look at me?"

"Yes."

"Well, what do you suppose she thought?"

He had a bad taste in his mouth. His tongue slid out and rested at the side like it was sore. "Look here, I told you I'd make a decision about the opium and let you know." He took one last look at the world outside our little well of darkness. Then he decided to proceed. "The thing of it is, if I help you there'll be consequences."

"That what you been avoiding all this time?"

"A community can stand only so much corruption. Let me put that another way. A community can stand only a certain sort of corruption. When it's systematic, citizens are content to run down City Hall and let it drop. Different story if a cop is doing it for love."

A little light from a neighboring house spilled over us. A maid about my age was cleaning the inside of a window. When I caught her watching, she just smiled at me nicely and her eyes said wouldn't she like to have my chance. It was the drama she envied.

Duffield lowered his voice. "Different story if a cop is doing it for love like Bernie Dunne—slugging drunks with his nightstick and nipping their wads. Then forking out a bundle for pearl-embroidered shawls, white kid gloves, and a Missal to match, so's Fanny Stilts looks swell when she goes to Mass. A community won't be elevated to poetical thoughts or raise a subscription for a pair of star-crossed sneak thieves."

Bernie Dunne is dead and Fanny Stilts wears a stunning pair of crutches. I said, "Can't you take a tin of opium and sell it on the quiet?"

"I can't do anything in this town in secret. If I break the law the whole town will know. If I do this for you, I'm going to have to skip town for good. Understand?" There was an edge to his words he wanted me to feel. "That's what I mean by consequences."

"I see."

"How would you like that?"

It was all I could do to stay on my feet. "I see," I said.

"You might have to slope too," he said.

My heart hammered. Did he mean we should elope together? I decided now was not the time to tell him my true feelings. "I guess I can take the consequences, if you can," I said, choosing my words.

He nodded like we had made an agreement. He didn't kiss me or anything. I searched his face to see what this would mean for his wife and any other older women he had a sentimental attachment to. He had an expression on his face like he didn't much care for himself, or me either, seeing the way we were prepared to behave toward people less fortunate than ourselves. I began to dislike myself too. I felt more glee than anyone should feel, ever. It was hard to hide all of it.

"Tomorrow, then," he said, and walked off.

I was so excited I couldn't go home. I coasted around town and got well-and-trulied. Sometimes when I'm gonged I get a wonderful coldness of the brain and feel a little superior to other mortals, as if someone is patting me on the back and telling me to have confidence in my own powers. That night I felt like I governed the town, and the stars, too.

FIFTEEN

About a hundred mourners jammed the Presbyterian hall for Sadie Marx's funeral service. The Catholics and Jews waited outside, silent and solemn, alongside Izzy Wink and Olive Ptoots and Annie Paddock. They were anxious to keep from the Christian ladies in the hall the fact that Sadie was acquainted with common hookers like themselves, lest it leave a stain on her memory, but to demonstrate the depth of their grief, and their decency, they had gotten themselves up in any amount of exquisite veils and vast volumes of black lace. Annie and Olly resembled brides in black; little Izzy Wink looked like an imp of hell making her first Holy Communion.

When I saw the crowd that showed up I realized some people grow in stature once they're dead. People talked about Sadie Marx like she was a comet or something, the kind of thing you only meet with once in a life. Ricardo Lara, who made strange stylish hats for her from ideas she sketched, had kept her drawings, seeing they were so unusual; Callaghan the stockbroker remembered sharp remarks she'd made on particular mining stocks; death improved her in everyone's eyes but mine. She *was* a sort of comet. You watched the spectacle from a distance. Even the times she would keep you in fits of laughter an hour or more, it always left a part of you cold. You knew you were nothing to her but an audience. Look at the way she swelled around the kitchen of the lake hotel preaching her gospel to the scrubbers. What was she doing there?

Six firemen carried the casket from the hall to the plumed hearse, six carriages of girls followed the hearse to the Protestant graveyard; and if there is anything more melancholy in this world than a brand-new cemetery, it's a brand-new cemetery that's filling up fast. From our graveyard you can look out over the town below and watch the world go on without you. The hoisting works of the mines are just nothing, the mine tailings and the immense piles of cordwood that fire the engines kill everything else. If your eyes drift from the burial of your friend, you can watch Lilliputians with ropes tackle a huge stack of square-set timbers, or lay track around the stamp mills. As the minister spoke a few words over the grave, I noticed Mama standing apart from the other mourners behind a tree. She appeared to be wearing all the clothes she owned, probably to hide how dirty she was. Then the minister was done and we threw earth on the casket: Mrs. Bird first, with Giz as her esquire, holding her arm in case she staggered, on account of grief or liquor; then Cordelia; then Ness; then me. When people left the graveside I stayed awhile till Ness took my arm and led me away. Just then Cordelia dropped to her knees and refused to leave. She beat her fists on the ground and cried till her throat was raw.

Once when I was eight, a mad dog ambushed me and scared me out of my skin. I got around it, but it followed me and barked and barked and barked. Just when I thought the scare was over and I was safe, the dog leaped up and gripped my hood between its teeth and hung there awhile, back of me. I remember the peculiar silence, and the dog hanging there, and the feeling at the back of my neck. When Cordelia howled at the graveside it hit me the same way. It's the kind of sensation it's still there ten minutes later.

After the funeral reception Ness went to meet Dig Squiers and that crowd in the Boule d'Or, and I watched her go with a vast deal of complacency. I was expecting Duffield that night, and I wanted to tell Ness she needn't worry herself; pretty soon the lush under my bed would be sitting safe and snug in the station house and pretty soon after that we'd have ourselves a buster of a saloon, and could retire. Mrs. Bird started two new girls that day to replace Sadie Marx and Genevieve. I took them to a saloon on C Street and got tight all afternoon. We were just discussing the death rate when Cordelia showed up; Ness had sent her to get me, by hack. There was trouble at the saloon, was all Cordelia would say. Inside the carriage she huddled under a blanket and outshivered a sail. She was having a miscarriage, she said. She's had more miscarriages than Justice, Cordelia; she has them wonderfully.

I expect you've been in an ice cream saloon when everyone is gabbing and dinging their spoons on their glasses and creating a ferocious din and then there's a sudden upset of some sort and everyone stops to see what the matter is. The silence is immense. That's the size of silence there was in the Empress. The gang of kids was there—the Chinese boy and the fat girl, the nervous kid that kept pulling at his pants, and the one that walked as though he had a disease of the groin. The kid with no face, he was bossing the show. They had tied Pontius to a chair and they were spelling each other, using his head to smash beer glasses. The boys in the saloon didn't interfere any. They had their Colts, but if you shot one of them kids it'd be the last thing you did; the rest of the gang would nail you for it. Every so often the kid with no face would go up to one of the boys and swipe his glass of lager and the fellow wouldn't say a word. Then the kid would take and smash the glass all over the fat pimp. Pontius had a hump like a cat, he didn't want the pieces of glass to get down the back of his shirt. At first I was afraid he'd notice me, but when someone's whacking your nut with beer glasses you probably don't see too far.

From just inside the door I watched the diseased-looking kid saw the buttons off Pontius's waistcoat with a knife (like there was diamond in them after all) while Ness tipped me to what she knew. Seemed the kids had found Pontius late afternoon lying doggo in the cellar of Frank Clement's bar; they'd been kicking him up and down D Street since then. He wouldn't tell them what they wanted to know, kept raising himself to his knees and crawling away from them. He'd dragged himself into the Empress a half-hour back, Ness said out of the side of her mouth. "He's come here on purpose, I reckon. Only the cops can save him now," she said.

"Did you send for them?"

"I sent for them an hour back but they didn't show up yet. They'd turn out for you; if you asked them, that is."

I didn't say anything; I decided to watch for a while before I made any decisions.

"We can do this all day," the kid with no face tells Pontius, clipping his head with a tumbler. "You sing out anytime you want to tell us where the bundle is."

Then the kid stands back, takes in the saloon, goes up to Alec Jewell, the English photographer. Jewell wears a sarcastic mustache and belongs to a religious fellowship called the Mortalists. They believe that you die. I mean, they don't believe anything extra. Sundays, they get together and celebrate their belief with hymns of thanks in a room above the Antelope restaurant. I don't know why they pick Sundays, but anyhow.

The kid with no face says to him, "You using your shooter?"

Right away the other kids bunch up on Jewell and the diseased kid hits him in the kidneys, not *too* hard, just enough to spill a note out of him.

"You hear me, bo?"

"I hear you."

"I'm only asking a loan of something you ain't using."

"Here," Alec Jewell goes. He gives the kid his piece. Then he says, "You're already wearing a gun."

The kid's voice hasn't broken yet; it comes and goes. "I like to use someone else's shooter when I kill my man," he says. "Sometimes I have someone else pull the trigger too." He waves the gun in front of Jewell. "You don't mind, do you?"

"No," the photographer manages to say. He wants to say something sharper than that but he can't come it.

"That's mighty white of you. Mind if I shoot you?"

Jewell doesn't want to die, but he doesn't want to seem unhelpful either. "I gave you the gun, didn't I?"

"Yes, you did. I could shoot the shine right out a your eyes."

"That's right."

"I got a better idea. Take off your drawers."

Alec wants to say no, you've crowded me too far this time. Instead he peels and stands there naked. That mustache don't look so sarcastic now. The kid tells Alec to put the drawers over Pontius's face, and Alec walks over there sort of on his toes.

Pontius is wearing his cream coat—he still looks like a stuck-up pimp—and he shies away from them underpants. But once they are over his head he is just nothing, and the kid puts the shooter to his head and fires.

Twice. Three times. Each time I turn away in case I see his brains all over someone else's face, but each time I turn back the pimp is still sitting there, with those drawers over his head. The kid is aiming to miss, I suppose; he's trying to scare Pontius out of his mind. Pontius can feel the gun at his head, but he can't see anything, and every time the gun goes off he is deafened, and sick with terror. The fourth time he gets to his feet and yowls and it's hideous, you can't see his face. He's hobbled to the chair, he can't go very far, and when he settles back down he starts in heaving. His guts are in earnest to get out of there; they try and try till the kid smacks his head with the butt of the gun, and that does the trick. His guts decide to stay put. I'm thinking, Go ahead, kid. Do it. Make me rich.

"Won't you do something?" Ness says. "It's awful just to stand here and watch."

The kid puts the shooter to the fat pimp's head and says, "I reckon it's this way, Pontius. I got two bullets in this here Colt, and I'm going to blow your brains out barring you tell us whereabouts you stowed the bundle. Now, you're probably thinking, That's a pretty good one! You're thinking, If they blow my brains out, what's the percentage in that? They won't ever find out where I cached the swag. They're playing a losing hand. Well, they're your brains. They'll be spread all over them pants, you miscalculate."

But Pontius knows that soon as he tells the kids where the lush is, they will do what they like with him. That's why he hasn't leaked yet. So now the kid with no face hands the pistol to the nervous kid, the one that keeps pulling at his pants and picking his nose. "Dingo, take this gun and stick it on him." Then he says to Pontius, "Don't believe you was ever introduced to Dingo."

He shakes his head, with those underpants on.

"Dingo here's a new chum. He ain't done the business yet. He ain't croaked a girl, even."

Dingo's a bluff, sure, but he doesn't know that; what if he gets carried away and pulls the trigger?

Dingo says, "Want me to kill him?"

"You want to be our chum, don't you?"

"Guess so."

"You don't want to be our pal then up and say so, we can end our 'sociation forthwith."

"I can plug him okay, you sure that's what you want all right."

"You don't wipe *someone* out you can't be one of us. That's how we run this mob. Now this is your chance. Stick that piece in Pontius's ear, pal. Go ahead."

"Like that?"

Dingo is shaking like an engine. He puts the shooter in the pimp's ear, and the boys in the saloon are expecting their shirts or their glasses to be splashed with blood or brains any moment now. They make noises like you never heard before.

"Got it right in his ear."

"That's upper-class, bub. Pontius don't sing out, you got to pull the trigger. Do you hear him sing?"

"No."

"Do you hear him sing?"

"No."

That's when the kid with no face punches Dingo, hard. "Blow his pimp brains out."

"I will."

"Go ahead, buddy!"

I almost yell, Go ahead, buddy!

Dingo yells, "You hear me, Pontius?" His face is screwed up and he's shying away so that when he fires the gun he won't get any of the pimp over him. If he did he would cry, or go mad, or something.

"Put a torpedo in his brain," the kid tells him.

"I will."

"Slip him the sweet one."

"I will!"

"Shoot, you gump, or give me the gun."

We are all cringing away from the bullet we expect when Pontius stands and points at nobody in particular and shouts, "She's got it! That bitch there has got it. Remember who told you, kids, remember it was me that brought you here. That double-crossing bitch has got the loot under her bed. Go look if you don't believe me."

The space around shrinks away from me. I've never felt so alone. Then there's an immense explosion and the plate-glass windows of the saloon break like a wave, and bury half of the boys under the thundering surf.

SIXTEEN

The smell of gunfire blew in through the smashed windows and about twelve policemen piled into the saloon, yelling at everyone to put their hands up. The kids were as surprised as anyone. They had ducked to shelter themselves from the bullets and the glass; next thing they knew, the cops were sticking pistols in their faces and putting bracelets on them. Only the diseased kid got away; he ran downstairs and out the back. This all happened in a matter of seconds; then Duffield walked in, coat loose around his shoulders, as though we'd gone and spoiled his night at the opera.

He was a little mellow. He whirled off his coat, flung it over the back of a chair, and sat down. "Gen'lemen; these officers are middle-aged, underpaid, and married. Don't try their patience."

The boys stared at him, shocked and cut. One man was dripping blood from his face onto the floor, but they all waited patiently while the cops corralled the kids into the hurry-up wagon. Then Duffield told them to clear the bar and the glass-spittled boys went outside, wiping themselves with handkerchiefs.

Pontius was still tied to the chair with Alec Jewell's underpants over his face. Duffield took no notice of him. He told his cops to search the rooms downstairs; he had information the bundle was under one of the girls' beds, he said. They found it in a minute. One carried the crate and six of them surrounded it, guns drawn, like it was a stagecoach treasure box; they huddled it onto the police wagon, came back for Pontius. Throughout the proceedings Duffield didn't look at me once; he wore his police-chief face right along.

Downstairs in our room Ness and I didn't say much. My bed had been pulled about when the cops frisked the place. There were bandboxes and shoes lying about just any old how, as though anything that was worth anything had been taken away, and I got a silly tear in my eye. I missed the opium something awful; I had to remind myself it was in a safer place. I didn't say anything to Ness about my hopes; I wanted to wait till it was a sure thing. Instead I asked how her meet with Dig Squiers went. Good, she said. She wouldn't be drawn, but the mention of his name was enough to put some deep color into her skin, like they'd given each other some pretty solemn assurances.

Seeing the Empress was closed, it was arranged we could drop into the Delta next door to pull some jobs, and jesus, it was something. The walls were sweating, the band was reckless, the boys were at the jumping-off place, and Sally Clocker was out of her mind and pretty near out of her bodice. I said she was a sweet girl and we all loved her heaps; I said the gents must be fascinated by her endearing young charms without she exhibited them in full. All the time I was jollying her, I could see Ness working a handsome silver-haired gent. As they moved toward the dance floor, Ed Stainback appeared and took her arm. Ness paled and apologized to the silver-haired gent and let Edgar lead her through the press of the crowd to buy her something at the bar.

Stainback is small and has those long arms, and he kept his head down while he explained to her the depth of his emotions.

He isn't a violent man, he's a well-doing locksmith of good standing in the community. All the same, I didn't like the way he was holding her by the wrist. I saw him sneak something out of his pocket and hold it down by his side out of sight. I suspected it was a weapon of some kind but even though I was only four yards away I couldn't stop what happened. The saloon was so jammed I only *saw* a part of it. I don't know if Ness screamed. If she did, I didn't hear her; that's how noisy it was. I tried to push through two fellows to get to her but I spilled their drinks and one of them laid ahold of me. As I struggled to free myself, Stainback went for Nessie's face with what looked like a razor and she blocked it with her bare arm. A long slit opened, like a slash in the sleeve of a cream dress, showing the crimson beneath.

That's when Arthur Griffiths—the man who was holding me—saw what I was screaming about. He's small and wide, and his fists are fat, but solid. Suddenly Stainback was mustached with blood and his nose seemed to slide to the side like it hadn't been stuck on right. He held on to Nessie's hair like grim death, though. He'd gotten ahold of what he wanted and he would not let go. Before Arthur Griffiths could punch him again he dropped to his knees with Nessie's hair in his fist. Ness bent over double and Stainback slashed upward with the razor. He cut her chin open. Maybe I was hysterical but I thought I saw the white of her bone, and after that I don't remember anything very clearly.

Arthur Griffiths kicked all the air out of Stainback and left him along the street a piece. We brought Ness home, made her sandwiches, and fussed over her until the doctor came. Then I sat in the darkness of the saloon and let my thoughts think themselves while the wind blew through the nonexistent windows. It was shutting time; the boys were starting back to their lousy lodging rooms and overcrowded beds. When it gets to that hour, those among them that have not taken liquor enough to disguise their bedmate or the great big tackety boots he'll be wearing are liable to get grouchy and slambang British foreign policy in China, or their pal, or both. Ed Stainback was on the road right outside the Empress; two fellows on their way home toyed with his carcass as he lay in the dirt, almost past movement, but they didn't see any fun in him.

Toward midnight a carriage arrived for me, and the driver gave me an invite from Duffield to join him at his club. It was the interview I'd been expecting—I supposed he would ask me to elope with him and I would have to give him the mitten. I popped in to see how Ness was before I went, and hold her hand. The doctor was not much older than us, wore his hair with a natty center parting and his teeth likewise. Ness had been bled white, so the sewing looked real grisly, and the doc had stitched up her chin and under her chin. He said she would mend well, but it looked like a bad-drawn beard to me.

She'd been dosed with opium; her eyes were pretty faraway. "Them kids," she said dreamily. "They're going to be awful sore when they get out of the jug. You think they might have it in for you?" She stared at the paper on the wall and its design of tobacco-colored flowers. "Duffield's probably thought of that, though." She seemed to be wishing someone had given as much consideration to *her* safety and well-being.

"Duffield's invited me to his club," I said. I wanted to say "I promise with all my heart I'll make you rich and happy." Instead I said, "Don't worry. I'll be back soon." But I put as much feeling into it.

On the way to the club I sat beside the carriage driver. A suck of wind got ahold of my thoughts, lifted them fifty feet high, and scattered them all over the mountain. When I arrived, it was all I could do to piece my smile together.

"We won't be disturbed here," Duffield said, showing me into the club's library. He looked like a man that wouldn't know a gag if he got off a good one and you laughed at it, and a man as solemn as that generally means to propose.

A small coal fire was burning. The coal was from Chile, he said, making small talk; I said they had good coal in Chile and he dipped his head toward me as though acknowledging a fellow connoisseur. The atmosphere of a library didn't suit the energy of his character; he walked as if he wished he was wearing slippers so he could pad about and make less noise. I took a seat, at his invitation, one of those oxblood leather chairs built for rich old men to doze away their boozy lives in. I sat on the edge. He squared his shoulders in that proud way he had of showing off his missing arm, and started.

SEVENTEEN

"I've been thinking about canal laborers, of late. They grizzle their backs and bust their knees building her, and if it breaks their hearts, too, it's all one to the canal. There's not much pride left in a navvy after a hard winter, I expect, and I been learning some lessons too, of late. I was rather full of myself till I fell in love this time," he said. "You'd of heard me toot my toot as good as the next man. Now?" He shook his head; not now.

I'd never seen him as tense as this; I was almost frightened for him. After he mended the fire he crossed to a sideboard to fix us a couple of brandies, still holding the poker in the only hand he's got. He didn't know what to do with it so he rested it upon a silver tray of small sherry glasses. It caused a good deal of distress and shakiness among the glasses but no ultimate loss.

"Frankly, it's humiliating," he said, "but I realize I want to spend all my time in the company of one woman. I never did feel that way about Mrs. Duffield. It's been a revelation, I can tell you." He handed me a brandy. He was shivering, the smallest sort of tremble, like a sheet of water. "We're going to leave town tonight. We'll make the Bay before the New York boat sails Friday."

I had to be careful. He had the boodle. "Tonight? I can't be ready that fast," I said. "Besides, Ness is lying sick-abed and Mama is in shantytown in a perilous state."

He took a sip of brandy. "No, I mean Margaret and me are leaving town."

"Margaret?"

"Mrs. Messenger." It was a good fire and Duffield took off his jacket, as though the formality of a gentleman's club was too much for him. He wanted to lounge around in his shirt like he was at home, with the extra shirt sleeve folded around his stump as smart and neat as a store clerk does up a package with string. "You mean you didn't know?"

"No."

"You surprise me." Then he went and sat down. "It started as a regulation affair. I would take her to Murray's Melodeon," he said, blushing in apology. "We talked a little afterward but only to be polite and put a better gloss on the thing. As time went on we chatted more and more. She's no more interesting than you or I but I could listen to her talk about anything. Curtains. And feel just musical. It was me that made her come to the Missionary Fathers' ball that night. I guess husbands are the most romantic of men, when they start on an affair, anyhow; I wanted to stand beside her in public. You know? I wanted to hear her asides on the people we ran into, or the buffet. Anyhow, it was a mistake. That's when the rumors started flying around."

"What did Mrs. Duffield think?"

"She hadn't fixed her suspicions on anyone, but she knew her husband was all adrift. She began to talk about taking the children away to her sister's for a while. I don't suppose it was wise or even kind of me but I decided to throw dust in her eyes and the eyes of the public by taking you to the theater. The bigger the scandal, the better, I thought. It was harder than I'd imagined it would be, that first night at the theater. I wanted to make a big show. But I didn't like making a fool of my wife, or you either for the matter of that. Then we went for ice cream and you made it plain you couldn't ever care for me, and that suited me perfectly."

That first evening I'd imagined his coldness toward me was because he had to bite back his true feelings. It was just the opposite. It was his conscience telling on him. What was his scheme when you looked at it? It was to deceive Mrs. Duffield for a few months while he tried to figure out what to do; and rubbishy as his plan was, he hadn't scrupled to use me as a part of it. I was a flash-girl. He hadn't given me that much thought. It made me mad I hadn't seen through it all. I'd heard the tale about their affair before I saw them. Every day, practically, I'd heard the talk around. But that's just it—it had gotten so stale I hadn't bothered to listen.

"When we were sitting up with Sadie Marx in the funeral parlor," I said, "Mrs. Messenger was there. And something happened that I didn't see, that sent her diving into her bag for candy."

"Mrs. Duffield caught Margaret and I," he said, "exchanging a look. She was taken aback but she didn't know what to make of it."

"That why you followed me to the vacant lot?"

"It certainly helped to draw Mrs. Duffield's attention from Mrs. Messenger."

"I foxed the trail, huh?" That was the night the maid had seen us from the window and wished she could have been me.

"But what good did it do? You didn't think Mrs. Duffield would get sore you were having an affair with me?"

"A woman can feel a little superior to a husband who has a silly infatuation with a girl half his age. She can expect the sympathy of her friends. If she'd ever found out about Mrs. Messenger she wouldn't have called on her friends. She wouldn't have gone outdoors. Mrs. Duffield is a beautiful woman and Margaret"—he paused—"is not. She's older than Mrs. Duffield and looks a little comical. Mrs. Duffield might have been inclined to take the thing as a slight on her personality."

I went and helped myself to another brandy. I didn't see any reason to be polite, and I drink more when I'm angry. Duffield moved in his leather chair; it creaked like boots in snow. "She's going to find out about Mrs. Messenger pretty soon," I said.

"I'm sorry about that."

He didn't get my point. "What changed?" I said.

"After we went to see your mother in shantytown, when we were in your room at the Empress, you made it pretty clear you knew about my affair. You said something I took as a threat."

"I like that!"

"Then you asked me to help you fence the *gow*. I thought you were shaking me down." He got up and went to mend the fire, even though there was nothing wrong with it. "That's when I knew I had to straighten things up and get out of town." He tonged some coals onto the fire.

"I only hope you haven't let me down over the opium, too."

The fire was a small bank of smoky black coals. He put the tongs down and faced around. "I did what I could."

The smell of dead cigars is more sensuous than anything I

know. It seems to promise everything. "I hope you haven't let me down," I repeated, holding on to my insides.

The poker was hanging on a fire stand. When he picked it up it made a small *ching*. "After we gathered up the kids and caged them, first thing my officers wanted to know was how they could fence the stuff. What their share of the divvy was going to be. Cops"—he shrugged—"I've seen murals in a saloon with more conscience. I told them, 'Go ahead.' I told them I look forward to eating some Chinese pork dumplings and trying to figure out whose balls they are."

"What's this you're giving me?"

He stuck the poker into the black belly of the fire. "Pontius lifted the *gow* from a Chinese boat in the Bay. It's Li Yun, some of the best stuff you can get. The Chinese company who owned the merchandise didn't go to the police to make their complaint, not having any existence as persons in the eyes of the law. They talked to Harry Fan instead." He let go of the poker. It stayed where it was, sticking out of the fire like an arrow.

"Harry Fan?"

"He's the boss of a San Francisco mob."

"Don't get gay with me. I know who Harry Fan is." He once gave a girlfriend of ours chloroform, then skinned her face.

"It was Harry Fan who hired the gang of kids to get after Pontius. He's promised them a thousand dollars and a little harbor boat if they bring back the lush."

A tear of sweat ran down my spine. "It's worth a whole lot of dingbats," I said. "Who you aiming to sell it to?"

"When people hear Harry Fan's name it takes all the tuck out of them."

"You trying to tell me nobody will buy the goods."

"Nobody on this coast."

He drew the poker out of the fire, hung it up without a sound, and sat down. Everything in that room was so solid it was hard to believe all my hopes had been an illusion. Out of the black coals a solitary flame jumped up and started waving. For a long while the fire blew that single flame from its black puffed-out cheeks, like a cherub that blows winds on a map. We didn't speak a word for about an hour. That isn't a manner of speaking, there was a clock. It announced the quarters and the halves with one of those chimes whose voice has been soaked in fine port for forty years. It was rich, mature, discreet, well content. I was none of those things. I had no standing in society and no purpose in life: I wasn't looking forward to going outside. I sat and listened to the clock, paralyzed. In the end I shifted in my seat and cleared my throat to forewarn him I was going to speak. "Give the opium to me. I'll sell it."

After a deep moment of silence he said, "It's gone."

"Where?"

"The desert, about eighty miles from here, place by the name of Sand Springs. I sent Pontius there, with an escort guard of three policemen. I couldn't send him for trial without sending you, too, seeing as you received the stolen goods and hid them. I told my men to handcuff him to the swag."

"Sand Springs?"

"It's a station on the stage line to Salt Lake City and the States, three days travel from here. It's abandoned right now on account of the Indian depredations, and midway of an ugly piece of desert."

"Won't the cops make off with the swag?"

"If they did I wouldn't miss them, but I don't think they'll chance it. I told the jailer to turn the gang of kids loose after a couple days; they can create all the mayhem they like in that howling desert. It's what it was made for. If you want a piece of the pandemonium, you know where the drug is."

"You said you'd help me."

"I saved your life this evening. I also broke the law for you: I ought to have given the opium back to the kids, or the Chinese business men who own it."

I had the feeling that, after I went, he would breathe a sigh of relief, then pack. I sat there another twenty minutes and let rage eat up every last piece of me in a ravenous silence. By the time I got up to go, I'd concluded to make Sand Springs before the kids did.

EIGHTEEN

Outside I took up as little sidewalk as I could, even though it was dark and late and pretty much deserted. I didn't want anyone to see me now I'd been flung out of power.

Ed Stainback was still lying on the road outside the Empress. A wagon rolled up, just as I got there, and lit him with its lamps. His face was slick as paint, like it might slip off, and the driver drove around him, leery like. I went to have a closer look. I was worldless too, almost as much as he was.

Two of his fingers were broken and no part of him could move excepting his peepers. His mouth had dribbled blood that had mixed with the floury dust and made little crumbs of cake around his mouth, as if he was an untidy eater; but he still had an air about him. His eyes had the hardness of a cardinal in his final hour who has gotten used to being right about everything and doesn't much relish Death or any surprises it might bring.

"Why did you do that to Ness?" I said. "'Cause she ate up all your savings?"

"Ness could take every dime I got," he said.

"What then?"

"She told me she was going to quit."

"And you can't allow that."

The cardinal closed his eyes, as though he was patiently

considering some objection to a point of doctrine that had been made a thousand times already. "No, I can't." When he opened his eyes again he said, "Sooner see her dead."

"Why should you care?" I said. "You're bankrupt."

If he could have moved he would have waved this objection away as immaterial. "I'll kill her stone dead."

I almost kicked dirt in his face only I reckoned it would give me no satisfaction. After I had settled in my mind there was nothing I could do that *would* satisfy me completely, I stepped on his broken finger with the sharp heel of my boot, watched his face silently scream for a minute, then went inside.

The bedroom was all pulled around. It would have been awfully woebegone even without Ness looking so poorly. I drew up a chair to the side of her bed.

"What did he say?" she asked.

"Oh, nothing. He's leaving town with Mrs. Messenger."

She'd heard the rumors same as everyone else.

"I didn't love him anyway," I said.

"I'm sorry just the same." She knew better than anyone how the gals would snigger over this.

There was a plate on the floor by her bed, with some orange peel on it and a few triangles of egg sandwich. She asked me to hand her the plate. The sandwiches had curled up a little at the sides. She took one and looked at it, all three sides. She put it to her mouth but didn't bite.

I said, "Ed Stainback's still lying on the road out there."

"He tried to cut my throat."

"He means to try again."

"Should I go somewhere else?"

"Where?" I said.

166

"I don't know. Sacramento? Placerville?"

"He'd follow you. He's dead set." The population of California and Nevada is maybe a hundred thousand; you'd find a girl with a stitched-up chin sooner than a big church.

"He's a maniac," she said. She snapped that out as much as she could without opening her mouth too much. She didn't want to trouble her stitches. "If the cops had any concern for law and order they'd cage him."

"He's lost about everything he owned," I said. "In the cold light of day nobody will blame Ed Stainback much."

She knew that. Her cheeks sank. She turned away and considered her sorry circumstances.

I took my time. "We could light out for the States."

She gave that a good deal of consideration. "He could follow us there. Couldn't he?"

"He's broke. You can't cross that fifty-mile desert without supplies and a mule to carry them."

"He would try it," she said. "He's insane."

"He'd die just the same."

Ness bit the knuckle of her index finger white but I could tell by her eyes I'd made a strike. From here in the far west all the way to the States is two thousand miles across a wilderness of wolves and Indians and sagebrush desert; it's a journey of four months by wagon and you can't do it bankrupt.

"It would cost considerable," she said.

"It most certainly would."

"Four mules, a wagon, stores. What do you reckon, eight hundred dollars?"

"I guess."

"How would we afford it?" She meant how could *I* afford it.

"Duffield's sending three cops out to Sand Springs to dump the opium and Pontius along. They'll handcuff Pontius and leave him to die there. The boodle is ours if we want to go and lift it. You can have half shares in it. More than half. And out of my share I'll pay a half of what you ante up for the trip." In case that wasn't clear, I said, "I think we should go halves on everything."

Her nails ticked against the head-board of the bed. "What about the Indian depredations?"

"The Indians stopped molesting people two months back. They got other things to do now. You think you can be easy in your mind here when Ed Stainback's on the cut?"

"Then there's those kids."

"I don't see where they come in."

"They'll get after the loot, won't they?"

"No," I lied. "Duffield is sending them back to the water-front, where they belong."

One last thing was troubling her. She tried to say what it was with the minimum of emotion. "I can't leave Dig Squiers without saying goodbye at least." Then she stared straight ahead while the tin lantern decorated her face and night-dress with spots. She was pretty as anything when you couldn't see her chin.

"Pay him a visit tomorrow."

"He'll see what happened to me," she said. She could barely allow herself to imagine what judgment he'd pass on her. The thought stood on the outside of her eyes.

"I know," I said.

"It's not that I'm vain," she said, though her voice broke in two when she said it. "It's just that he'll want to know why

Stainback did it." She stared hard ahead, to keep her tears back. She kept her head perfectly still.

"Well," I said, "what difference does it make? You're going to the States. You're done with him anyway."

She considered the question for two long minutes. "I suppose," she said. She gave the tiniest of nods, enough to spill the tears down her face.

PART TWO

ONE

Next morning I wanted to skin out first thing but Ness was a
heavy drag; I needed a snifter with a couple drops in it to tranquilize my nerves. First she put some shiny salve on her wound,
as if she wasn't fit to be seen out, and rustled about the bedroom
for an hour deciding what cosmetics she would take on the trip.
It was after one before we bought ourselves a wagon and
supplies, and Ness made everyone agree to buy things back, at
the same price we had paid, if we failed of going. Then, when
we got home, she asked the bar-tender for paper and ink and
wrote a letter to Dig. She sent Cordelia with it.

To remind her that some of us have obligations in life besides ourselves, I took her to shantytown. Ness was already a
lurid white after the blood she'd lost, but when she saw Mama in
these new circumstances she turned a color, well, it was the
color of wallpaper paste, near as I can describe it. Mama and five
fellows who had scalded-pink faces and legs they had borrowed
for the afternoon were sharing a bottle of forty-rod whiskey.
They were pentecostal. They spoke in strange tongues and
understood one another perfectly. Two of them, that didn't
know a pick from a shovel and had very likely never lifted anything heavier than a skirt, sang songs about the gold-diggins
with tears of nostalgia in their eyes. Mama gave herself more

airs than ever; even when she fell on her backside she sat there and reigned over her subjects, and they let her.

It's hard to watch someone you love turn into a poor copy of a human being. I have tried everything I know to remind her of her better self. I have warned her of the consequences to her sanity, frightened her with examples of drunkards who have died before their time, told her I love her, or I hate her, or I'm ashamed of her, or all those things in the same conversation. It's hopeless. She still has feelings but she can't always lay her hands on them, or not for long enough at a time. Anyhow, we lured her to the Empress by promising anything she asked for; we had no idea what she was asking for, we just said sure, drove her to D Street, sat her in the saloon, and stood her drinks.

At half past three our outfit showed up—a wagon and four mules packed with the supplies we had ordered—and a little later Cordelia arrived to say that Dig was asleep in his room at the Hotel d'Afrique after driving back from Placerville overnight with a wagon full of fresh flowers, and nothing could roust him up. Ness sent her to try again, and we started stowing our plunder in the wagon. It was Mrs. Bird who reminded me about the piano I'd hauled from the Bay and put in store. She offered ninety dollars and two crates of London Jockey Club gin for it. I told the barkeep to carry the booze to the wagon and to make sure Mama noticed him. Her pimp was beside her, begging her to stay. She was talking to him the way kids do before they know any words, but when she saw the liquor her eyes and ears perked up like a dog's. She was still listening to the hard jangle of the last gin crate landing on the wagon-bed after it had died away, the way you might consider the last note of a concert.

That's where I was when Cordelia arrived with a letter from Dig Squiers: I was in the saloon with Mama. Ness was outside superintending two men who were packing the wagon. Through the new plate-glass window the glaziers were hoisting into place I saw her open the letter from Dig. After she had studied it out, she asked Cordelia some questions. Cordelia couldn't answer them, not to Nessie's satisfaction anyway. I saw Nessie's eyes needle with the coming on of tears. I didn't want to give her time to dwell on it. I helped Mama out of the saloon and put her on a mattress in the wagon, then I climbed onto the box, took the reins, and at a quarter after four we made tracks.

At the corner of E Street I drove past the diseased-looking kid. I was scared Ness would see him. She wouldn't adventure her savings on a trip across the continent if she knew the gang of kids would be right behind us, soon as the rest of them were turned loose, anyway; and the kid had that peculiar shamed way of dragging himself along like he had bad sores under his pants, you couldn't miss him; but Ness was walking on the blind side of the wagon and didn't notice. She was doubtful enough as it was.

All the way down the steep grade of Six Mile Canyon to the sagebrush flat of the Carson Valley, where we joined the wagon road and pushed on in the dry, engine-hot heat of the afternoon, Ness walked like I was leading her into an ambush. From time to time Mama would yell at the world from the back of the wagon, and Cordelia followed behind, carrying Sadie Marx's lovebirds, like some kind of hoodoo. There was nothing to lighten our mood until we camped in the shelter of some cotton-woods along the Carson River, and a crowd of Snake Indians paid us a visit to swap some of their fish.

Now, here's the best piece of advice you will ever get in my experience, if you wish to live in peace with the Indian nations and travel through their lands alive. Gingersnaps. Indians have a sweet tooth worse than any people on earth. We gave them gingersnaps enough for twenty men, women, and children; they gave us two fish. They wore rabbit skins, these Indians, or nothing at all, and had cunning bows and arrows, but Ness would have nothing to do with them. After they decamped, she bedded down and I stayed up to think over the struggles of the day. I'd had no way to make Ness quit on that town except by using every last ounce of my willpower, so I was pretty tense; but after I hit the missy and gin I began to relax, feel my achievement, and spread myself a little.

Next thing I knew I was walking through the desert with two coyotes at my heels. I knew it wasn't a dream because I could barely see and there was a wind on my face. The coyotes didn't appear vicious; they acted like they were seeing me off their property or something. Well, if you don't know where you are, it's hard to find your way back home. Any direction you go in might be the wrong one. That tires you out pretty good, and I dropped onto one knee to rest. One of the coyotes got so close to my face I could smell his breath. I tried to push him away and missed, rested awhile on all fours. Sleep crept up and extinguished me. After I'd been out a little while, it seemed as though someone was trying to pinch my arm. I heard myself yelling, opened my eyes to see the coyotes back away.

I still didn't know where I was going but I set off anyway. Out of nowhere I saw a light. It was Ness holding a lantern. I walked toward her and all of a sudden it was like putting my foot through something that wasn't there. I don't know what all

I hit before I wound up lying on my back with my leg snagged in a bush above. It seemed there was a river between me and Ness and I had dropped down onto the bank. I wondered why Ness hadn't warned me; I even wondered if she'd been playing a trick on me, but she probably supposed I would notice the geographical feature myself. She called out to me and held up her light and I waded into the water. Halfway across I got so weary I had a yen to lie down on the riverbed that I couldn't resist. Unlucky for me, the bed was under some water and wasn't as soft and welcoming as I'd imagined it would be. I couldn't go to sleep because I had water in my mouth and nose, and Ness had to haul me out of there. It was a hard fight, for either the strong hands of the river or my sodden clothes seemed to drag me back.

TWO

You know how, after a big drunk, your friends sometimes speak to you as though you're a perfectly ordinary, decent human being, except they look at your ear and smile weakly when you speak to them? Well, after breakfasting on some of that I followed the others into the Twenty-Six-Mile Desert, ashamed to be alive.

The road was littered with the skeletons of wagons, furniture, overcoats, hats, and all sorts of ironmongery. Seeing the stuff people had discarded to make things easier for their animals, we knew we were in for a dreadful *jornada*, and I wished I wasn't so thirsty before I'd even started. The dry desert wind was rough on my throat and everything was burning hot: the harness of the mules if you rode, your shoes if you walked. The thousands of pretty clouds were perfectly useless; they occupied no more of the vast blue sky than a thousand handkerchiefs in a field, and the sun blazed without let or hindrance. We had brought some water but it tasted bad, and nobody we passed would sell us any.

They were all going the other way; a few small advance parties, they said, of a much larger emigration. They had left the jumping-off towns in Missouri and Nebraska three months back, at the beginning of spring, glad to leave the war behind them. It was all anybody talked about, they said. They made it sound like a war between heaven and hell; and I tramped along, trying to picture how the States would look by the time we got there. After a couple hours, Ness noticed we were being followed by two Indians on foot. They wore old-fashioned top hats and carried the stalks of some river bulrushes, which they peeled and sucked. It was infuriating to watch if you were as thirsty as we were. The sun started to spit hot oil, and when we stopped to noon, each of the Indians made a shelter out of poles and brush. Ness, Cordelia, and I took refuge from the heat under our wagon and talked about whether to open fire on them. We gave it a lot of consideration, but they had done us no harm yet and it might make matters worse. It was hard to concentrate on the discussion on account of the jingling and scraping above our heads. Mama kept shifting crates of liquor about.

I went to see what she was at. She was on her knees in the back of the wagon, picking out bottles of gin, tasting them, then putting them back in the crate. Her hands were shaking and she was sweating like a tunnel.

It's hard to be alone with Mama. It's as though she's always busy in her mind, or gone. Either way it makes no difference whether you're there or not, you feel kind of extra. I said, "What you looking for?"

"Gin."

"That's a whole crate of gin."

She handed me a bottle. It was water, with maybe just a molecule of the gin that still coated the inside of the bottle. Another half a dozen were the same. It was sad. I mean, it was sad we couldn't get indignant about it. We could hardly exclaim, "What sort of a person would do a thing like this?" It was a reminder of other embarrassments that we had to keep quiet about. It was a special sort of humiliation—it sank down below the skin and stayed there—while the two of us carried on with a silent, systematic search of the crates. At last I struck hard liquor; five bottles in all.

After she got some of it inside her, I said, "Do you know where you are?"

She shook her head. She'd been in the wagon since Virginia City. "No."

"Ain't you going to look?"

The scenery outside was something a volcano had spewed black rocks and ash over. "Is it an allegory?" she said.

"No. It's a desert."

"Is it in my brain? I'll cut my throat if this is in my brain."

"No. It's a desert in Nevada."

The brush had the color of a used-up broom. But once Mama knew it wasn't a scene from her imagination, she got out and looked around like she was in a botanical garden.

In the afternoon we pushed on. The Indians followed and camped next to us that evening, out of pistol range. Here's another piece of advice you won't find in the guidebooks. There's a thorn bush here that's plentiful. Well, don't use it for fires. It cuts your hands first-rate and it burns like fresh shit. Dig a pit and burn the sagebrush: sagebrush goes up like a paint shop. Once our fire was in good health we didn't let the Indians crowd us a bit. Mama got shiny with drink and recalled how she used to read stories about noble savages when she was a girl in Scotland. Little did she know, she said, looking around at the hellish ash-heap of a desert and the hat-and-trouser Indians, that she would live to see the real thing. By and by she was telling us all about Edinburgh and its top-notch castle, its grand assembly rooms and its gala occasions; then, as the sun dropped in the western sky, she gave us a song she'd heard Peggy Moffat sing one night outside a waterfront bar in the foggy port of Leith. Mama said Peggy Moffat was a handsome lass that had gotten coarse with the years and had a reputation among the men of the port as a hard case.

STARBANK GREEN

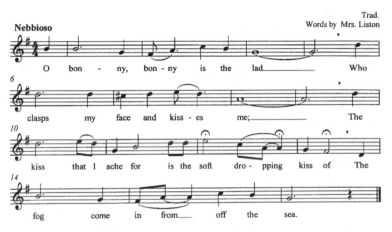

Nebbioso

Trad.
Words by Mrs. Liston

O bon - ny, bon - ny is the lad_____ Who
clasps my face and kiss - es me;_____ The
kiss that I ache for is the soft dro - pping kiss of The
fog come in from___ off the sea.

He lays me down upon the grass
The bluebells stand around our bed;
Of all your sheets and linen the finest that I know of
Is the fog come in from off the sea.

A sailor gave to me a gown
He said it never would decay;
He gave it to me to keep me reminded of
The night on Starbank Green we lay.

O, I will wear my pretty gown
And paint my lips a carmine red;
On Starbank Green I'll lie on the cold-fingered grass
As the fog comes in and covers me.

You will have heard a good many folks that won't sing a note if they can stretch it into three; Mama sang each note pure as a pearl and let each word come out at its own insistence; she didn't lard the statements with sadness, she wanted the facts to ring out clear and true. The fire kept up an accompaniment, popping and cracking; and by the time she had finished her tale of being deceived and abandoned, my idea of Mama had crumbled to dust and another one had been raised in its place.

Why, I wondered, would the accomplished daughter of a doting father visit a waterfront bar in the port of Leith and pick up with the Peggy Moffats of this world? Then I remembered, when I was young, how I had overheard a private conversation of gents, speculating in careful tones as to why Mama could be so beastly to the maids, because it transcended reason, don't you know. As a matter of fact, there were so many clues of that kind it's a wonder I had managed to overlook them all. How many times did she accuse someone in local society of spreading malicious gossip about her? She would scream at her husbands and fling out of rooms and take to her bed for days. Then she would gather around her all the other social misfits, and plot her revenge. The more I thought about all those months she spent expelling her venom, the more obvious it became that if she ever lived among Edinburgh's elite it was as a maid, and if there *had* been a Captain McQueen in the true history of her life he'd married someone his social equal.

I knew I wouldn't be able to sleep that night so I volunteered for picket duty with Ness. It was one of those times you are so intoxicated by an idea you need some liquor to sober you up. I stared into the darkness so long and so hard I forgot Ness was right beside me. When I remembered her it felt only right to ask her a question, out of charity. She seemed so alone. "Are you missing Dig?" I said gently.

"I shan't dwell on it," she said.

"What did you tell him in your letter?"

"I asked him to come with us."

"Oh," I said, "you did?"

"He said the war in the States wasn't making anyone more tolerant toward colored folks, what he heard; he would think long and hard before he went anywhere so perilous to our lives and injurious to our hopes." We listened to the fire going off like a firecracker, just the two of us. "That broke *my* nose," she said.

Two coyotes called back and forth to each other, talking above our heads.

"I think Mama was a maid when she was young," I said.

For a moment even the coyotes seemed curious. "I wondered where she got the song," Ness said.

"I always knew something was running her. I used to think she was taking instructions on how to behave from someone she consulted in secret. She would disappear into her bedroom and reappear in a different personality." I took a sip from my silver flask. "How does she do it, though? I mean she appears to *believe* she's a lady. Same time, she knows for a fact she's not."

"Maybe that's why she's intoxicated all day," Ness said. "So it's easier to deceive herself."

A wolf that had been hiding nearby suddenly let its voice loose for twenty seconds, and the coyotes buttoned it.

"You know," I said, "I reckon you are dead right."

"About what?"

"Mama."

"I'd forgotten about that. The wolf put it right out of my mind. What did I say?"

"It's all clear now. I don't think I'll sleep at all tonight. I want to think about Mama some more. I want to think about this all night. Isn't it amazing that human beings *can* deceive themselves? How is that possible? What if I was the one that showed people how it was done? I think I could too." I had the feeling the answer was just around the corner of my mind somewhere.

Ness shivered. "I keep seeing savages crawling toward us."

"What d'you suppose they want from us?" I giggled. "Our hair?"

"I don't see what we have that's of any use to them. If it was grub they wanted they would just right out ask for it. They want something, though."

Even so, along about four, she fell asleep. That didn't bother me at all; I had taken the perfect amount of booze and the perfect amount of missy; I was just dandy. The only small little niggling unease I had was when I remembered I'd gone a-wandering the night before. I didn't want to do that again with those Indians so close, so I got aboard the wagon, dug out Sadie Marx's handcuffs, and cuffed myself to a wagon wheel. I felt as good as if I'd invented something. The peace of mind was wonderful. This way I could get gonged and know where to look for myself afterward. All our supplies were in the wagon anyway and I wasn't liable to fall asleep, knowing those Indians might attack, so I took a right good dose and let my thoughts dwell on Mama.

That time I doubled the Horn alone, I met an acquaintance of Mama on board ship who suggested I make her character the subject of a scientific treatise. Well, maybe I took him more seriously than he meant it, but it's a great consolation when you're shipping alone to have a large purpose in life, and I was only ten. I kept it up for years. Every other month I would jot down little incidents; like the time I ran into Mama on the beach at Valparaiso where she was walking with Mr. Kingston, the English consul. Her mouth fell open, her eyes got positively slushy, and she hugged me like she hadn't seen me in months— rather than at lunch. Then she held me away from her so she could have ample room to enjoy the sight of me, and her face shut. "Oh, it's you," she said, like I'd deceived her. "I thought you were someone else." I wrote an account of the incident that contained a good deal of humor and philosophy; but four years later I abandoned the whole thing. You couldn't watch her crawl across the floor toward the sideboard where Ernesto Márquez kept the booze and imagine any such human being was worth wasting ink on. But now—do you see?—this new discovery appeared to be the explanation for how she worked. I could even think about fixing her.

"Wake up, dummy." Cordelia was shaking me.

I wakened with a start. I was pleasantly dim, the way you should be the morning after a bender, and I was still handcuffed to the wagon all right. I had a serenity that came from something very like omniscience. I didn't know everything but I knew where I'd been the last few hours, and that was every bit as good.

"My, look at the bracelets!" Cordelia said. "I knew nobody trusted you much. I didn't realize you had the same low opinion of yourself."

I sat up in such a way as to suggest that handcuffs didn't call for any special explanation, but it was hard to look debonair. "What's all up?" I said.

"Notice anything?"

As far as I could tell we were in the same place we'd camped last night. "No," I said. I couldn't hear anything but the wind. "Everything seems pretty quiet."

She threw a look at that dirty black piece of desert behind her. "That's because the Indians pinched our mules."

THREE

You will spend anywhere from $150 to $200 for a mule, but they'll be worth the same price you paid when you reach journey's end and then you can sell them. If you lose them, well, if you lose them you won't make journey's end anyway so you won't feel your loss. The most of the trip here we had taken the stage road; according to our guidebook there was a station a half-mile off, and Ness and I set out to scare up some help. On the way we met a lad on a burro. He had beautiful long eyelashes and a shy smile.

"We're in a heap of trouble," I said. "We think some Indians copped our mules."

He frowned. "You are in a heap of trouble if you've lost your mules."

"You got any ideas?"

"I know the Indians up ahead were burning stage stations back in April."

After a little I said, "We've lost our mules, bub. How people are fixed up ahead don't interest us any, we'll likely die before we get there. Now, if you can help us at all we'd be obliged."

He lowered his heavy eyelids and watched me from behind them. "It's polite to ask a person their name," he said.

"I'm sorry. What's your name?"

"Alias."

"Alias, huh?"

"I have a gnostic name too," he said.

"What's your gnostic name?"

"It's a secret. You want to know why the Indians are sore?"

"If you feel like telling us."

"Last winter I camped near Roberts Creek Station, a couple hundred miles along the line there. The Indians would go in the stables and wash the mule shit in those willow baskets they got, about the way a placer miner pans for gold."

"Why did they do that, Alias?"

"Sometimes the mules would pass some barley pearls."

"They picked out barley from the shit?"

"They didn't have a smitch to eat otherwise," he said.

"Jesus. What did they used to eat, winters, before Americans got here?"

"Bunch grass grows here some places. Used to be the Indian women gathered the seeds and made cakes out of it, laid them up for the winter. Then the stage line came. Sixteen mules every station, station every twelve miles. The stock used up all the bunch grass. Never used to be horses or mules in this country, not one. The Indians walk."

"That don't make a bit of sense," I said, after I thought about it. "Why they taken our mules, then?"

He frowned and blushed at the same time. "I suppose someone already told you I have a mental disorder."

"No."

"Then why don't you believe me?" Under his embarrassment he was seething.

I looked toward the station. "Any stage-company boys here?"

"They slid out. No stage been through here in three months."

When we got back to our wagon, Mama was in discussions with the two top-hatted Indians. They wore Navy Colt revolvers in their belts and were pretty fat-looking. They said they were number-one expert trackers and offered to find our four mules. They wanted pay of a sack of gingersnaps, and cartridges for their shooters, two boxes apiece. I wondered if they were out of ammunition; but supposing they were, shooting them wouldn't bring our mules back. We agreed to the price and they struck for some low hills about two hundred yards away, came back with the mules in a minute.

The going was hard and choppy that day, as bad as cobblestones at times. The Indians followed us with the ammunition we'd given them. They had enough now to wipe us out plenty, and I skinned the mules till they were raw. Listen here, you can't steal mules except they concur. They were fly to the joke. I mean it, they practically laughed in our faces when the Indians brought them back.

A little before sundown, after two days eating desert, we spotted some cottonwoods marking the path of a river and gave a yell. They were green, the cottonwoods, a fresh lime green; in the dirt of the desert they looked as fine as a cold beer. We picketed the mules to the wagon wheels that night and set a watch: Mama and Cordelia. Come morning, the mules were gone. The two Indians appeared, wearing their six-shooters, and offered to find our critters if we would let them keep two. That was too high a price so we searched for them ourselves all morning. Eventually the Indians got tired of hanging around and threatened to evaporate, and we came to terms. They kept Buell and Pope and surrendered McClellan and Grant. When I hitched them to the wagon, McClellan and Grant gave me the dickens of a look, sidelong but cool enough, as much as to say I could blacksnake them if I chose, I could hurt their bodies and embitter their minds, but they would endure it and get me back.

By the time we set off, Mama was soused and sweating like a cook, so we stowed her in the wagon. Ness drove; Cordelia and I walked. The plain was miserable, but the river bottom was lush with cottonwoods and willows, and grasses with feathers and fur collars. We took some of the bulrushes along, to suck and ease the soreness in our throats, and the Indians followed in a leisurely style with their mules. They hadn't wiped us out so far; maybe it was more convenient for them in this heat if we hauled their supplies for a while. I fired a couple of shots at them but they were too far away, and I wasn't popular with anyone when they fired back. Then Cordelia decided she wanted to ride in the wagon. She put her hand to her forehead and swooned. When she did it for the fourth time I hollered to Ness to halt, took a spade out the back of the wagon, and batted her with it. Cordelia held her elbow and yowled. I said if we bust the mules we were done for. She wanted to know how come Isobel got to lay about sick all the time, and I hit her again before Ness tore the spade out of my hands.

"Don't take it out on her," Ness yelled. "You got us into this mess."

"You can't blame me for the Indians."

"It was your idea to come into this desert in the first place."

"We came this way to give Ed Stainback the cold shake, remember?"

"If I'd known we'd be trailed every step of the way by Indians I don't think I'd of started out."

I couldn't believe my ears. "You want to backtrack?"

"I have put most all my savings into this outfit, Dol, and I am counting on the money I get from selling the mules and wagon to start fresh. We already lost two mules. Seems to me we might do better to turn around and make for the Bay. I don't want to get scalped and left by the roadside, do you?"

I flung down the spade. "Well, I'm not one to throw up the sponge first thing that goes wrong. Why don't I go find us some help?"

I had no idea where I was going; I was so mad I couldn't think, hardly. My brain had swollen up like a barrel in the sun; I thought I would bust my hoops. Nessie's arguments were dreadful. I mean, the Indians didn't appear to be the scalping sort, but if they were, they could nail us whether we pressed on or turned around; and she just had to mention her savings, of course. After a short while I happened upon Ragtown. I took it for an illusion at first, seeing it had no purpose there, but then I looked closer. It was at a crossroads in the wilderness; about fifty shanties, some built of canvas, others made of poles and brush. There was a chophouse, a clairvoyant doctor, some gambling tables, a couple of tent saloons, and some hardened drunks with purple-red faces and eyes that were in moist, stinging earnest. It was a deadfall in the desert to rob travelers coming and going, though the fancy-gals weren't much of a temptation to sin. Two of them were having a shindy with knives as I arrived. They probably earned their keep as decoys. You plank down a dollar expecting nothing worse than a dose of the clap and *whack*—if you wake up you've learned a lesson, you don't wake up, who cares?

The emigrants from the States stop here to wash their duds

in the Carson River before climbing out of the bottom to spread their wash on the tall, spindly sage that grows tall as a tree here. They were all from Illinois, the ones I chinned with, bar a plasterer from Terre Haute, a Milwaukee policeman with a sly, humorous face, and a runaway boy. He was the sort of street boy gets illustrated on a piece of sheet music; he was too cute for anything. He had bright elfin eyes and a knowledgeable ass.

After I had scouted the settlement I walked into Hookers tent saloon and said I was looking for a killer. The boys said Galletly was a good killer when soaked but he'd been teetotal three days, and recommended Lunas June. I found Lunas alone outside his shanty, fretting over a garden he was raising in the desert and dreadful low in spirits. He was dosing himself with Benedict's Specific. The bottle said it was a certain remedy for "Cancers, Colds, Liver Complaints, Delirium Tremens, Female Weakness, and Scaly Eruptions." Lunas had no great hopes of it as the doctors couldn't say what ailed him, although in his opinion it was a species of gout that attacked the brain. I told him he had nothing of the kind. He had a melancholia, I told him, and I had the cure. I said I would give it to him if he would get after some Indians for us, and he promised to do that first thing tomorrow.

The mule-thieving Indians were cooking fish by the river when I got back to camp. Ness was keeping an eye on them while Cordelia watched the lovebirds murder each other. She'd named them Sadie and Alice for our two dead chums. Well, they may have had the appearance of goody-goody sisters in white cloaks and hoods, but Alice was a killer. Sadie was crouched on the floor of the cage, blood spotting her pure white breast. She was wounded close to her wing; she could neither fly nor defend herself. Off and on Alice would fly down and pitch into her, then return to her perch and spread herself. She didn't make a sound, that was the awfulest part. Cordelia was horrified but she couldn't stop watching; she gorged herself on it till her eyes popped.

When I went up to Ness she didn't look at me.

I said, "What we need is someone who'll give those Indians the fright of their lives."

Then I said, "You don't mean to camp here, do you? There's a place ahead they got wood and water, must be thirty, forty people camped there. And I found us someone who will give those Indians rats."

I don't even know that she heard me.

I said, "I'm sorry I yelled at you."

"You found someone who will chase them Indians?" She had these two white spots high in her cheeks that she gets when she's mad, but at least she was talking to me.

"A killer, they tell me."

"You suppose he's a good one?"

"I hope so," I said.

"I don't suppose the men he's slain can write him a reference." She was so stiff I couldn't tell if that was a crack or not. "Be nice to have some company when we camp. Those Indians won't bother up a whole bunch of us, I reckon."

We arrived in Ragtown almost friends again, and come evening we cruised about the attractions of the shanty settlement. Cordelia wanted her future told and it turned out she had savings, so we went looking for the fortune-teller and found her in one of the saloons. She had long, thick, black hair; on her arms, I mean. She was hairy as a buffalo. She'd lost an eye, along with the skin of half her face, in some fire she had failed to foresee, but Cordelia had so much faith in her that her self-belief revived, and cunning lit up her solitary eye. She promised Cordelia she'd meet her husband soon but felt awful faint when pressed for details, and was only revived when Cordelia spent an extra two bits to get her a medicinal brandy. Then she was able to furnish Cordelia with her future husband's name and an address in Pittsburgh.

Next morning I called on Lunas June and gave him a bottle of Black Drop as his fee. That left just one bottle for myself but I reckoned it was worth the sacrifice if he could rid us of those Indians. I told him he would be cheerful and recovered inside a week, then I took him to where the thieves were camped and he banged away at them. They could do nothing with their revolvers against his rifle and decided to slope with their plunder. As they made their escape, one of the Indians turned and howled like a wolf. He was telling me it was him that made the coyotes fade out the other night, and letting me know how ignorant I was. It unnerved me at first, but then I remembered he'd fooled the coyotes, too, and didn't feel so bad.

FOUR

After Ragtown we followed the river, south and east. It was flat as a plate. You couldn't see more than a few miles because the plate turned upward at the rim. Nothing besides that, just a vast sea of sky.

We met a couple of Snake women along the way, gathering the seeds of some bunch grass. Each stand was a consolidation of a thousand tiny blond curls about this size—*v*—that seemed to be suspended in air. The Snake women wore smock dresses with skirts over them, and wicker hats that had no brim. They moved among the bunches, whacking the seeds into hand-baskets then emptying those into the large willow baskets they packed on their backs. They looked like daughter- and mother-in-law, the two of them. The mother-in-law smiled, the daughter-in-law scowled and tried to ignore us. When McClellan decided to help himself to the bunch grass, the daughter-in-law flew in with a stick and yelled at us. It got pretty nasty after Cordelia laid into the Indian girl for calling her a disgusting word, though how Cordelia knew that, when she doesn't speak the Snake language, only the fairies can tell you.

Next day I was driving; Ness and I didn't mention the fact but we both knew Sand Springs was up ahead. Too much depended on it, I suppose. Almost as soon as we left Redman's

Station, the river disappeared and we headed into bad-looking land surrounded by low mountains that rose a little above the plain, like alligators with their heads above the water. The scrub was the color of dried blood until it pinched out, then the land was just dirt for a spell. In the end we came to a dreary plain of mud that looked like the dried-up bottom of a lake, and the mules came to a dead halt. I whipped them till my arm was sore and weary. They didn't protest and they didn't shift either. It was eerie.

Ness said, "Maybe we ought to turn back. Don't you think we should turn back?"

"Turn back now when we're so close?"

"I never saw the mules this way before."

The mud had a salt-white scum. "Jesus," I said. "You're worse than the Israelites in the desert who longed for the melons and cucumbers they had when they were slaves in Egypt. What did we leave behind in Virginia City?" She turned away from me so I wouldn't see Dig Squiers in her eyes. I said, "Ed Stainback, that's what."

"I don't want to have the mules give out," she said. "That's all the capital I have. It's little enough as it is."

She went up to McClellan and pulled at his bridle, like she meant to turn him around. I lashed out with the whip. The mules bellowed and Ness screamed.

"Even the poor dumb beasts think we ought to turn back," Ness yelled. There were tears in her voice like I'd nipped her with the whip. "They likely can't smell water. I heard mules won't venture into bad-looking country without they can smell water."

"Ness, a mule can smell water inside a mile, and that's good smelling. If you suppose they can smell the *absence* of the article at distances greater than that, well, you can believe it if you like but you'll excuse me."

After you deliver a snapper like that you feel just immortal, especially if you slam a door afterward; the best I could do was hop off the wagon and take out, past the mules, into that barren waste. I didn't look back. It was like stepping into old dry cake two feet deep, that's what the mud was like. The salt crusted my face and cracked my throat; and after a while a mirage appeared, a huge creature that dragged itself along on its belly and sucked the good out of everything. It was like an immense apparition of Terror or Panic. I didn't care; I marched on, regardless.

After an hour or more I turned to see if Ness and the rest of the outfit had followed. There they were, quarter of a mile back, frazzled-looking, as though they'd followed me only after a terrible argument among themselves. Toward eleven I spotted Sand Springs Station off to the left, built of smooth black stones and standing out pretty good against some sand. There was some green shrub and grass around it, first of that color I'd seen in two days.

It was awfully quiet. No sign of Pontius or the cops. Nothing that said they were here, nothing that said either way. I walked up to it, then all around. Back of it was a horseshoe of low patchy-skinned mountains and a hill made all of sand, with a spine as smooth and keen as a panther. Outside the station—at the open doorway—was ash, grease, bones, tripe, bottles, all in a mux. It was where the station-hands had flung their garbage, when they were around. Back of me Ness yelled something I couldn't make out. Her voice was harsh and ugly.

I said, "How's that?" So was mine. It was sore to talk. The desert had sandpapered our throats.

Ness put her hand to her neck and said, "You see any water?"

I shook my head. "Not yet."

I stepped inside the station—into the stable part, first of all—I wasn't liable to find anyone in there anyway so it wasn't too bad if I didn't. The faraway stone wall was chinked with light, and the shit in there didn't hardly smell at all. It was old and dry, except some horse manure in the corner that looked and smelled like yesterday maybe. Then I turned into the store room between the stables and the living quarters. It had the remains of a woodpile, and the end of a haystack that was soiled with scraps of food and a rusty saw. My insides yawed to one side then the other, like an unsteady basin of water. There was only one room left. Through an open doorway I could see the good plank floor of the parlor room. I stood there and listened.

Nothing.

I bet ordinarily it would have been as neat as a sewing card. The floor was good, and the fireplace; the walls were plastered and you could hang up what things you wanted on pegs. It would have been a comfortable kitchen parlor till the coppers had arrived. Now there were empty wine bottles, a bottle of Royale Grenadian rum, and the remains of purple-stained lemons in the pot they'd used to make their punch. Butchered pieces of sheep were scattered here and there. They could've slaughtered the animal outside in the corral but they didn't; probably they were bingo'd and did it here for the fun of the thing, to top off the spree. That's how cops enjoy themselves, the soreheads; one of them had even shit on the floor. It was in between the bottles of Bass Pale Ale.

The remains of the sheep were black with death, I thought, but when I walked in several thousand flies rose up with a dreadful drone of criticism. I would have screamed but I swallowed something and wanted to gag. I backed out of there, into the store room, and leaned my head against the wall, and suddenly I felt so tired and weary of it all I can't tell you, I wanted to lie down and sleep in the leavings of the haystack. I couldn't stand to see Ness now that all my hopes had been dashed, so I went deeper into the station and found a well, enclosed by the station wall but roofless. The water was warm and salty. I kept taking little sips, hating it and then wanting more. It eased the soreness in your throat, then inflamed it. When I couldn't stand it anymore, I went out to tell the girls I'd found water.

The wind here dries out your eyes so you want to cry but can't, and I saw Ness sitting on the wall of the corral. She pointed to an abandoned wagon on the other side of the corral that looked like it had been sitting there who knows how long, ten years, maybe. If something dies out here, the desert will oftentimes mummify the skin and preserve it; it was that way with the wagon. The canvas bonnet had tightened over the bows like skin stretched over a rib cage, real thin. Ness led me around two sides of the corral toward the relic of a wagon, then she helped me balance on a ledge of the corral wall so I could look inside.

Pontius was kneeling slouched over the rum crate like it was a too-small table, hands in front of him handcuffed together and attached to the crate somehow. He was asleep; he would sag and droop then bounce up and wake. When he saw us his head snapped up. He'd been expecting the kids. I could tell by the relief on his face. But there was still a smear of panic left behind; and, before he let anything out, I took Ness by the arm and pulled her away a good ten yards.

I said, "That's the opium, all right."

Ness said, "How do you make this out?"

"What?"

"Why didn't the cops take the boodle and slide?"

They were terrified of the kids, that's why, but I couldn't tell Ness that. I said, "They have wives, I suppose."

"They could get better ones in the States with a fortune like that."

"I guess we ought to leave it where it is, if you think the cops know something."

"I'm trying to figure out what they know, that's all."

My throat had turned into a meat grinder. I couldn't make anything sound attractive. "Don't you think you deserve it? You spent all your money outfitting the company, you deserve half the booty at least. More than half, I suppose." Then I said, "That's all the capital we need right there to buy our saloon. We'll be rich as hallelujah."

"What do we do with the pimp? We don't want him along."

I hadn't thought about that. After a minute I said, "We could shoot him."

Ness looked off to one side. The sand hill was two hundred feet high. It looked like it had blown in from the Sahara. "You can't kill a man and take money that don't belong to you," she said.

"It does belong to me," I wanted to say. But I knew that would sound childish. "I don't see why not," I said.

Ness stared at my left shoulder, to avoid the difficulty of looking at me. "You'd be alone for the rest of your life."

"I'm alone now." I might as well have slapped her in the face. She folded her arms to keep from slapping me back. "Anyone can raise obstacles, Ness. You got a better idea?"

"We could leave him behind."

Most of my anger eased away. "I guess so," I said. "We could handcuff him to the machinery of the well." I pictured the kids finding him. That would keep them occupied for a while. "When do we roll out?"

She turned her face away from the wind. "We can bait the mules and lay by till sundown. There's an ugly piece of desert ahead. It'll be cooler when night comes, we can cross it then."

We watered the mules and had smoked oysters and beans for dinner. I couldn't eat. There was no way of knowing how far behind us the kids were; I could only see a few miles back. They might be pretty close for what I knew. I took some missy and listened to Mama give the scenery a sneering notice. She was drinking gin—on account of the water being so bad, she said—and I joined her. I needed to brace myself up before I tackled Pontius. I took a hammer with me. Ness said to yell if I needed any help but I wanted to be alone with him in case he said anything about kids.

The first thing he said was, "We ought to cut dirt before the kids get here. What's the hold-up?" His voice was all stony, not having had any water for a couple days.

"No hold-up."

"What we waiting for?"

"Night." He probably saw as much terror in my eyes as I saw in his. His were slippy-looking, like they might drop out.

A pimp is all the time feeling you out to see what you don't want to tell him; it's his job. "I got to hand it to you," he said, scanning me. "The funk you're in, I'm amazed you got the grit to hang around and wait for them."

Ness turned up with a tin cup. "I brought him some water."

I put the tin cup right to his lips and told him to drink. He took a couple gulps, winced, and tried to drink some more. Ness didn't go, she waited till he was done.

"Want some more?" she asked Pontius.

"More? My tongue was all swollen before I drank that stuff. Now it's too big for my mouth. Get me some booze, for Christ's sake."

"I don't think that'll help," Ness said, "but I will if you want me to."

Still she didn't go. She stood there and talked about the thirst you suffer in this desert, the grip it gets of your throat. She said she was amazed. She ran on some about the supplies we'd brought and how—if it was to do over again—she'd be a lot wiser. More water and less of everything else. Why she thought Pontius would be interested in her observations, or what possible use she imagined they would be to him, did not appear. She was just talking.

When at last she went, Pontius said, "She's as cool as the price of an ice company. She couldn't be any cooler if she wasn't in any danger at all." Then he added, "That she knew about, anyway."

Either I shot him on the spot or I had to think of something. It didn't matter if it wasn't too bright; I had to stop him from blowing on me to Ness. Before I had begun to get an idea, Ness came back with a little gin.

"Obliged," Pontius said. "I don't want to lose the use of my tongue. Only thing I got left."

"The guidebook says there's better water at Cold Springs," I said. "We could dump him there." Ness looked at me askance. I didn't offer her any explanation for my change of heart. What could I say? I didn't even know what face to put on it. I swallowed the back of my tongue. "Wouldn't hurt us any."

Ness held out a hand to get her cup back. "Well; I can stand his company till tomorrow, I reckon."

The rest of the day I shied about Sand Springs on my own. The sickish feeling I had just inside my ribs didn't budge. I told myself I'd lied to Ness about the kids for her own good, but I knew she wouldn't see it that way. Toward sundown I crept aboard the abandoned wagon, to hide from myself. Pontius was being tortured by the position he was kneeling in; and his face kept banging onto the crate; but every now and then, when he could drag himself out of his pain, he would wink at me. He thought he owned me now.

"There's the key to the handcuffs," he said, nodding toward it.

The cops had left it right beside him, just to annoy him. Maybe he expected me to release him, I don't know. I picked it up and put it in my purse.

After dark Ness came and said, "Dol? We got to get under way now. What you doing in there?"

By the light of her lantern the canvas had a touch of yellow about it, like old hard foot skin. I called back, "Hitch up one of the mules to this old relic. I'll stay here and guard the opium."

Ness knew something was amiss but she hooked up one of the mules and the wagon pulled out with a jerk. As we rattled along, I would begin to imagine we were alone, me and Pontius, and feel almost comfortable. Then Ness would speak to the mules and I would get a sudden flush all over my body that reminded me of being twelve, the shame I felt when I would wet the bed and wouldn't tell the maids. I would sleep in the same sheets the following night. My body would warm them and stir up the smell of old pee. It was sad, the smell, but it was warm and clinging, and I knew that nobody would find out what I'd done while I was occupying the bed. It was the days I dreaded. What if someone came in my room when I wasn't there and stripped it? That's why it was comforting to be with Pontius. He was like the warm dry pissy sheets that I crawled into, to be alone with the shame.

The wagon shuddered and creaked along; I took some missy and sank into myself. By and by I got to fancying we were traveling through a region of ash-heaps and black hills on the way to the Underworld. The driver appeared to know the way pretty well and the mules were keeping their thoughts to themselves. They pushed on, slow but steady. Somehow it wasn't a surprise when some riders overhauled us, firing pistols, and the wagon came to a halt. It was as if we'd arrived at the Gates to Hades.

"Well," I heard Ness say, "you boys want something?"

"We'd appreciate the society of you ladies."

"Why, you scared me most to death firing them shooters," Ness said. "Who in the mischief are you?"

"Soldiers."

"I can see that much," Ness said. "Won't you tell me your names?"

They didn't want to be as friendly as all that. Instead one of them said, "You ladies alone?"

Ness said, "I ain't so alone. I have a six-shooter."

"Why you so suspicious?"

"You boys look more ashamed of yourselves than a sheep-killing dog," Ness told them, "that's why."

"You want to know who we are—I'll tell you who we are." This one had the sneering upper-class drawl of a nineteen-year-old with a pet mustache and a rich mamma that spoiled him when she remembered to. "We're a detachment of Colonel Patrick E. Connor's Third Regiment California Volunteers. We are detailed to protect the stage road, to insure the safe delivery of mails and the safe transportation of silver from the mines of Virginia City to the U.S. Treasury for the duration of this war. We have been sent here to awe and chastise the Indians."

"The three of you?"

He drew his sword with an icy ring. "Don't get gay with me, you bitch. I won't get many opportunities to use this sword."

"I got this gun, remember."

"You keep telling me you have. I can take it off you and stick it up your cunt, if you like."

"There's no call for language, Lieutenant," someone else piped up.

"Dry up, Jansen."

"This young lady don't want the company of three loused-up soldiers."

"I said dry up."

"We can barely stand our own company tonight, don't see why we should inflict it on other people."

A gun roared. Then there was a noise like meringues being flattened under something heavy.

"Nobody listens to me. I said dry up, didn't I? I told you twice."

"No use yelling at him now, Lieutenant," another voice nagged. "You killed him. You killed Corporal Jansen."

"Don't you start, Eckels."

"Oh, gee whiz. He's dead. He's as dead as a mackerel."

"Well, miss," the lieutenant said, "I trust you will know me better the next time." He said it as though that was giving it to Ness pretty good, and rode on.

Eckels continued to whine. "Poor Jansen. He was alive not two minutes ago, and now he's dead. Oh, gee. Little did he know when he shaved this morning he would get put to bed with a shovel."

I heard a spade being dragged along the ground, then biting into the earth; and Eckels boo-hoo'd something woeful, like he was digging his own grave. From inside the wagon it sounded almost comical. It was hard to believe there was a dead body out there when there'd been so little drama.

Ness said, "Where's the rest of your regiment? That boy of a lieutenant rode out here with just you two?"

"Regiment's six miles back. He brought us out here on account of some kids."

"Kids?"

"They snuck into camp after sundown. We were playing cards, me and Jansen, when we heard a commotion in the lieutenant's tent and looked in. The kids had stuck a pistol up his ass. They wanted to know if he'd come across a rum crate packed with opium."

"Why didn't you shoot them?"

"We didn't like to do that, miss, seeing the lieutenant had a gun in his ass-hole. The kids had been eating this Chinese drug, keeps you awake night and day. They were pretty jumpy without anyone pointing pistols at them. They went when they were done funning. Course, the lieutenant didn't like we'd seen him with his pants down. He wanted to get even with them kids, took us with him so we'd see him do it. How'd he suppose we'd find them in the dark?" The noise of digging stopped. "We probably passed them way back." He started in again. "Though I guess he didn't care much who he raped." There was the dirty whisper of earth falling on stones and brush.

Ness said, "I thought there must be some reason the cops left the booty at Sand Springs, I said as much to Dol. Well, here it is. They knew the kids were coming. Dol, will you come and help?" Ness shouted.

I couldn't move.

"Dol!"

The moon didn't illumine the scene any; the dead man was just a darker shape than everything around him. Ness was helping Eckels dig. He was a tall, stalky fellow with a stooped back and low, weak knees; he dug with a skill that made you think he'd been a gravedigger all his years. Ness, on the other hand, didn't appear to know how a shovel worked. Her technic was to put it into the ground to the depth of a fingernail, then let the dirt slide off it while she looked around and wondered where to put it. "No wonder the coppers got sore," she said. "All that lovely boodle they were afraid to touch, and nothing to look forward to besides starting home to torment their wives."

I was glad she couldn't see me in the dark. I said, "I don't understand why Duffield lied to me."

"It's hard to explain," Ness said in a tight voice.

I said, "He definitely told me he was sending those kids to San Francisco under guard."

Cordelia hissed at us and said, "Listen!" She was holding up a lantern. You might have supposed it was the wind squealing and squalling in a narrow place, but it was too many notes out to be the wind and the more you listened the more you could hear a drum. It sounded like a dead band.

"That the kids?" Ness asked.

"How should I know?" Eckels said.

We listened to the eerie noise some more. I counted five instruments, one for each kid. They were telling Pontius they were coming for him, I reckoned. "Let's clear," I said.

Eckels threw down his spade in disgust. "Won't you at least help me bury my friend?"

All of Ness's shoveling had only shifted a spoonful of dirt. I ripped the spade from her and commenced to dig. We planted Corporal Jansen and zipped. It was good and deep where we laid his head, but his boots stuck out.

FIVE

Ever been chased by a tall storm? There was one night the Fair Maid of Perth was driven back to San Diego and the waves followed faster than we could run from them, smacked the backside of the ship with claps that made her jolt forward. The same running from the kids—it was terrifying how slowly we fled. My heart beat faster than the mules could walk. And then the noise we made: the jingle of the harnesses, the wagon creeping over small stones, our own breathing; it wasn't much in the way of din but it was enough so we couldn't hear the kids and know if they were closing or not. Then, when the mules halted and wouldn't budge, and we could hear the kids, that was worse.

We weren't the only night travelers. Three colored iron-foundry laborers, who were running from New Albany, Indiana, to escape the wrath of the local Irish, stopped to answer our questions about water ahead. Later we met a train of wagons that didn't appear to notice us even when they looked our way. I mean, I'm sure it was a good idea to cross the desert under cover of night; same time, what we saw by the light of our lamps was the sort of phantasmagoria you might sweat up lying in a sickbed delirium. Whole teams of oxen lay dead together where they'd dropped, their skin dried and preserved in the desert air. Horses lay in their harness, graves had head-boards with names scratched on them too fast to read a foot away. I saw a white scorpion skitter across an abandoned skillet, and in the gray before dawn we came across a bed with a bridal dress laid out on it. I sat down on the bed, weary and sore, like I would never get up.

When I did get back on my feet it was morning. I followed the others to Middlegate (two dirt hills nose to nose), where they had stopped to fill their water kegs in the creek. I was leaning back against the wheel of the old wagon when I spotted the gang of kids—maybe an hour behind us, stirring up the dirt of the barren plain. I said we better lighten our load before we got going again. I had the feeling Ness wasn't speaking to me; but she tumbled some trunks into the creek bottom, two of mine and one of her own, while I watered the mules.

I was standing next to McClellan, who had his nose in a bucket and was up to his eyes in water, when Ness tried to un-hitch him.

"We better leave this old wagon behind," she said.

"What about the swag?"

"The poor mules are all wore out; the less dead weight they have to haul the better."

I said, "Dead weight?"

"The kids won't bother us if we leave them their swag."

My throat was sore even before I started shouting. "We can't just give up. We got several hundred pounds of something that's more valuable per ounce than gold."

"You don't know when you're beat, that's your problem."

I yelled myself hoarse. "I got my mother to think about, I can't let myself get beat. I carried her out of shantytown on my back, and if I fall she falls harder. Somehow I got to get to the States and set us up in a business of some kind whether you come in on it or not, and that dirt is the only chance I got. I wish I *could* dump everything, I wish I had nothing to weigh me down, but unlike some people I could mention I didn't abandon my mother."

It was like I'd killed something. Ness left me standing there and went down to the creek bottom. I watched her stuff her bonnet with green cottonwood leaves, to keep her cool on the journey ahead.

I yelled down to her, "What do you say?"

She didn't look up at me. "What'll we do if the mules give out?" she said.

"Tell Cordelia to dump those lovebirds," I said.

In the end she gave in. "You can put the opium in the good wagon."

"Pardon me?"

"You can put the opium in the good wagon." She carried on filling her bonnet with leaves like I wasn't there, and there was nothing else for me to do except take myself off. I found a claw hammer among the tools we had brought along and went to separate Pontius from the rum crate. His handcuffs had a hoop linking the two halves and through this hoop the cops had nailed a piece of wood about six inches long by five inches broad. It was an unhandy piece of work but they had done it with passionate feeling; it was hard to shift. I laid into that bit of wood like I didn't care if I missed now and then; I was grinding these furious noises out of my throat. Pontius was scared of what I'd do next. He thought I'd nail him soon as I had the loot.

"I know you lied to her," he said.

"Shut your trap!"

"You lied to your best friend."

"Shut your head!"

"I can smooth it," he said.

"I'd just as soon shoot you. That'd be the smoothest thing."

"I'll tell her Duffield *did* send those kids to Dabu under guard, but the cops sold themselves to Harry Fan."

I stopped hammering. "How would you know that?"

"I'll tell her the cops that took me to Sand Springs were fly to it. They knew they would get their bit when they got home, that's the reason they had a jam. Every cop but Duffield is licking the sugar off a Harry Fan's fingers. They were blowing about it, I'll say."

You know when someone you don't like makes you feel better? You're so swimmy with gratitude you loathe yourself. Ten blows bust the wooden block and he was free.

If I could have taken the crate without him seeing me, I would have done.

"Take it," he said. "It's all yours."

Those two fat faces of his cramped his smile.

Outside I didn't want anyone to notice me either, Ness especially. In the other wagon I hid it under some gunnysacks full of clothes.

After Middlegate the land turned raggedy. The bunch grass was barely a foot high; each piece stood up like a blond shaving brush. Ness walked alongside the mules, I walked behind the wagon with Pontius. He'd had no water for two days and was like to fail, so I gave him some of mine. It was as though I had a monstrous fat baby to look out for all of a sudden. He was wearing those bracelets, so I was obliged to hold the canteen to his mouth. One of the times I was feeding him like that, Ness looked around and caught me. Three hours or more we tramped onward through that hard-looking country, glancing behind us every few minutes to see where the kids were. I tried to walk fast and light so my sore feet would touch the ground the smallest amount possible, but I got too weary and weak for that. The mules were worse than us: by the time we struck Cold Springs stage station they were trembling in their joints. Mama soaked her hankie in the stream and bathed Pontius's face, firing me looks as she did so, like she was giving me a lesson in how to look after a man. I was hurting so bad I could have laughed at her. I sat on my butt and eased my shoes off. Then I leaned on my elbows and held my feet in mid-air, and for a few precious moments there was no pain. It was as good as dying. My body departed and I was a soul in bliss.

"Here they come," Ness said.

You could have pulled me apart like a wishbone.

"Let's get scarce," Ness said.

By the time I crushed my feet into my shoes, the others had hit the trail. I took a look back a ways. About a mile off, below a lemon-colored hill, I could see the kids and hear snatches of the racket they were making. They carried a drum, guitar, accordion, fiddle, banjo; nothing else, just their shooters. It was terrifying: I mean, even Snake Indians don't venture out into the desert without canteens and some poles to build a shelter; that gang of waterfront kids ought to been dying of thirst like everyone else in the desert, or shading themselves in the brush like the Indians and the rabbits. I stood and watched them in a sort of wonder, then lamed out after the others. The first steps I took I walked on the outsides of my feet but I couldn't go fast enough that way, so I gritted my teeth and stepped on the cut-up meat of them. I was last, and I was falling farther behind when Ness stopped the wagon and signaled me to catch up.

"Will you help me?" she said when I fetched up. "The opium. We got to heave it overboard."

The kids were maybe half a mile back, yelling and popping their pistols.

I said, "But we decided about that."

Ness said, "We can't go any farther. Look!"

I don't know what sort of Indians they were. They had American pants and boots but their chests were bare and they wore their hair in braids. They were about fifty yards ahead, ten of them, plundering the wagons they had ambushed in a surly silence, like longshoremen on the graft. The road all around the wagons was white with feathers, the air was thick with them; the Indians had emptied mattresses of their stuffing and were filling them with swag, while their mules and horses looked upon the snowy scene in a sort of dim person's bafflement. Well, you know me: I was raised on pandemonium. I started to the Indian massacre with a crate of London Jockey Club gin. Nobody tried to stop me. Mama and Cordelia stood with their mouths open, not sure what you were supposed to do when you ran into Indian trouble, and Pontius tried to look like he could do plenty if only his hands weren't tied. I had taken a dose of missy, which right away soothed the pain in my feet. I was glad of that; you don't want to walk up to a gang of Indians on the job, looking like you've just wet yourself.

Among the dead was an eight-year-old girl with an arrow in her back. I saw an Indian bend down, lift her head, and peel her scalp. The flesh and the blood were two different colors, the inside and outside of a strawberry. As he was hanging it in his belt he looked at me. I almost got an electric shock from it, he was so live'd up after the skin he'd lifted. He stepped up to me and grabbed my hair. The storm of feathers was rather other-worldly, so I was surprised the Indian was so real, the smell and all that. He wiped off his dirty knife on my arm and yanked me till I knelt on the ground; he was about to let loose with a war cry when some of the feathers and down got into the back of his throat and made him gag. He tried to cough them out, once, twice, three times, but no go—they wouldn't shift. When he finally picked them out of his mouth with his fingers I knew he didn't have it in him to hush me, not after that. Some fellows could of done it but not this party, he would of felt foolish. His face was spattered with elderberry pimples; and even though he was almost naked he appeared to be burdened by a heavy over-coat. I was still holding the crate of gin. I told him his friends could have it if they saw off the kids that were after us.

The kids had stopped a hundred yards away. They were whooping and getting their guns off and spatting their bare backsides at the Indians. The Indians didn't seem the least both-ered by them, and they looked *us* over like lions that are full. They already had more booty than they could carry and only wanted to make off with it in peace. I begged them to save us from the kids, but it was hard to put any feeling into it when they appeared to regard me as a different species.

They talked it over in Indian and apparently came to an agreement. The pimple-faced Indian said we could come with them. "No wagon," he said. "Just mules."

I said, "You want us to leave our wagon?"

"We headed thataway, see? No good for wagon." He was pointing to the nearby hills. "Just mules. You got two nice mules. Got to hurry. Sooner we get up there, sooner we can eat."

I told the others to unhitch the animals and grab what things they wanted. We tumbled all our belongings out of the wagon, and in a few panic-stricken moments we tried to decide what things were precious to us. I put a bottle of Black Drop in my pocket and a precious fossil belonging to Mama that I'd carried all the way around the Horn. Ness filled a gunny sack, Cordelia grabbed the birdcage, I lifted the rum crate. It was too heavy, and I had to put it down twice before I'd gone twenty yards. When Pontius offered to take it, I undid his handcuffs; he shouldered the boodle like a sea chest, and we shinned out with the Indians.

SIX

I supposed the Indians were bandits who got along by pillaging on the road. It was only when we were following in their footsteps that I began to wonder what they would do with their plunder. We were headed up into a mountain wilderness: who would want a white book-muslin dress a sweet Methodist girl might wear to a revival, or a pile of sheets? It was as if they had taken anything the mules could easily carry, out of greed, without asking themselves what they could sell.

It was a hard climb. Fear put us out of breath as much as the exercise. The kids were a few hundred yards below us, and we were following ten banditti into country we didn't know. Every so often the Indians looked behind to see if the kids were coming on; then, more than halfway up the mountain, they stopped to wait for them. They didn't bother to hide themselves. The kids appeared around a turn of the path, hauling the fat girl up a steep part. Just as they stopped, half-blind, to recover their breath, the Indians gave them a blizzard with their rifles, two volleys. The nervous kid they called Dingo hit the dirt; the others left him for dead and retreated down the hill.

It was when we were safe from the kids that I got uneasy about the Indians. They didn't exhibit any affection for us before or after the skirmish. I'm not saying they had gone to any great trouble to save our lives—they enjoyed the shooting—but why were they tolerating us unless we could serve some purpose? In spite of that our spirits rose. The higher we climbed, the more the hill was covered with a small humorous tree that looked like a cross between a pine and a broccoli, and after the barrenness of the desert the mountains seemed young and alive. There were lemony butterflies browsing on the brush, purple daisies, a jaggy nettle with a white, poppyish flower, and a bird that shammed a broken wing and dragged herself along the ground, so you would know she had a baby somewhere in the neighborhood that was easier meat than her.

Mothers.

Once we were over the brow of the hill we struck south, staying close to the spine of the mountain range. We made a halt in a hollow and filled our canteens from a spring the Indians showed us. Our mules were looking poorly after traveling without rest for a day. The pimple-faced Indian found some of that good bunch grass—*wai*, he called it—and went to feed Grant. Then he took out his bowie knife, dug it into the animal's throat, and sawed a little. Ness screamed. The mule held still and tried to keep its feet but its strength went at the knees. Ness took her gun out and put her arm around McClellan like he was the only thing she had in the world and screamed at the Indians to keep away from her. The mule killer let the animal bleed to death then hauled him away a few yards and went to work butchering him. They didn't cook him; they ate him raw. I don't know if there are certain parts of a mule that are better eating than others but the bandits didn't argue over it. I guess they each got a piece they liked.

We stood there the whole time with shooters in hand in case they tried to rob us some more, but they had gotten all they wanted. After they went, it was difficult to stir from there. We were shocked. When you looked at the smear of blood where the mule had been dragged through the brush, and the general carnage, it was a surprise to find ourselves alive. We took stock, had some water, and got moving. What a crew we were, the five of us; we staggered about up there like castaways from a shipwreck clinging to our few worldly belongings. Pontius carried the crate of opium, Mama had a sack that clinked with a couple of gin bottles, and Cordelia had the birdcage. Please don't tell me it was all the poor unloved girl had to show for her life. It was still annoying. If she wanted us all to know she was thinking of Sadie Marx she could have told us now and again, she didn't have to slosh around the wilderness with a stupid symbol of her eternal friendship that she could hardly carry. It was pretty rough on the lovebirds, too; they got jogged up and down for hours on end. When her arms would get too sore she would fling the cage to the ground.

It wasn't long before it dawned on everyone we were going nowhere. We were leaving the kids behind us but also the only road in several hundred miles, and we'd be out of food inside two days. Seeing there was so little to drive us on, Mama got polluted with gin and started to lag behind, and Pontius lagged with her. Around four o'clock we stopped and made camp, the sort of cold camp you make when you have no fire and little food. I filled my mouth with dry crackers. After Pontius and Mama had shared their small amount of rations with each other, he took her aside and told her of my falsehood to Ness. Mama made it clear they were talking about me, in exactly the same way as a girl in the school yard trying to make another girl jealous. He told her I'd lied to Ness about the kids (I imagine), and Mama put her hand to her neck in shock. Then he explained how he could save my honor. She handed him some shiny-eyed adoration and looked at me like I scarcely deserved such kindness, though she didn't doubt Pontius was doing it more on her account than mine. Directly the pantomime was over, they came back and loaded Ness up with the tale about the cops and Harry Fan.

Later, Ness sidled up to me and offered me a piece of jerky. She wanted to make up—I wanted to make up—I was about to tell her I was sorry for what I'd said about her and her mother, but Pontius came up behind her right then and tipped me a wink, like he was glad to have brought us together again. She saw the expression on my face and turned to see what I was looking at—Pontius and his puffed-up smile. I carried on the conversation with a queasy feeling in my stomach, and when it got dark I crept away by myself. I took some painkiller but it didn't make me feel any better. That's a lie. Of course it made me feel better—it always does—but deep inside I felt thin, and cold, and deceitful, like rotten ice.

When I wakened at first light the hills were still colorless; Cordelia was burying one of the lovebirds, while Alice hopped around her cage. We had to decide what direction to go in— north and run into the kids, or south with no object. We went south, slowly, and before evening we were out of food. At the edge of a mountain divided from the next mountain by a pass, Cordelia said, "What's that?" Crossing the pass east to west was a beaten road, rutted and scored and shined by wagon wheels. It raised our hopes, but we followed it down the pass with a dismal feeling that we were probably being fooled. Maybe halfway down we started up some sage hens that creaked like they hadn't flown for a while and needed to have their wings oiled. That seemed to say there hadn't been any traffic on the road in a year or two; and I broke in two like a cracker, just as quiet as a cracker.

It wasn't as though we decided to camp there, we just gave out and lay down. Toward evening some Snake Indians appeared, returning home from the day's hunt with a couple rats hanging at their belts, or a cottontail rabbit. They were old-time Indians, nothing at all like the banditti: some of them were naked and some wore rabbit-skin robes. They spoke to us in Indian and passed us up when they didn't understand us. Another hour we let the road torment us with the hope that something would pass. Nothing. Mama tanked up on her last bottle of gin, and I staved off hunger with some opiate. It was Cordelia who eventually said, "Them Indians got food." Seemed as though Ness would rather starve, but Cordelia kept pecking at her, and it was agreed to give it a show.

The first family of Indians indicated by signs that they didn't welcome our company, and Ness wanted to quit right there. But Cordelia had less pride. If she knew nothing else, that girl, she knew how to make a nuisance of herself; her life had depended on it. The next family of Indians was camped next a mountain-stream. Their half-hut was an al fresco sort of affair: a half-circle inclosure built of piñon branches and brush, maybe four feet high. They had a cook fire and a kettle boiling, and a view all the way down to the barren flat at the foot of the mountain. Beyond that they could see the next mountain range, veiled right now by the shadow of a cloud.

They were two families mixed up, by the looks of them. One man was making a quiver for his arrows out of rabbit skin; his feet were black with pitch. A half-naked older woman with a necklace of shells sat cross-legged with a stone in her lap, grinding seeds. A young woman with a flat face heated stones on the fire, then dropped them into a willow basket full of seeds and tossed them together to roast the seeds. She wasn't overjoyed to see us, five more mouths to feed. Any rate, she didn't take the hint after Cordelia had been sociable with her ten minutes or more. I think they argued over whether to feed us or no. An older man seemed to be saying "Give them some chuck," but the flat-face female got riley and pointed to two little kids. One was a boy of five she called over. He stood up to her breast and she fed him her nipple. Then she pulled him away, scooped some porridgy mixture onto her fingers, and pushed it into his mouth. After she'd petted him with two mouthfuls she signaled for us to sit, said something to her kid to placate him, and started back cooking.

It was more naked than Mrs. Bird's parlor, that inclosure. I didn't know where to look. The Indian beside me had a broad face and scarred cheeks. He wasn't handsome in the usual way; I don't know if he was handsome in the Indian way, he was just gorgeous. He dipped his fingers in a bowl of food and offered me his fingers to lick. Shyly I held his hand by the wrist and brought it to my mouth. They were big and bony, his fingers, and covered in mush; I licked them and licked in between them. All the time his eyes were wonderful—a little startled. When I finally took his fingers out of my mouth, I had to remind myself this was just the Indian way; as far as he was concerned I'd just taken food from him. But my face was as hot as though I'd kissed him.

Then I saw that everyone was staring at me as though I'd put my tongue in his mouth in front of his wife and child. His wife in particular was looking at me like that, and this naked eight-year-old girl stood up, her kid mouth and kid eyes wide open in shock. That's when I twigged that the gorgeous Indian had been showing me how to eat; he'd expected me to do it with my own fingers, not his.

Ness and Cordelia, they stopped chewing their food, waited to see if the Indians would order us out of camp or what the up-shot would be, but the Indians decided to forget about it. They didn't like our mule, though; he fairly pitched into some of that frizzy-haired grass that was growing nearby: you could hear the rip of the grass and the wet of his tongue, like nobody had ever taught him not to eat with his mouth open. I took him away and picketed him out of sight. When I got back, Mama was alive with liquor and playing with the Indian girl. She showed Mama her doll and how she carried it in a cradle board on her back like a real papoose. Mama admired it a whole lot so the girl fetched out a rabbit coat she kept stowed away. It was the cunningest article you ever saw. The rabbit skins were twisted and then worked together into a long robe that fell to her knees, and she wore it for special occasions (we supposed) because after she put it on she acted out the steps of an Indian dance, a grave, slow shuffle.

Suddenly Mama was in her element. She started teaching the girl how to do a Scotch dance, a sort of Highland fling. The Indians didn't like to see the girl played this way, but Mama and Pontius clapped as she danced and gave her so much attention they whipped her up into a frenzy. You know when you're thirteen and you have a hopeless crush on a ship's lieutenant who loves his wife? You hurt and ache and feel puny all day. After a while you forget you loved him, you just feel sick. Well, that's what my childhood was like, and I wasn't going to sit there and watch Mama be sweet to a little girl she didn't even know.

I went back to the stream and took a dose of missy. I took enough to make a street-girl feel good. Pretty soon I could hear everything clear as can be. I heard a creature come out of the night somewhere above and drink from the arroyo, both of us alone in the darkness.

SEVEN

We awoke next morning to find the Indians had gone. There was the remains of a fire, and outside the hut two different kinds of shit, ours and the Indians. After a breakfast of some berries we found, we drifted down the ghostly old wagon road to the sagebrush flat. Pontius had the rum crate on his shoulder and led the way, like we could depend on him.

You might suppose such a barren plain wouldn't be much of a habitat for anything, but you'd be surprised. Say you're an antelope browsing on a stand of sage and a bunch of Indians are hunting you, you'll see them sneaking up on that nude plain for about an hour. You find it tough being an antelope here, don't try Chicago. On the other hand, if your native habitat is Chicago and you have made out to hide your expensive liaisons downtown from your wife in the suburbs, don't get a big head. Try laying a gay-girl on these bald, naked plains and keeping it from your loved one and traveling companion. That would be something.

Bob Valentine had been fired by a manufactory of reapers in Chicago. He was traveling with his wife, Lucinda, her sister Mrs. Tinker, and Mrs. Tinker's latest husband, Bert, as well as assorted kids and the Fleishacker boys. Mr. Valentine had bought a map of a station agent for half a dollar, seven hundred miles back on the Bear River, and followed its directions faithfully. The camping places on the road west had been so crowded most evenings they had risen early to get ahead of the other emigrants; same thing yesterday, but this time they had found themselves traveling alone, not just for a few miles but all day. They showed us their map, and all hands agreed this must be an old road the migration had used in years gone by. If we followed it east for twenty miles or so, Mr. Valentine said, we would join up again with the stage road to the States, the one we had left after the Indian massacre.

Valentine was a small, chesty fellow who used his every inch to best advantage. He was most always up on his toes when he talked; up and down, up and down. When he listened, the tip of his tongue poked out and rested on his upper lip like a tiny tortoise head. Pontius still wore enough rings on his fingers to leave no doubt as to his profession, and Mama stood right beside him and flashed Valentine some choice smiles. She was out of liquor. I had a dreadful premonition she would try to sell herself, so I pulled from my sack the enormous fossil I had taken on my travels as a keepsake of her, and said, "You could always sell this, Mama." It looked like the egg of some gigantic extinct bird. Then I said to the Valentines, "We're running low on necessities. You can probably see we're in bad case."

Valentine had bright baby-blue eyes that took in every detail of our circumstances. "Say, what is that?" he said.

"Like to buy it?" Mama said. "It's a fossil my dead husband resurrected in the Gobi Desert."

"I've kept it safe for her," I said, "since I don't know when."

"What do you say to this thing, Tinker?" Valentine winked at Mama. "Mr. Tinker's a fossils sharp."

Mr. Tinker had bad lungs. He coughed into his handkerchief and said, "Wouldn't the boys in the Smithsonian like to get their hands on that."

"Is that so?" All the time he was talking, Valentine was running over Mama's shape with the tail of his eye. "Well now, Tinker, what would be the figure for a thing like that?"

"Oh, now, I really couldn't say for sure. Twenty-five dollars? A collector might give more."

"I'd sell it for some hard liquor," Mama said and laughed, as though she'd made a joke. "Or any kind of painkiller you have. I'm in mortal agony."

"I don't want to swindle you," Tinker said. "I'm afraid we're rather low on currency. Why don't you keep it till you strike somewhere they'll appreciate a find like that?"

"Tinker, offer the lady a figure that won't make her blush," Valentine said.

Tinker got terribly uncomfortable. He couldn't afford to pay what it was worth but he didn't want to gouge her either; he was in a bad pinch for a person with character. "I really can't offer you anything like its value. I don't know, fifteen dollars? I should say it was worth a good deal more, but that's all we can spare, I'm afraid. And I don't know if Mrs. Tinker would go *that* high."

"Fifteen dollars is no use to me, sonny." She'd told him what she would sell out for, painkiller or hard liquor; she didn't know how to say it again. Tinker said he was just as glad; he'd as leave not buy at all as pay a price that would make him feel ashamed, so that was that, they said their goodbyes and pushed on.

After we'd walked three miles or so Mama called a halt. She said she was too sick to continue. In the full stare of the sun we all waited while Pontius walked off and returned with Mr.

Valentine riding a mule. Goodness knows what excuse he'd given his wife, but even if she didn't see right through it, she would have a pretty clear view of things from the hills above that naked plain. We could see Valentine coming for an hour. He had all that time to think it over. He didn't employ much in the way of cunning either. He gave Mama some food and three black pint bottles of medicinal brandy, then they went and lay behind a weakly piece of sagebrush about the size of a lettuce. When he climbed back on his mule to start back to his folks, he had the air of someone who perhaps expected to meet with some insinuations upon his return, but evidently believed he'd be protected in the trials that lay ahead by his character and intelligence. It was a pretty large piece of self-deception. If I knew how he managed it, I could write a book.

After she'd done the business Mama walked over to Pontius with a smile and flashed him her tit where Bob Valentine had bit her. It was the smuttiest thing I ever saw. After a fine meal you might have the shine of pork fat around your mouth, shows you enjoyed it. She was showing Pontius how satisfied the customer was; she was showing him the money. Pontius didn't need any more of the stuff now he had his paws on the rum crate, but I guess a pimp is a pimp all the way through. It's what makes him go. When he'd got after Valentine, he was a different character. He'd even walked in a different way, without any vanity, his mind fixed on what he was doing. Then after he brought the couple together he kept himself in the background, like a clerk at a ladies' underwear counter, eager to help. Then when she flashed him that bite he was transfixed. He had fat shoulders and a fat neck and was all bunched up ordinarily, but for those few moments he looked sort of light on his feet.

The rest of the tramp that day, I retired inside myself. Mama had banged a man for booze in front of all the girls. She was probably ashamed of herself, so she necked some of the brandy and was louder than usual. The other girls were extra quiet. For me, it was like the first time I saw Mama in Mrs. Liberty's flash-house or visited her in shantytown. You can't help thinking she's just pretending. You feel like giggling, but you don't want to let your panic out.

A heavy lump of lead sky thundered and lightened when we were midway across the plain, and a solid weight of rain turned the white plaster into gray cement. It was so heavy I could scarcely drag my skirt through it. After it cleared off, the plain had the smell of a dowsed fire and our feet smacked in the sucking mud. We practically had to carry the mule. We made a halt when we reached the next range of hills, left the road, and climbed till we found somewhere we could fill our canteens with water. When we were settled, Pontius came around with a bottle of Mama's brandy and dispensed it like it was a special sort of medicine. He moved from girl to girl and handled the three of us in a different way, like he knew what made each of us go.

I could see Ness wanted to speak to me, but I wouldn't let her catch my eye. She came over anyway, hairbrush in hand, and knelt beside me, still damp after the rain.

"Poor Isobel," she said. "She needed to get some booze, I suppose, but I didn't know where to look. Worse for you, I expect."

"I don't let her affect me much."

"It was a pretty big racket they made."

"I put myself to sleep when she acts that way."

Ness peered at me the way she peers into darkness. "You have to, I suppose."

"It's something I've learned over the years or I'd a died of embarrassment. I don't like to see her with a pimp, though. She's too old for that game. She can't see it, of course, she's deluded. When she's all used up, he'll lose her on the road somewhere."

Ness was holding her matted hair out like it was piece of raw wool right off a sheep's back. "She drinks the same way my pa done. It's hard to watch someone poison theirselves day after day. You can't get the poison out of their grip because they think it's their medicine and they'll die without it. It's a mystery."

The sun was low and squeezed out a lemony light. The sky was a smoky blue gray. Across the plain, where we'd camped last night, Indians were lighting their cookfires. I said, "I got to save her somehow."

"How?"

"I have to find out how to work him, I suppose."

On the gray plain below, three antelope feeding on sage stopped suddenly and looked over their shoulders.

"People are stubborn," Ness said. "You won't change her."

"I'm as stubborn as her. I won't give up."

Ness let the hairbrush drop to her lap. "It's like the night you got chased by them coyotes and lay down halfway across the Carson River. When I asked you why in the world you did that, you said you wanted to sleep on the bed of the river. You'd be kind of puffy by now, if I hadn't a noticed you were gone. You'd be considerable of a corpse." She dragged her hairbrush through a snag in her hair. "That didn't change you any."

I suppose she was trying to get me back for the sorry pass I had led her to, but you have to strain the comparison pretty far to make me look like my mother. Mama is not in any way a rational or responsible creature, which is why I have to look out for her, and she drinks whether she wants to or not. Me, I get varnished because that's how I enjoy my own company. The odd occasion I overstep—so what? I'd be the first to admit it: my judgment is out sometimes, but I don't set out to annihilate myself. I take missy for the pleasure of the sensations it gives me and the largeness of the thoughts.

"You didn't ought to of said that, Ness. I wish you'd given it some more thought before you opened your trap."

Ness stood up and just then the antelope on the flat below evaporated. Their tails flashed till they were out of sight. Ten minutes later we saw what had disturbed them. From the foot of the hills opposite, moving across the plain, were four figures so small you could say nothing about them for sure. They were directly opposite us, maybe twelve miles away, maybe ten, heading toward us on a straight line. Likely they had been watching us all day from the mountains that overlooked the plain. We followed their progress until night fell and they stopped on that bare desert. Then, at first light, we slung our thin sacks over our shoulders, and slid.

EIGHT

All day we fled, though whenever we looked back there was
no sign of the kids. Late afternoon we spotted in the distance
the telegraph poles that gave away the line of the stage road,
and soon after that we met with a body of emigrants camped
by a limp river. Passing through the encampment, we came to
Reese River stage station and the beginnings of a hopeful new
settlement that has crept up around the depot, called
Jacobsville. Cordelia was starved and offered to lay out some
of her savings so we could put up at Nieri's hotel and eat
something hot.

After Salt Lake City, Nieri's is the first roadhouse in about
five hundred miles. You won't understand how a saloon could
fail in such a location until you get there, all dragged out and
thirsting for refreshment, and meet Adolfo Nieri. He's as idle as
a constitutional monarch, and a ton weight; no part of him
works except his mind, which is busy with a deep depression.
Order a drink and he just hoods his fat eyelids at you; it took
him an hour to get someone to come and fix us some grub.
Afterward we went outside where the Jacobsville boys were
hanging around the stage depot. There are about thirty of them,
camped in shanties by the river, who have come here on account
of the silver discovery nearby. They are the sort who write

home to their sisters and sing comical songs, after a snootful, in harmonies of three parts; and they were expecting mail this evening.

Now that the 3rd Regiment California Volunteers was guarding the stage road from Indian depredations, Mr. Ben Holiday & associates had agreed to restock the whole line with agents, mules, and teamsters; and the first stagecoach in four months was imminent. It was hard to get excited about that when I was all the time thinking the kids would get here in a few hours, prance in, and grab the opium. But Ness seemed to manage. She shared in the boys' anticipation so much I couldn't stand it. I went to the river, where Mama was sitting on the rum crate, drinking.

I said, "You going to let him pimp you?"

She plumed herself. "If he treats me right."

"He's a pimp. He ain't dippy about you. He'll look after a pack of cards better."

"Jealous?"

"Of what?"

You know the man that does the three-shell trick where you have to guess which shell the pea's under? He knows something you don't but he doesn't want to sicken you, so he tries to keep the smile in his cheeks from getting to his mouth too often. Mama smiled like that and said, "He's promised me a share of the booty."

"How could he refuse you? Why, you're just as sweet as the last dab of honey in the jar. Did he say how much he'll give you?"

"I'll put in a word for you," she said. "I will use my pull the best I can."

Thistles grow by the river, huge ones in the shape of serpents, which have purple heads. When they die the heads lose their color, turn into frowzy straw hats. I cut myself pulling the head off one. I said, "You fucked him yet?"

"No."

I was feeling cruel. "Did you try?"

She leaned her arms on the rum crate as if it was a nifty new piece of furniture she'd bought and she wanted you to admire it. "I don't need to, dear."

I sloshed back to the hotel and spent my last dingbats for a couple of drinks. Two drinks is like getting into a bath that'll be cold in a minute. Nursing the second, I went upstairs to my bedroom and waited for the stagecoach, standing at the window. The Jacobsville boys were facing in the direction of a set of hills that resembled smoky green pyramids, but the way the land lay you couldn't see the road even a quarter-mile off. The first anyone knew of the stage was the horn. Then came the racket of the coach itself, the grinding of the wheel boxes; and at last—with a flash air of having raced all the way instead of making a good quantity of miles with everyone aboard asleep including the driver—the stage roared up and dropped its ballast of mail and passengers. The Jacobsville boys whooped and cheered like billy-o. Generally city girls have more things to get worked up over; Cordelia was metropolitan about the thing but Ness behaved like a back-country farmer's daughter, overwhelmed with more feelings than she understood. Then she caught herself, looked around at other people, and tried to copy them.

The passengers were long-haired, rich young men, stage-crazy after days cooped up together, who rammed through the door below my window into Nieri's saloon, followed by the Jacobsville boys. They packed as much noise into the space of ten minutes as sailors on a two-days' riot and slung the drinks themselves. I had just poked out onto the staircase when two men were belched out downstairs. It was Pontius and some young fellow; they came upstairs, went into Pontius's room, and dickered. There was the distinct chunk of metal weights and I heard them argue over the price of something that was quoted on the San Francisco stock exchange: opium, I supposed. I happened to be leaning on my doorpost when the young fellow came out of the bedroom—fair-haired, purple-cheeked, fruit-skinned—flushed with excitement over the deal. He clattered downstairs and Pontius came out of the bedroom, sporting a fine new Army Colt.

He seemed now to regard the opium as entirely his; I wanted to check him in some way, but I didn't have the nerve right then.

"Come with me on a job," he said. "I can't take Isobel." He tapped his head. "You can't trust her to remember anything."

I followed him to the river, where he wrapped the boodle in a sheet he'd stolen from the hotel. Then he hoisted it onto his shoulder and jerked his head to say I should follow him. Mama put on a front like I needn't give myself ideas but she didn't like to be thrown off her seat and it bothered her she was being left behind.

Pontius didn't cross the bridge, he stayed on the left-hand side of the river so as to go around the encampment of emigrants. On the other side, suppers were being cooked and chores done. Nobody noticed us until, right at the outskirts of camp, a young woman came down to the river to wash dishes. A fish surfaced and thrashed, like the water was too warm and it wanted out. "Don't look too healthy," the young woman said. "All sorts of strange fish in there. That river don't meet the sea, they reckon."

We waded the stream and climbed up the other bank.

"What's your name?"

"Jean Manlove."

"Jean Manlove, you see this crate? I want you to take it, put it in your wagon."

She yelled out, "Les!"

Les showed up and Pontius explained the same thing to him. Les had plenty courage for all he was so odd-appearing; Pontius had to tell him not to be brave, there was nothing to be gained by it. He said if they didn't take the crate, he would put a hole in them. Their wagon had a motto painted on the side: PERSEVERE. Pontius said it wouldn't be too clever to run away, he would find them in a minute, and he shoved the opium in the back of their wagon. It was diked out like a bedroom inside. Clothes were hung up on hooks, and so was a towel and a looking-glass. On a hook above the bed was a picture that was curtained, as though it was something lurid.

I said, "On your honeymoon?"

"No."

"Looks like it. What's the smutty picture?"

She opened the curtain. "Our mother. She died last year." She certainly looked dead; she had that accusing stare.

"You only got one mother between you?"

"He's my brother."

He said he slept under the wagon. Pontius said, "You can both sleep in here tonight, you hear?"

On the way back I said to Pontius, "When it comes to the divvy, I want half."

"I'm going to the hotel and hole up. You know where to find me if you want to be some use."

"I got to know how we're going to split up the loot first."

"How about we divide it into four? One share for every kid we croak."

"Prime," I said. Then I headed for the noise of the celebrations in Jacobsville, the jubilee they were having on account of the stagecoach and the mail it had brought them. It was only when I got there and waded into some strong liquor that I realized how rattled I was. From the beginning Pontius had behaved as if he could work me to his own ends, and it seemed he'd been right. He'd borrowed me for a while. And if he finally got his hands on the swag he'd likely leave me behind. I tried to imagine what it would be like if all my hopes flatted out and I was no better off than when I set out. It didn't bear thinking about. The Jacobsville boys pulled me here and there, and I just let them; they told me the history of the settlement and projected its future, and I submitted to their humorous tales without complaint. I was trying to figure out what I would have to do to hook Pontius.

By the time you get here Jacobsville will be a good-going town. Nothing is visible as yet excepting ropes and pegs sketching out the streets and lots, but the boys expect to sell out to hotels and builders when word gets abroad about the bonanza here. One of the Reese River station hands was prospecting in those cool-looking mountains when he struck silver, and a sample has been taken to Virginia City to be assayed and whooped up; until prospectors come here, and grocery stores and saloons, the Jacobsville boys are mere speculators. They buy and sell their city blocks while sleeping in tents and shanties. They play poker for streets all night, fret the days away, and go on almighty benders. Nothing nerves you up worse than being *almost* rich, I suppose.

They were mortal by the time I arrived. I was in no mood for boisterous spirits, but soon as I took their booze I was obliged to listen to them spoil each other's jokes. One of them wanted me to help him write a girl he'd knocked up back in Camden, New Jersey; he proposed we go to Nieri's, where we could be more alone. He was the kind you like to be alone with. He had black, black eyes and a smile that took about a minute to develop. In Nieri's he scrupled over his choice of words, for, being a free-thinker, he would not intrust the ruined girl to the care of God, not for anything. In the end he decided it would be a harmless deceit if he ventured to trust that the Eternal Mind of the Universe would guide the skirt through the dark and hopeless days ahead. I suggested that *grim* had a better sound than *dark*—grim and hopeless days ahead. Then I coaxed him into buying a bottle of wine, and we moseyed back to the shindig just as Ness and Cordelia were going back to the hotel for the night.

I stood in front of Ness and said, "Did Cordelia say anything to these boys about what's in the rum crate?" I thought it might get hairy if they knew how much money was sitting there. They might want it for themselves.

Ness shook her head. "I warned her," she said, edging around me. "If one person loses their life over that boodle it's too many. Let the kids walk in and take it. They got more right to it than anyone, what I know about it."

I watched her all the way back to the hotel. I watched her till she closed the door behind her. Then I loaded the bottle of wine with the last of my missy and for an hour or so I watched the Jacobsville boys dance with one another. There was a shiver inside of me somewhere that couldn't get out. I was all alone in the world but I wasn't going to quit. There's no quit *in* me or I would have given up when I was ten. If I had to fuck Pontius, so be it, and I stood up, holding my bottle of drugged wine, and sashayed off.

NINE

I used up the wine and fetched up in a thorn bush. It scratched my eyes and face pretty good but it was comfortable enough once you relaxed, so I lay there and gave myself over to sad reflections on the way certain parties run away from their responsibilities. Next thing I knew I was crossing the bridge and wandering among the encampment of travelers.

The bonnets of the wagons shuddered in the wind. Around a fire a girl with a flushed face was curled up beside her mother like she was having a pretty hectic dream. Her mother looked worried but very neat. I lay down beside them and watched the Big Dipper, but then I remembered waking up with the Chinese girl and how she hadn't liked it. Anyway, the ground was hard and beginning to be chilly so I stood up, dusted myself down, and started for Nieri's. As I crossed the bridge I saw an apparition of a young woman caught in a thorn bush, naked. She tried to escape and the thorn bush crackled in ecstasy.

Adolfo Nieri was still in the saloon so I sat down directly opposite and stared in his face. He was too busy being miserable to take much offense, and by and by we got comfortable sitting there. You won't find better company than Adolfo Nieri if you want to be alone. He reminded me of a waterfront bar I knew in

San Francisco by the name of Dead Marines. It's the sort of shop where they don't appreciate your company, they want to drink their poison in peace and quiet. Piled up all over the place like lobster traps are fifty or sixty cages with macaws in them; the macaws don't say an awful lot and you wonder why until the tide comes in and the sea rises through the plank floor of the bar, up over the bottom of the cages. None of the customers appear to notice the development, but the macaws sit on the highest perches and grow dreadful quiet. Sit with Adolfo Nieri long enough and you will be up to your ankles in water.

Mama looked quite pretty, sleeping on the stairs. Her head was resting on her arm, and her long neck showed to advantage. On her fattest finger was a big ugly ring Pontius had given her. In one bedroom upstairs Ness and Cordelia were asleep, or letting on to be; in the other one Pontius was sitting at the end of a bed watching at the window, on the look-out for the kids. It seemed as if the back of my dress was heavy with water and I was dragging this dirty tail of skirt behind me. My skirt wasn't wet at all but it seemed that way—I was gonged, remember. I went and sat on Pontius's bed.

After a while I said, "I reckon there's something comforting about vile circumstances, don't you?"

He had his back to me.

"Once I woke up in a hooker's crib with Esmé Jennings," I continued. "I didn't know her from Mrs. Lincoln when I fetched around, but it turned out to be her crib. So we smoked some hop and told each other sea stories."

I leaned back on my arms and the mattress made a frog noise. He didn't face around.

"I wish you'd fuck me," I said.

He heard that all right. The stones of the wall were listening now, every one of them.

"Well?" I said. "Would you like to?"

"I'd sooner choke a girl than fuck her."

My cheeks were ringing like he'd slapped me in the face. I stood up and started to peel my clothes. It was the dirtiest thing I'd ever done. What if he turned his nose up at me?

"Won't you even look at me?" I said sweetly. "I'm naked as a worm."

I could tell by the back of his neck that he almost faced about. "I got other things on my mind right now." He was keeping watch.

"I reckon you might get carried away fucking a girl. And you wouldn't like that. Am I right?"

"I might get carried away choking a girl." His throat was thick with it. "And nobody would know about it afterward."

I leaned all my weight on one foot. The floorboards noticed and creaked. "You wouldn't croak me, would you?"

"You're just nothing to me."

I dipped my voice in little girl and molasses and said, "Will you look at me if I call you daddy?"

That turned him. He faced around and looked me over, every inch. His eyes were shiny with a gluttonous love. He was thinking about the asses we could lead by the nose, the two of us, the way he led Bob Valentine.

"You want me to be your daddy, I got to know you love me, don't I?"

"Well," I said, "I could show you if you like."

"Can you do it quick?"

I knelt beside the bed, unbuttoned his pants, and started in. He didn't seem to like it or he didn't want to like it, and nothing happened for a while. Then I must've done something or said something or touched him by mistake in some way that stirred him, because he all of a sudden stood up, thick and tall. Seemed he wasn't so different from other men after all. I pushed him back so he was laying on the bed, because here's a piece of advice if you ever have to screw someone you loathe: sit on top and do it that way. You don't need to look at him and it's more hygienic.

I rose and dropped on his cock; hard; rose and dropped, like getting even. I wasn't certain who I was getting even with; I mean, I was sore at Ness for turning her back on me and I was mad at Mama for confusing everything, and he kept one eye on the door and a pistol in his hand. I slapped him and said, "Move!" I was hardly on the bed and I wanted he should shift. "Move!" I said, and belted him again. When he was more on the bed I started in again. I think his prick was inflamed; every time I rose and dropped he winced like it was sore. At first I supposed I was hitting him because I didn't like doing what I was doing, but then suddenly I did like it, I liked fucking him plenty and I liked hurting him too, and I just let my back hair down. I didn't care what anyone thought, I didn't care what I thought. I didn't even think it was loathsome anymore. I mean it was loathsome, sure, it was loathsome as two lepers fucking, but what do the lepers care? I was riding him real hard, me and the mattress bellowing like a couple of sea lions, when suddenly the wall seemed to cave.

It was Ness. She almost tore the door off its hinges; it was like she'd come to save me. Maybe from the noise I'd been making she'd supposed he was hurting me or something, and then she saw me sitting on top of him, touching my monkey. We didn't say anything. After she went, Pontius and I finished the job. Then he flung me off and took his place watching at the window.

When you sleep with someone you despise, well, it's interesting, I suppose. It's interesting you can do it, but I don't recommend afterward. I kept perfectly still in case the mattress made a frog noise.

Pontius said, "I'm going to see the Manloves are all right, hear?"

"Yes."

After I heard his footsteps disappear across the bridge, I dozed off for a little and was awakened by a noise outside. I got out of bed and dressed—that's when I noticed he'd taken my gun with him. I went downstairs, into the saloon. Adolfo Nieri was still sitting there. Most of him was nodding off but his mind kept nudging him awake. We were both looking at each other when the door opened, slowly, and a face appeared back of the door. It scanned the room like a thief. Nieri had a lantern on the table in front of him and I was in its light, so we all three could see one another. Eventually the party behind the door decided there was no call for secrecy and walked in, gun in hand. It was the Chinese kid, with the fat girl at his back. It must have been four in the morning but they were wide-awake extra, you could see the drug working their faces. He was wearing a slight frown as though his mind was a shoal of piranhas that kept changing direction and he wanted it to stop.

I didn't want to be alone with them so I was glad of the disturbance upstairs. Any company at all, even noise. The other two kids had climbed through the windows. They were scaring Ness and Cordelia out of their beds. When they drove them down into the saloon, I couldn't look at Ness, I was so ashamed.

The kid with no face bossed the scene. He tackled Nieri first. Adolfo tried to show by his fatness and humility that he was someone you could depend on to give you the straight goods; he said Pontius had come downstairs an hour or so back and let himself out. The kid with no face said good, where was he now? Adolfo had fast eyes you noticed because the rest of him was slow. He said he wasn't going to fan around, the plain truth was he didn't know. Then he looked at the kids with that doughy face of his. You might have supposed nothing could shift the sadness there until the kid with no face dislocated his jaw. He used a full bottle of wine, and Adolfo dropped onto his hands and knees and moo'd in agony. The kids held one another back until Adolfo had gotten over the first fresh pain, then the fat girl booted him on the chin.

The kid with no face turned to me and said, "I don't know why we bust *his* jaw. He don't know nothing."

I said I wished I did know where he was, the bastard. I said the bastard played us for mugs then took out. I said we didn't like the bastard any more than they did. I said I hoped there was enough of him to go around.

The Chinese kid grabbed my hair and the other three lamped me so hard and so fast I dropped to the floor. I didn't throw up any difficulties: I lay there like a good girl while they kicked me in the tits, the ribs, everywhere. The kid who always dragged himself around like he had the clap, he annoyed my ear with his bare naked feet. They were hard and horny and I thought I would gag, until he bust my lip with his heel. I suppose I looked just frightful, because Ness split out in a terrible sob. Maybe now she'd appreciate the sacrifices I made for others, and I rolled onto my back so she could see my face better. But the kids weren't done. They picked me up and said what they'd do to me if I didn't take them to Pontius. If I really didn't know where he was that was just too bad, they said, I was a goner. They dragged me out of Nieri's and did all sorts of things that made me not want them anywhere near me. So long as I kept moving right along, they left me alone.

It wasn't dawn yet but one or two of the campers were awake, the cooks or the ones that couldn't sleep. I saw a fire getting kicked into life but no great stir; the tails of horses, canvas beating in the wind. On the outskirts of camp I came to a dead halt. I said it was one of these three wagons, I didn't know which, and I couldn't tell them no matter what they did to me. They hit me a couple more licks and left me on the ground. I knelt there with my arms over my head till I heard a piece of metal snap shut. The diseased-looking kid had climbed onto the tongue of a wagon and caught his hand in a steel trap. An old woman had set it there, to keep Death from sneaking up on her in the night, I suppose, but she still hadn't been able to sleep, she was at the back of the wagon in her nightgown, watching the dawn. The kid screamed and got off his gun any old how and the Chinese kid went to his aid. The old woman had a back that was hooped, she snuck up on them around the side of her wagon; she didn't waste a shot on the diseased-looking kid, she wiped out the Chinese kid and retired to reload.

The kid with no face and the fat girl, they knew now that Pontius was aboard the *Persevere*. The kid found a tin of kerosene oil; she got a shovelful of live coals from a bivouac fire. Inside a wagon, what can you see? How do you defend yourself? All those kids did, they built a fire under the tongue of the wagon out of what materials they could find, dosed it with the kerosene, and tossed the coals over it. It was only a matter of time, I reckoned, before Pontius ran out of there screaming for mercy. The kid with no face and the fat girl fed the fire with a bottle of spirits and some sheets, and eventually the Manloves jumped out and ran. The wagon was fairly ablaze. The kid with no face went right up to it, then found somewhere he could cover Pontius when he bolted.

But it appeared Pontius had chosen to die like a heathen in a funeral pyre and there was nothing anyone could do about it. All I could think about was the booty going up in a black cloud of smoke and how the kids had fouled things up. "What a waste!" I kept thinking. The kid with no face got impatient too—he shot the diseased-looking kid to put him out of his misery and stop the hollering. It didn't work. It put the diseased-looking kid out of *his* misery but not the kid with no face; he looked like he might tear himself in two, and he ran up to the burning wagon. He tried to look inside but it was too hot; in frustration he emptied his load into the back of the wagon then threw his shooter in after, just for good measure. After a little it exploded.

There was a bunch of mules and horses nearby and the fire was getting on their nerves. They were pulling at their picket pins and one or two had pulled free, and the kid lost his temper with them. He tore a burning sheet from the fire he'd set under the wagon and walked toward the animals, whirling it over his head. Two horses moved toward him, rearing and struggling; it seemed odd they would move *toward* him. Suddenly they scattered and Pontius was there in their midst; he stepped up to the kid and shot him, three bullets at arm's length.

TEN

He shot the fat girl as she waded loudly through the stream, and started back to Jacobsville directly the river shut up. He wanted to make his getaway fast. There was a wagon ablaze and four corpses lying about; the scene wasn't going to look any better ten minutes from now. The unburied bodies of four kids might begin to take on the appearance of an atrocity, and sooner or later somebody would get overcurious about the rum crate. The eyes of the Chinese kid were perfectly still. I unclasped his hand and took his Colt Dragoon, stripped him of a flask of shot and cartridges, and followed Pontius through the camping place. Children who stared at us got pulled away by their older sisters.

It was barely an hour after sun-up, if that. Around the depot there were Indian women who'd come down from the hills with baskets of berries on their heads. The emigrants were swapping with them and trading with the station agent in currency. There was something of the stir you might expect of a regular plaza, only people were frowning and distracted-looking. It was a while before I realized that was on account of the shooting they'd heard two minutes ago. They seemed to know we had something to do with it. Pontius found three mules the station agent was willing to part with, and started packing them. I didn't help much. My face was numb, my hands were swollen; I felt as though I'd been rolled in nettles. There was blood stuck to the hair on the back of my head that had dried and turned into taffy. Mama watched us from the doorway of the hotel, then she came out with her sack of belongings and handed it to Pontius. Instantly, there flashed on my mind a picture of me sitting on top of Pontius, naked, and my skin flared up like I'd touched something poisonous and come out in a burning red rash.

"Ness wants to see you," Mama said.

I wanted to keep my eye on the rum crate. Same time, I wanted to get out of the light and escape the way Mama was looking at me. I was inflamed from head to toe. "What about?" I said.

"Don't ask me." As I started to the hotel, Mama said, "She's had her stitches out. One of the Jacobsville boys was a doctor back in the States."

Inside the saloon I was astonished how little blood there was on the floor, considering what the kids had done to Nieri and me. There were about six spots that could have been anyone's. I examined myself in the bar mirror, gave my face a cat's wash, and started upstairs. Soon as I put my foot on the fifth step I got the most awful gone feeling in my stomach. I heard Ness stiffen upstairs and go quiet, get herself ready to face me. You wouldn't believe what I can hear. When I was ten I came home to our house in Buenos Aires and I knew when I stepped inside the door that Mama had gone. There was someone rattling about in the kitchen but somehow I knew the rest of the house was empty. I didn't even go upstairs to look for her, I went straight into the kitchen, though Connie the cook used to yell if I ever so much as poked my nose in there. Not that time. She paled when she saw me and dried her hands on her apron. She chopped a banana for me and sprinkled sugar over it, then sat me down and told me the news. Later I went into Mama's bedroom—she wasn't there to forbid me—and examined all sorts of jewelry and treasures I'd never seen before. I read love letters from men I could barely remember, and toyed with the clothes she hadn't bothered to take. I held them to my face so I could inhale her scent, and then I sat with them in my lap. I didn't want anything she didn't. I didn't actually turn my nose up at them but that was the feeling I had; that, and wanting to cry.

Those last few steps I thought over what I would say to Ness, and what she would say to me, and how I would answer her; I couldn't make up my mind what face to put on: humble or hard. When I went into the bedroom I realized my face was too swollen to have any expression at all, that I could choose.

She knew I was there but didn't face around. I was scared to say anything because then the conversation would begin. "I hear you got your stitches out," I said in the end.

She turned and peered at me like she was looking around a corner. Then she touched her chin with the pad of one finger, where she'd scraped her beard off. "I'm awful red around the chin. I'm hoping it'll calm down before I get back to Virginia City."

"Virginia City?"

She buried her cheek in her shoulder. "Let me clean your face. Sit on that bed."

The mattress cringed when I sat on it and made that frog

noise; I almost bounced right up. Ness went to get hot water and some liniment. The whole time she was away I held my ass tight so it wouldn't sink into the mattress and make it squeak. She came back with a basin, put it on the floor, and started in.

"I wired the stage that's due tonight," she said, "to find out if they had any free berths and if they would take up a way passenger. They said they would."

She waited for me to say something but fists were punching the inside of my throat.

"Then I asked the station agent what he would give for our mule," she went on. "He said a hundred and ten dollars."

I was surprised it was that much.

"Course, I wouldn't want to hog it all," she said.

I could hear my breathing, I could hear her breathing. "I guess you're entitled to half," I said.

"Half?" She probably supposed she was entitled to more. "I suppose that's fair." She started to dab the top of my head. "I'm sorry I saw you with the pimp last night."

"You'd think you'd never gone to bed with a man before."

"It's none of my business who you screw," she said. "It was along of the din you were making that I came to see if he was hurting you. When I bust in, you stopped what you were doing," she said, "and sneered at me."

It was like someone peeled my scalp, that was the sensation I had.

I said, "Why would I sneer at you?"

"I don't know."

"I sneered at you? You sure? How did I sneer? Can you describe the way I sneered?"

"Like you were immortal, at least."

It's bad when somebody tells you something you've done and you can't account for yourself. It's humiliating. "I don't know why I did that," I said.

She pushed my head down. "Remember the wedding at the Lake Hotel, and I said I wanted to square it and run a dry-goods store?" She was nipping the cuts on my skull. "You didn't actually look down your nose at me that night, but you spoke to me like I didn't have a particle of imagination."

"Will you stop talking like I do nothing but sneer?"

She left off anointing my head. "It's you that don't have an imagination, Dol. You don't foresee danger. You don't see the trouble you're in when it's staring you in the face. And after it's happened it's just something gone by."

I went to the window. Somehow I knew for a certainty that Mama and Pontius had skinned out, but I let it sink in for a couple of minutes. By now the berry baskets of the Indians had a picked-over appearance, and the women looked miserable. One of them wore a necklace made of tin cans. After all the excitement and whiz of trading, all they had gotten in exchange for their fruit was some flour and some canned goods, and they looked as though they would be glad to swap everything back so they could do it over again.

"I just hope you've learned something from this experience," Ness said. "Will you take the stage home? I'd be glad of your company." She didn't mean she'd be awfully glad, just that she didn't want me to feel like an outcast.

"I think I'd be nervous all the time in case I sneered at you," I said with stupid sarcasm.

"What's that supposed to mean?"

"I daresay you won't miss me. Anyway, I got to get after Mama."

"She's gone?"

"With the pimp. While I was in here being lectured on my morals, they took their chance and cut out."

I could practically hear Ness try to keep her temper. "You don't have to chase after her."

I was seething myself. "Yes I do, Ness. Yes I do."

ELEVEN

Ness gave me fifty dollars for my share of the mule and I bought a hand-cart, ham, coffee, and beans. There was no missy to be had anywhere and Nieri wouldn't sell me any booze. His face was so sore it was painful for him to sit at his table and drink, never mind stand up and walk to his bar. Cordelia decided to come with me and chipped in her small savings. She gave the lovebird and cage to Ness for safe keeping. I said whyn't she take the stage and keep Ness company; but her future husband was waiting for her in Pittsburgh, she said, and Ness could look after herself.

All the way to the foot of the pyramid-shaped hills I imagined Ness was watching me, and didn't dare to falter or look around. The hand-cart was hard labor. My arms were trembling before I started up the mountain road, but I had a clear purpose to drive me onward, and a Colt Dragoon to accomplish it. Whatever grief or trouble it caused me, I was going to find my mother and separate her from that pimp.

It was over a thousand feet, the ascent, maybe two; it would have taken three or four hours, ordinarily. It was a lot longer with a hand-cart; after less than an hour my back hurt, my neck was sore, and my arms wanted to drop off. I asked Cordelia to take a turn, but her doctors had advised her against physical labor in case it caused a fallen womb. When we stopped to rest, all I could see was the large amount of mountain still to climb, and Cordelia's hair. She wears it coiled over her ears like muffs, in the style that is fashionable among females who scrape up a personality by steady opposition to public opinion, and I would willingly have chopped her head off. We halted at the summit to glance down at Jacobsville, then headed off along a gentle path on that mountain roof-top. With every step I took my insides unraveled like row after row of knitting, as if every mile from Ness was a mile in the wrong direction. By evening I was all ripped out.

Next day I dropped into a fever of some kind. My nose ran and so did my eyes. I started to sweat. Cordelia kept asking what ailed me. I had no idea. On board a ship once I saw a sheep after a bad squall—that's how puny I felt. An hour or more before noon I wandered off the road and hid from the sun under some brush. I didn't sleep. Mostly I tossed and turned the way you do when you're tormented by hot, sticky sheets. Other times I was cold right through. I began to wish I had some missy and asked Cordelia to get me some. I was lying all curled up and my voice came out in a bad-tempered whine I scarcely recognized as me. That's when I realized I was suffering for want of a dose. Cordelia put her boot on my side and seemed to want me to roll over so she could see my face. I didn't mind, even when she kicked me in the back a little; I don't think I could have stood anything kinder. She bent over me; I could feel her there; then she pushed my hair behind my ear. Maybe she enjoyed the way she could do what she liked with me or maybe she wanted me to listen better. "Huh!" she said. "This is the girl who reckoned she was better than me."

I still do, I thought.

"You make me sick," she spat out.

For hours on end I couldn't remember the start of a thought by the time I got to the end of it. My bones ached, and my muscles; I rubbed my face into the dirt to get some comfort. I was soaked in all sorts of fears and horrors. There's the sweat of hard labor and the sweat of bad dreams; this was like something dirty running its fingers through my hair. And it got worse. To get some relief I crawled across to my hand-cart, raised myself, and struck my forehead, hard, against the corner edge five times. After that I fell asleep, and woke up to the smell of potatoes and onions, frying.

Two men were camped nearby. There was a little touch of sleep in their coughs and in the quiet gaps between talking. At first light they pulled out. They tipped their hats to me as they passed, almost out of superstition more than courtesy. I was wet as a barman's apron; I daresay I was quite a sight. I found a creek and washed the best I could, my hair particular, then sat down and watched the day come over the valley to the south. There wasn't much to it: two low mountain ranges running north to south; between them a vast sage flat. Nothing else, no tricks. But you couldn't tire of it. In the edge of morning the ice-green sage had a sort of shyness about it—a grayness. Then, little by little, the colors grew. The sky got bluer; the hot, dry plain was cool and bright and tingled like a field of snow. I noticed the insides of my nostrils were aching; either the air was too pure or I wasn't used to breathing in so deep. But it made me feel good clean down my back.

The boodle had stirred up something ugly in me and clouded my thoughts. All the time it had been in my possession I knew deep down it wasn't mine, and wanted it all the more. But now it was gone for good I was clearer in my mind, and stronger. I had to save Mama: that's all, nothing else. Before breakfast I bathed in the stream again, to wash the bad dreams out of my hair, then I ate breakfast with an appetite I hadn't had in goodness knows how long and even felt a little hungry afterward. When we set out, I felt like a different person for the first few miles, till the hand-cart started to stretch me like the rack.

Cordelia still wouldn't help, so I didn't give her any food, and along about noon the following day she fainted. I promised to give her some chuck if she pushed the barrow all afternoon. She nearly died but it schooled her and I got no trouble after that. Against the tide of emigrants we climbed up tall Nevada mountains, covered with firs whose branches were like candelabra hung with tracery, and down the other side to a barren flat. Then up another mountain. Often I got to wondering how different things would have been if I'd shot Pontius when we had the chance, back at Sand Springs. Sometimes I thought that same thing all day, trudged along with nothing in mind but murder. At least once a day I would try to find out how far ahead of us they were and I always got the same answer.

"I'm surprised we're only two days behind," Cordelia said. We were climbing our fourth mountain in four days and had stopped to rest.

"The mules are packing all their plunder. They have to walk the same as us." I had just stuck a knife into a blister and was letting it ooze.

"They don't have to carry anything," Cordelia complained.

"The mules do. A mule can only go so far without water and grass and rest, and there's only so many camping spots they can find those things. We just have to be patient. Sooner or later one of those mules will get sick or lame or something. We'll see how tough they are then."

Cordelia looked at my foot, skeptical-like, and said, "You think their mules will let 'em down, huh?"

"Those mules will break down before I do." I forced my feet into my boots and stood up. It was like walking on thorns. I had sores on my hands and my arms were almost too stiff to pick up the hand-cart; but I pushed on, leading by example, showing Cordelia I have a will nothing can break.

We were maybe nineteen days out of Jacobsville when we left behind those high Nevada mountains belted with regulation pine and struck out into Mormon territory. That part of Utah has hills and buttes of strange shapes. There are black cones, white pyramids, mountains with domes; it's hard to believe. Same time, everything is clean as salt, and dry. You feel your lungs. The back of your neck goes tight. Late one afternoon, the road dropped into a dried-up river, maybe half a mile wide and a hundred feet down, which led to a riverbed station. I went to buy some water, asked the station hand if a fellow dressed like a pimp had passed this way lately, with a female.

He nodded and walked away to the water barrels.

"When?" I said when I got there. "Can you remember?"

"Three days back."

Three days is a lot to catch up when every step you take makes your feet wince. "Three days ago, you say. Couldn't have been two days, by any chance?" I was almost in tears.

"Day before pay day," he said. He couldn't look me in the eye. "The dame wanted some brandy. I said we'd run out. Her man cut up pretty mean. I had to go get it for her. I'd hidden it somewhere none of the other hands could get any. I was saving it for myself."

"You sure this was three days ago?"

He handed me my canteen without answering. I walked back to where I'd left the hand-cart. Cordelia had gotten into conversation with a black cook who was fixing supper for the family he belonged to. Next thing she turned around and pointed at me. The cook had these showy tongs in his left hand so he could enjoy picking up those elegant rashers of ham, while his belly relaxed over the front of his pants. He took in our barrow and meager outfit, and his head sunk between his shoulders like a boy who's just been belted around the ear. Miserable, he gave Cordelia some hot biscuits and shoo'd her away.

What kept me going the next few days was that each step was agony and goaded me onward. When we made Salt Lake City, Cordelia set off to find a post office while I trudged on through town. The Mormons have trained water to run in streams up and down the streets; besides that, it doesn't look any different from other towns; frame houses and shade trees and stores. To the east there is a wall of huge black mountains that rise up from the level plain. They make the town feel pretty small. Some of them have hills at their foot that are two hundred feet high and look like their knuckles; they could be huge thrones for supernatural creatures out of the Book of Revelations. They never go away, but along Main Street you are sheltered from them some by the telegraph office and the liquor store and the fellows sitting outside with their feet up on goods boxes. On the other side of me a buggy crowded me to the edge of the road. It had cooled its speed deliberately to keep alongside of me. I just ignored it.

"Miss McQueen? It *is* you." It was Henderson the druggist, still carrying his wife's little dog in the crook of his arm and exactly the same as he looked back in San Francisco. He was a spry little man, but cold-eyed, who thought himself the equal of most physicians. He used to spend hours in Hardy's choosing the right gloves and the perfect material for curtains; and he fairly piled it on when he talked. "Now this is the most singular coincidence I ever struck. Only this morning I had the honor to be of service to *Mrs.* McQueen in the matter of a little misfortune that has felled her traveling companion. He had a typhoid fever, though a trifling one. What we generally classify as a walking typhoid. I made her some pills and gave her some blackberry tea, a wonderful specific for that particular complaint. She said they were intending to push on today and would it be injurious to the invalid to travel. I said, certainly not. I had other customers to attend to and I make a habit of being categorical in my opinions. They were taking the Bear River road to Fort Bridger"—he pointed to those black mountains—"and I said the sufferer would find the exercise and mountain air most beneficial."

I said, "Did Mrs. McQueen look well?"

"Splendid." He tightened the fingers of his natty new driving gloves where they join the palm so they fitted him nice and snug, and then pointed his chin at me. He was going to insist on everything being splendid today.

He was still talking when Cordelia arrived back and handed me a letter. It was directed to *Miss Dolina McQueen Salt Lake City Utah Territory* in large handwriting that took up every inch of the envelope. It was all I could do to keep my balance and wait till Henderson had gone, whereupon I stood exactly where I was, not trusting my legs to move, and pulled the letter apart.

My dearest Dol,

I take pen in hand to drop you a few lines and let you know I am still in the land of the living. Take care, Dol. Reports here are rife of Colonel Connor's regiment of Californians and what their true purpose is. People say they mean to exterminate the Snake Indians just as soon as they locate them. They will do it too for this is their chance, the Federal Government at this great crisis in the affairs of the nation will let them do it and say Good luck too. You travel that road with your eyes stretched, men who are sent to exterminate an Indian nation are liable to get a hectic in their blood and take liberties with anyone they meet.

Well, you will see I am back in Virginia City. Mrs. Johns boards me, the church friend of Dig's. Soon as I made it back I sat down and wrote him my whereabouts. I had no more than twenty-eight dollars to my name. You can imagine my Pride, you of all people. I started the letter four times and four times Pride et me up. It was like swallowing a pound of lard, mouthful after mouthful. But I finished it at last and when Dig called on me we talked and cried. I shall draw a veil over the sentimental scene or I will make you sick.

O Dol, I don't know why I ever doubted him. He was perfectly right not to venture his life on a trip to the States. Remember the colored iron-foundry laborers we met on the road that had been chased out of New Albany? These are scaly times in that part of the world. And you'll never guess what he did the day after you and I shoved out of Virginia City. He took Ed Stainback out of town and put a bullet in his leg so he wouldn't follow us. Well, there are momentous events taking place in Virginia City. Three weeks ago I started in selling lines of cosmetics! Dig staked me and I do a driving business. I retail to the gals and I begin now to get a name among the élite. I walk right up and knock their doors and show the maids my samples and they tell their employers. It has been just a few short weeks but I have about paid Dig back the principal he loaned me, business is so good. The interest I shall pay in due season.

I wonder if I will ever see you again. I wonder if you are alive. I cannot pretend that everything is easy here. I don't take it well when I am told how to pray and what to pray for, that is my own business, I reckon, and Dig had better learn it. But when I am apt to think of the old days and wish them back I read the poem you wrote for me. If anyone would want to know the sort of life we lived I would show them that poem for answer, for you describe it about right. It was a perfect Waste.

I will close now. If this reaches you, let me know that you are safe and be sure that you will find at this address

> *she who has the honor to subscribe herself*
> *your dear friend, Ness Boschert*

It seemed awfully cold somehow. Am I wrong? She passed over our adventure in considerable silence. She told me her news. She was happy. She had struck out on her own and she was thriving. She made no comparison between her present happiness and safety and the ruin she had faced before she separated from me; she left me to draw my own conclusions.

I sat down on the edge of the sidewalk before I toppled over. I was outside a store that had a club foot in its window. Beside the model of the club foot was a promise to build you a bespoke boot no matter how deformed you are, and I never felt so useless and fit for nothing in my life. Cordelia was pestering me to know Nessie's news. I dropped the letter at her feet, told her how near at hand Mama was, and dusted for the black mountains.

TWELVE

The next three days were uphill through rough mountain country. One canyon was two days long. It got hard to believe anything human mattered. It got hard to believe anything human existed after a while, even when you passed people by. The earth was red and there were pink pillars of rock hundreds of feet high standing shoulder to shoulder that had been fired at temperatures beyond conceiving.

Sometimes it seemed from what we were told that Mama might be four miles ahead, other times more like twelve. Then, fourth day out from Salt Lake City, going on for two o'clock, we found out a typhoid case had laid by at Bear River. Cordelia wanted to stop where we were; it had been a brutal day and she had sprained her ankle, but Bear River was only six miles away and I yelled at her until my throat was swollen. Maybe two hours later, on broken feet, we climbed a scrubby hill the shape of an ant mound and saw below us a fast, shallow river and—beyond that—a large camping ground where a quantity of covered wagons were parked.

It was a sight for sore eyes. Bear River had all the coolness and spangle of water fresh from cold mountains, and the frisky grass had a sheen where the wild flax grew, like a blue undercoat. I stood there and gave myself time to take it all in. I wanted to memorize it—the place I found my mother and got her back. She had had the convenience of mules but I'd followed her just the same, for four hundred miles and almost thirty days, with nothing to keep me going but force of will. I walked downhill to sit in the shallow water and resurrect my legs, then I loaded my Colt Dragoon. It had an Indian skirmish engraved on the cylinder and was heftier than a gun you'd see in a saloon. It was like something that had been used in battle, and I started to the toll bridge across the river with every confidence. My skirt was soaked but it was hot and blowy; a perfect drying day, I said to myself.

"What about me?" Cordelia yelled.

"What about you?"

She was so weary her legs folded and she let herself drop onto a stump that was narrower than her backside. It would have been awfully sore if she'd missed it; but it hit her hard and square and she sat up straight in surprise. "I don't like your chances. What'll I do if you don't come back?"

"You'll find some other outfit to handicap."

I walked across the bridge, past the stage station, and turned into the cool of the wood that fringed the river on the other side. I picked my way through cottonwoods and willows, and mud pools of water left behind after the river had gotten over its bottoms, until I found a tree I could stand behind while I looked out over the camping ground.

I suppose I expected a quiet, busy camp; people cooking, washing, or mending; young girls sent on berrying parties while their mothers rolled out pie crusts. Instead the entire community of emigrants was having a celebration. There were maybe forty or fifty of them, all in the very pink of fashion, parasols enough for the promenade deck of a steamboat. I don't know what had possessed them, but at half past four of an afternoon a band was playing "Speed the Plow" and a couple were dancing down the middle while the other couples clapped in time. Spectators stood around and gossiped. If the ladies didn't hold on to their hats, the wind knocked them off their heads, and some stretchy young lad whose shoulders were stooped with youth might go chasing after it. Of course, the lady might be obliged to retrieve it herself, if she was middle-aged, and then make light of it.

They had every appearance of being well-off lunatics. Why would you decide to have a dance out here in Indian country? But it meant I had the wood to myself. There were no boys traipsing through it to draw water from the river, or pinching the flossiest fruit from the currant bushes. I followed the loop of the river until I couldn't hear the band hardly at all. The wind was blowing the other way. Here, the wagons were backed up to the edge of the wood, canvases drawn tight at the back with puckering string, all bar one. Its stores of grub and household items had been put out to air and a boy of about fourteen was lounging against the wagon tongue. He had a musket; I guess he'd been left behind as a picket, to raise an alarm if need be. I stepped out of the wood, walked right up, and said howdy.

Right away I saw he was a good-hearted middle-class boy keen to serve some higher purpose, so I said I was looking for my mama, who was being held against her will by a bad character. The boy with the musket had hair his mother had cut. She'd given him a fringe that hid a low forehead and came down to his eyebrows. He puffed up with the justice of my cause and showed me where I could find them. As I headed off there, I hardly cared what happened to me. On all sides the canvas of the wagons boomed and rattled in the wind; it was like walking the deck of a brig that has crowded on any amount of sail. It was a day of reckoning. As if I wanted to tell myself I meant business I showed my teeth, and noticed how dry and tight the skin was around my forehead. It would be a dreadful thing to take a person's life. But what else could I do? When I ran out of arguments I would have to use my Colt.

I'd tried my whole life to make her see sense, but she thinks she knows what she's doing, she supposes she's in control of her affairs, she doesn't imagine for a minute that she's a hopeless drunkard. She told me there was a time—this was in Valparaiso—when she didn't touch the stuff for two whole months; she offered that as proof that she wasn't *obliged* to liquor up. If she happened to decide every morning in life that she would take a snort, it was only because it settled her stomach and gave her the strength to take a little lunch, and then the nerve to look in a mirror.

From maybe thirty yards away I spotted them under the shade of a cottonwood tree and, in spite of everything, I wondered if this time I could hit upon the words that would undo her self-deception and help her see the truth about herself. Duffield once told me he saw a coffin opened that had lain in the crypt of a chapel twenty years. He said the corpse was as life-like as the day he was buried: hair combed, teeth bared, face composed, if a little off-color. But as they were maneuvering the open coffin back to its resting place, someone lost his balance and the coffin dropped about a foot onto the stone floor.

Right away the head fell off and the entire body under the shroud disappeared in a cloud of dust. I mean to say, if a change has been coming, all it takes sometimes is a small upset or accident. As I headed toward them, I could feel a tiny amount of hope in my throat, just enough to choke on.

The wind was catching the trees by the river and pulling their hair, tugging them one way then the other. Pontius was lying wrapped in a sheet. Mama must have warned him I was coming because he hauled himself up onto the rum crate they were using as a table and pointed his gun at me. He'd lost maybe half a stone in weight, shitting. His face was wet, and the blues of his eyes had weak points and holes; but what he lacked in steadiness of aim he more than made up for in his willingness to shoot.

I said, "I wouldn't have known you two were alive only I ran into Henderson the druggist back in Salt Lake City. He looks like he's made a barrel of money." Pontius was sweating hard. It was difficult to tell how much he understood. "Can we go somewhere and talk, Mama?"

A brown skirt and white shirt-waist gave her the sober appearance of a good manager and matron, but I knew she didn't like sick people and the burden they placed on her. She stood up, brushed the knees of her skirt, keen to cut out. "She wants to speak to me in private, Billy," she said to Pontius.

"I heard her."

"I won't be long," she snapped.

"Go ahead," he said with the remains of his voice.

She would feel better about leaving him on his own if they quarreled first. "Every time I look at him he makes me feel like

I've got a dead rat in my gut. Do you hear me? I'm saying you make me feel like I have a dead rat in my gut. I've had nothing to look at these last few days but your miserable face." She turned up her nose. "And I'm afraid there's a definite smell." She poured him a coffee and tried to hold her head away from the stench. "Lie down. I said *lie down*. I'll put the coffee here where you can reach it."

He kept me covered with that gun until I faced around and walked away, followed by Mama.

I was anxious to get our conversation off on the right foot seeing as, if it failed of its purpose, it might be the last we ever had. But I was weak with hunger and didn't trust myself to speak. Eventually, when we were crossing the ground where the lunatics were having their shindig, I said: "What's the occasion?"

"A wedding," Mama said. But she didn't give it a glance.

All the wedding party were overflowing with good spirits, barring the girls my age. While the dance band was having a rest break, the girls were wandering the park in close-headed groups of two, conjuring with each other. I guess they'd walked over a thousand miles from the States, eating nothing but bacon and beans, their figures had never been better and their hopes had likely been high. But then certain boys hadn't asked them to dance—or had shown themselves susceptible to the smiles of other (more shallow) girls—and now they were trying to decide if the boys ought to be given a second chance.

Mama marched through the festivities with her head down. I wanted to get off some witty and cynical remark about marriage that might cement our divisions, but I had walked fourteen miles that day and I was witless with nerves. I heard myself say, "It's the daisiest wedding. I hope the bride will be happy, don't you?"

"If she doesn't bother me, I don't care."

The bride was a small, stocky girl with white-blond hair. Her eyebrows were so white and blond her eyes looked bald. "Look, they built a table for the wedding feast." There was a long trestle table. I stopped to admire it for two seconds and then I had to run to catch up. "How on earth did they build that?"

I was giving her a sore head. "How should I know? We just got here."

"Did they use the side-boards of their wagons?"

She stopped outside the stage station. "Look, if it's *dinero* you're after, tell me how much you want and I'll ask him."

The inside of my throat closed. "I wouldn't touch his money."

"Then what *do* you want?" She was bewildered.

I wasn't ready to tell her yet. "That's what I came to talk about," I said lamely.

The station agent was holding out his hand to collect some dimes off a wagon driver that wanted to use his bridge. "Wait here till I buy some whiskey," she said. "No doubt he'll be charging fancy prices. They think they can ask what they like out here."

That's why the wedding celebrations had been just nothing to her, I realized, she'd had booze on her mind. The station agent sold her a bottle and she shoved for the nearest piece of wood, where she could feel more alone. She looked like an animal sneaking off with a piece of meat it has killed, to eat it on the sly. I left her alone for a little then I followed her into the wood. It was that time of year when plants are in the milk, you could smell it. Outside the wood some little girls were kiting through the tall grass in their wedding duds, screaming the way little girls do, for the fun of the thing. The screams went scaring though my blood.

"What's wrong?" I said. "Pontius don't like you to drink?"

She didn't like anyone to know the amount she used up but she couldn't say that, of course, so she nodded toward the wedding celebration. "I don't like the flats to see me. They look at you like you've got two heads."

"A wedding in Indian country," I said. "We could write a book of our travels, you and me." Somehow that sounded a little strained. It was the kind of thing an unhumorous person might say after traveling two days on a coach with you.

"We had some rocky times," she agreed.

"There was the earthquake in Talcahuano."

"We had a couple of earthquakes," Mama corrected me.

"And that flood in Los Angeles when the mud houses were washed away."

"The walls of those adobe houses were three feet thick. They were good strong buildings," she said, like she was setting someone straight on the matter. "But they melted like sugar lumps in that flood." She said that with a grave face; it gave her a lot of satisfaction and she smoothed her dress at the hips.

There was something cobwebby about that wood. Even when you kept absolutely still, you could feel the touch of it around you. Insects tickled your face, sticky plants clung to your skirt, trees reached down and touched your hair. "We certainly had some experiences," I said, my heart pounding. It surprised me just a little that she remembered we had a past; I was frightened she might decide to deny it at any moment. "Where do you miss most?"

"Valparaiso, I suppose." Right away she said the name, her carriage and demeanor became more ladylike; and she'd had the right amount of drink. She looked like she'd gotten something hairy out of her mind. "I miss the British Pacific squadron," she said. "I liked the way they told me all their woes. If they had any affairs of the heart I would undertake little commissions for them, or gather intelligence concerning their prospects." She glanced at her shawl, which had happened to slip, as though surprised to find some gent hadn't fixed it for her already. "I miss that."

Then she seemed to notice where she was and who she was with and fell silent. The light outside the wood was quieter now. Two little girls were still chasing each other through the grass. Every now and then a childish scream would just expire and die.

"You look wonderful," I said.

I just wanted her to go on talking. She held up her arms and looked at her outfit as if it wasn't hers. The neat brown skirt and shirt-waist gave her the appearance of a campaigner for temperance or equal rights for females. "It's practical," she said with a sour edge. "It's not something I would wear in society."

I didn't want her to think I was pouncing on her so I waited awhile. Then, as quietly as I could, I said, "So you still hope sometime to take your place in society?"

She was shocked I could think otherwise. "Well, of course I do."

"I'm glad about that. I'd begun to despair about you."

She frowned. "I don't intend to live this way forever." And she gave a little glance in the direction where she and Pontius had camped, as if worried he might overhear her.

"I'm going to square it," I said. It wasn't cold but I began to tremble a little. "I sort of have already." I was talking between my teeth. "I mean, I'm fit for company again. I quit taking missy. I won't have to sneak off on my own all the time and hide from people."

She leaned against a cottonwood with her hands (and the whiskey bottle) behind her back, letting on she was in a summery, almost girlish mood. But her face was grim. "How long did you quit for?"

"Over a month now."

"Couldn't you get any?"

"I didn't try," I said. "Been thirty-three days, about."

"I'm surprised," she said.

"Shows I can do it."

"Is it a strain?"

Once again the wedding crowd were dancing, I could hear the band playing a mazurka. I didn't like where she was leading the conversation so I said, "When do you suppose you'll be ready?"

"Ready?"

"To cross the river."

It was as if I had asked her when she was doomed to die. She stood there pinned to the cottonwood, her eyes dull and clouded with the hint of tears. "It's awful empty over there."

She looked so miserable I considered telling her I sometimes felt the same way. She managed to push herself away from the trunk and steered off through the wood. She let on she was taking in the flora and fauna. She didn't know how to make it look realistic, though; instead of stopping to admire something in particular, she just turned her head this way and that and kept right along, pulling her skirt through knee-high, taffy-dipped wood sorrel.

I caught her up in a bright patch of wood where you could stand your height without something fingering your hair. "We'll get used to it after a while," I murmured.

Even though there was a full yard between us, it was like we were touching, only it was more tender than that. We stayed that way for half a minute. Then something started to rile her and she turned away from me and put the whiskey bottle to her mouth. She kept one eye out in case I saw how much she was necking. The eye stuck out like a well-cooked trout's.

When she was through, I said, "It's only two years since you inaugurated Ernesto Márquez's dance hall. People said you danced like it was Paris."

Her eyes slid off in disgust. "None of them had *seen* Paris, my dear." Maybe she remembered that she hadn't, either; she stepped to one side and slapped away some tiny insects with excessive irritation, like they had ruined her life.

"I only meant it's not that long since we lived like ordinary people."

"Pardon me, but I have never been ordinary."

"Didn't you used to be a maid?" I didn't mean to be cruel; it just came out. Then I took half a step back and waited for her to crumble.

Her face got smaller and harder. "Who told you that? I was no such thing. I never heard such nonsense."

There was something so forbidding about her I backed down. "You're hard as nails when it comes right down to it," I said, shaken.

A piece away Pontius was calling "Isobel! Isobel!" My hand almost went to my pistol. I told myself not to panic just yet. "I wish you'd leave him," I said. "Pimps keep a girl the way some people keep a carriage, so they can spread themselves."

"That's all you know."

"You don't delude yourself he'll give you a share of the lucky, do you?"

From her silence I deduced that she did. Pontius called her name again. It had a woody sound to it and seemed much closer than before. She turned in his direction. She had half a mind to shout out to him.

"I'm trying to save you." There was a jitter in my voice. "I've walked five hundred miles. I don't think I can follow you any farther. I mean I'd be a fool to, I suppose. So I'm giving you a choice." My insides were clawing to get out like a sackful of kittens thrown in a canal. "It's him or me." I was almost crying with the childishness of what I'd said.

He was close now; we could hear him crashing about. He fell and picked himself up, talking to himself. It was stupid and comical how noisy he was, like a wild pig that has no idea someone's laying in ambush.

"Come with me," I said. "I don't care how you talk to me. You can be sarcastic. Anything. There's so much I want to ask you."

"Oh, for crying out loud, Dol. About what?"

"Our lives together."

She looked at me like I was a customer she'd served and she was waiting for me to go. "I probably won't remember much."

"You will if I help you."

She decided I was too strange for anything. "Pontius!" she called out.

He wasn't sweating when he arrived; the closeness of death had dried him out. The rum crate dropped from his hands and he put one arm against a tree to support himself. He looked like he was trying to push it over. I wanted to say, You prefer him to me? "Look," I said with a hole in my voice. "I understand the temptation of low company. It's nice sometimes to be cheap as six bits. With someone like him you needn't care what he thinks about you. You can loosen out. But will you for once in your life stop and think before you abandon yourself to Fate?"

She came down on me like a building. "I'm not ashamed of myself, if that's what you think. It's only natural I'd rather be with him than you. You? You've got a face like a sermon. It's like being thrown into a dungeon full of martyrs. And you're a hypocrite into the bargain."

"A hypocrite?"

"You tried to steal him the first chance you got."

"I was gonged."

"You were keen enough."

"Watch what you're saying. This gun could go off of its own accord."

"He says you wore him out."

"I'm warning you."

"He's still raw."

"You think I'm jealous of you?"

"You'd steal my skin if you could."

"I don't want to be you as long as I live."

"You keep trailing after me everywhere I go. I can't get rid of you. It's like you want to copy me."

"I'm nothing like you. I pity you, that's all. You disgust me, if anything. He disgusts me. Look at the ugly bastard, who could possibly want him?"

"You were desperate to have him."

The mistake I made was to aim at her feet. I aimed at her feet to demonstrate my contempt, but a Colt Dragoon is apt to kick, it seems; if you aim at the feet you're in danger of perfection.

THIRTEEN

My pistol was bigger than I could handle and in the booming silence that followed I found myself on my backside. The smell of gunpowder peppered the milkiness of the wood. When the bullet struck her, for two moments she looked the way people you love look when they are so mortally ill they only have strength for themselves. Their faces drop. They look like strangers. Then the bullet spun her around and dropped her on her face.

"I don't resemble you the least bit," I shouted.

As I scrabbled away crabwise, Pontius got his gun off; but I made it to my feet and ran. Branches caught my hair, thorns pulled my skirt. A bullet rattled the bulrushes just as I reached them. I whacked through the tules and waded the river like I was pushing people out of the way. On the other bank Cordelia shook her head at me, and that's when I realized I still had the gun in my hand that I shot my mother with. I could smell the powder on my skin and on my clothes.

You always suppose you're the heroine in the story of your life; the day you discover you're the monster, it's apt to come as a surprise. I hit the road alone—back the way I had come. I begged food and avoided questions. I imagined Justice was at my back and would want its vengeance and I hurried along, panicky but, same time, disgusted with myself for running away. Exhausted, I slept like I was six feet under that night and woke up feeling refreshed, till I remembered I was the girl who shot her mother. I continued on my way, too clear in my mind to hide from what I'd done. If only I could have been feverish, I thought. All day I would call myself a coward and a murderer—as if I only half believed it—then I would remember it was the truth; and each time I would feel a little more empty and desperate. At least I'm not as deluded as my mother, I told myself. I said that again and again, like chewing something when there's no taste in it. In the end I was so sick of myself I couldn't move; I sat down by the side of the emigrant road and watched trains of wagons pass till it got dark.

The road down Echo Canyon is brutal. It wears out the emigrants' nerves and their brakes; and it's busy, but even a quarter-mile away you can be entirely alone. I dug out a hole for myself beneath a rock. I decided to live as an outcast; I didn't deserve the society of others and we wouldn't understand each other anyway, I reckoned. There was a stream nearby, choked with willows and currant bushes, that was all I needed for food and water; and night-times I would creep near the road to scavenge among the things the emigrants dumped. There were more books than I could fit in my library, and a lovely illustration of "The Coy Shepherdess" all framed up. Often as I was picking over the garbage, the thought would come into my head, I'm a murderer. And then I would stamp on the glass that covered the illustration, or drop the book like it was a shitty cloth. All the time I tried to keep my mind distracted; I knew there was something worse about me than the fact I'd shot my mother, something even more shameful.

One dreadful day I read *Bleak House* by Charles Dickens.

It's all about London, and England, and a daughter that's born out of wedlock. There's going on two hundred characters and they die pretty regular; and Dickens, that's just his style, he fills up his fountain pen, the deathomaniac, and lets her rip. All the time I was reading it I was nauseated with fear; I read it fast, skipping over whole pages at a time. I couldn't concentrate. Something was eating me, something I was trying to ignore. Passages in the book that contained the author's finer feelings or passionate views sickened me. You shot your mother, I thought, what do you know about human sentiments? I tore out three hundred pages so I could get to the end quicker. Then I got ashamed of myself I had destroyed the book and started to dig a hole, to bury the torn part. As I was scratching away at the dirt with my fingers, I had one of those moments where you see yourself the way someone else might see you.

I knew I would have looked as mad as a marooned sailor. But the way I felt when I ripped that book apart seemed familiar, the way it didn't appease the rage I had; and I began to remember other times I might have appeared to be out of my mind. When I walked right up to that Indian massacre, just as serene as can be. When I lay down on the bed of Carson River. When I got gonged and chained myself to the wagon and preened myself on my genius. All that time I'd supposed I was a number-one smart girl who could see into the minds of others, and guide them. That was why I'd had the nerve to lead Ness into the desert, with an outfit paid for with her savings. When I thought of how I'd lied to her, and how I'd imagined I knew best, and how she'd been robbed on the journey of everything that was precious to her, I just shriveled. I might as well have clubbed her with my own hands.

The self-delusion reminded me of someone I didn't want to name, even to myself, even in the privacy of my mind. But other similarities kept occurring to me. When Mama was drinking it was as if other people weren't there, and, well, maybe that's what it was like for other people when I was gonged and wanted to be alone with my thoughts. She got so drunk she didn't know what she'd done; I climbed into little girls' beds. Then there was the way I'd sneered at Ness, the time she found me sitting on top of Pontius, that was the same sneer Mama had given me a hundred times, like she was so superior she lacked the vocabulary to explain herself to mortals. I stayed in my hole for a day, afraid of myself. I was scared I had an illness of the mind, some mental derangement I'd inherited from my mother. How could I have been so deceived in myself? Other people had known I was defective: Ness, for instance, had tried to warn me. She'd coyoted around the subject in a hinting sort of way, same as I'd done with Mama, afraid to say anything straight out.

Early that evening I noticed that I hadn't buried *Bleak House* properly, it was sticking out like the boots of that dead corporal. I pulled it up by its spine and was about to cremate it, when I saw a familiar figure on the road.

You can tell someone by their walk from quite a distance; Cordelia leans back and throws her feet forward in a particular way. She was with a train of wagons going west, and I decided to follow her, seeing she was the only person in this wilderness that I knew, and it was my twentieth birthday next day. Later I recognized one of the outfit as the bride from Bear River and I got to thinking this was the lunatic wedding crowd. The sort of people who can make trestle tables out of their wagons are the opposite of me; I imagined them sizing me up and seeing right away how worthless I was; but having camped near them that night, I trailed them again the next day.

Late in the evening that second day, the young people of the company gathered around a fire and chatted. The darker it got, the nearer I crept; I got so close I could almost make out what they were saying in spots. I was curious to know how nice young people behaved to each other. They didn't drink any liquor, far as I could see, so there were moments when the conversation and joking stopped and you could hear the night crowding their thoughts, then the powwow would continue with thickened voices. Cordelia was louder than the others; she had a fast way of talking, as though the more she said, the more chance there would be she'd say something that would make them like her. I was wondering how long they would stand her when a fellow, who'd been keeping shady all evening, took her aside. For all he seemed quiet and stand-backish, he had a way of pushing his fat paunch out like he was proud of it; and anyhow he offered her his arm and took her on a *paseo* along the stream, holding up a lantern to light her way.

I followed them the best I could. They walked a couple hundred yards and stopped and she faced him and put her arms behind her back like a coy shepherdess, only the majority of coy shepherdesses don't seem so pressed for time. He set the light down on the ground and they were hidden in the darkness for a good while. Her shirt was a little unbuttoned when they reappeared, like she'd been showing him her cancer. He piloted her back to camp and dowsed the light, and I sat behind a bush all night, wide-awake, making up my mind to turn myself in. I supposed I'd swing for what I'd done. What could I tell a court that would soften their hearts toward me—I shot at her feet? That seemed so careless of human life they would put me down for a—well, a monster. I *deserved* to be punished, that was the truth of it; and at least I could look someone in the face if we both knew I was going to hang. If you are sentenced to die by society, you still belong.

Sun-up caught me hiding behind a piece of scrub maybe thirty yards from their camp. I was sick afraid to hand myself over but after four days in the wilderness I couldn't stand to be alone with myself. I wanted to know if I was sane or not, that was the most important thing, but I was hungry, too; I hadn't eaten in a day, and soon as I heard the quiet clatter of a kettle being set over the coals, I stood up and walked toward the grove of quaking aspen where Cordelia's man was cooking breakfast. If you disturbed so much as a stone in that echoey canyon it got noticed, it was like you were being watched; Cordelia's fella heard me coming and looked up. He was the only one around. He was about twenty-seven, twenty-eight, had pop eyes that let in too much light and an endearing stutter of the eyelids. I reckoned he might be tougher than he looked, though, spite of that belly he coddled.

"I'm Dol McQueen," I told him. "I shot my mother."

He watched his oven close and steady. The bread was holed up in there and he meant to get the drop on it. "You're lucky," he said at last. "A back-country Missouri woman got all the bullet out of her. She was on the gain when we left her."

A minute later I stopped shaking. "You think I could go see her?"

He looked at me like I hadn't grasped the situation. "He'd put a bullet in you, for one thing." He pounced on his bread and set it to cool. "What'll you do now?"

"Wander off into the wilderness, I guess."

He nodded and started making the coffee. He was waiting for the mad person to go away. The wilderness didn't bear looking at. I said, "You need any help?"

He was listening to the coffee bubble like he was a deadly expert. "No. I'm just fine."

The wind stirred the grove. Each tree shivered beautifully. "I mean, if the outfit needs an extra hand."

"No, I don't think so."

He looked me up and down. I supposed he could see right through me. I wished I knew how to hide the parts that were broken. "I'd be company," I said.

He jumped the coffee and set it on the ground to rest. "You got the biggest idea of yourself of any girl I ever run across." The pale lids blinked. "You shot your own mother. Why would we need your help?"

"What about Cordelia?"

"What about her?"

They'd managed to find a berth for her. I said, "Can I speak to her?" The words tore half my throat out. It wasn't going to be easy, being sweet to Cordelia.

"There's the wagon she's sleeping in, right there."

From outside her wagon I said, "Cordelia? It's me."

"Uh-huh?"

"Can I speak to you?"

"I'm fixing my face," she yelled.

"What do you want me to do? Want me to go away?" There was the start of a wail in my voice.

"Will you for pete's sake give me five minutes?"

All around people were turning out of wagons and tents and heading to the stream to wash their faces and fill buckets. They looked staggered by their dreams. After fifteen minutes Cordelia appeared and said, "Well?"

"I been talking to the fella that's sweet on you."

She peeked around the edge of the wagon. "That's Arnold. He lets me sleep in his wagon. He sleeps in the tent." She tugged at the ends of her yellow hair as if it had been the subject of many compliments. "He certainly has a case. He's the worst in love man I ever saw."

"I saw the two of you kissing last night."

"I can't hardly fight him off," she gloated. "Just think—he fought in the war. He was a three-month volunteer with the Sixteenth Ohio. They were out in West Virginia with Tom Morris's brigade." She went and got herself a coffee and came back. She sipped from it as she fixed her hair. "He can tell some tales. When they got after the rebel army and were catching up to them, the butternuts were terrified; they left behind mattresses, trunks, wagons, they couldn't retreat fast enough, but the Union boys were cool as you like. They walked along by Cheat River singing 'On Jordan's Stormy Banks.' The cowardly secessionists stopped to face them in the end. They set up their dreadful rebel yell, fired their muskets—then skedaddled! The whole kit and tuck."

"Damn sesh." I wanted to show I was interested. "What did he do before the war?"

"He was a route agent, Columbus and Xenia railroad."

"I can picture him with a mailbag and satchel."

"I wasn't taken with his looks just right away. Do you think we look alike? People say you could take us for brother and sister." Cordelia has pop eyes and a small paunch. "I don't see the resemblance myself," she said.

"I can see why they might say it, though."

She looked at me with a face like a smacked ass. "You're not as pretty as you think, you know."

"Did I say I was pretty?"

"You act like you think you are," she said. She went to pee behind a rock.

I followed her. It wasn't the best time to ask anyone anything but what else could I do? It was either suck up to Cordelia or wander the world alone. "I slept over there last night," I said. "Well, I was too sick of myself to sleep; I lay there staring at the dark wondering if I was fit for human company or not." Cordelia wasn't at all curious to know where I'd spent the night; she didn't give it a second glance. "I know I don't deserve anything," I said. "I was hoping you might let me throw in with you. If I can be any use at all, I'd be only too willing."

"I don't see what earthly good you would be."

Cordelia had cost us more than finishing school.

I said, "You don't think there's *anything* I could do?"

"No."

"Cleopatra had a maid," I said.

Cordelia stood up. "Did she get in the way?"

She started back to camp.

"I won't go away," I shouted after her. "I'll follow you around like a bad smell."

She stopped and came back a few paces so she could keep it hushed. "Don't you understand? These are decent people. There are parts of the body they won't say the names of. I don't want to call you a bad word, Dol. You know yourself what you are."

"I'll make a nuisance of myself. I will tie myself to you like old tin cans. I used to know someone who was a champion at that."

She stared at me, eyes like raw, peeled onions. She saw now the trouble I could make, and without any shame she changed her tone and made a heartfelt, sentimental appeal. "I think he's the One, Dol. It's like I've found a long-lost brother." She hesitated, stole a look at Arnold, back a ways, and broke out in a garish blush, like she was about to make a confession. "He says he loves me body and soul." She faced me as if her breasts had enjoyed all the success that could have been hoped for them, and a languor dropped on her. It appeared she only had to think of Arnold and she could hardly stand; she had the loaded, intoxicated heaviness of a summer-evening bee. "You wouldn't spoil my one chance?" she wheedled. "He's just perfect."

And as though that was all that needed to be said on the matter, she headed back to Arnold, who was waiting for her before he dished up breakfast. They were the picture of self-contentment. Arnold saw to it that Cordelia had everything she needed before he set to eating, and then they ate mouthful after mouthful with their eyes shut. It gave them the appearance of a tiny religious sect. The Bear River bride had finished her breakfast; she sneaked a look at me as she washed her plates not twenty yards away. I suppose she wondered why I didn't go away if I had no business here. Only people who are crazy hang around like I was doing—the longer I stood there, humiliated by hope, the more murderous my thoughts became. Just then there was the slushy hiss of bacon hitting a frying pan; Arnold was cooking up some extra. I stood on my toes and ached for the smell to come by but it stepped around me. I tried to imagine what would happen if I crossed the stream and asked them one more time to take me and they said no, but even that was a better prospect than heading off into the wilderness. The earth here was red. It looked like a planet nobody lived on.

Cordelia had a loaf of bread under her arm as I arrived; she was buttering it. When she saw me, she cut off a buttered slice and handed it to Arnold, who took his knife and lifted a long streak of bacon out of the pan and onto the bread and sort of stirred the butter with it. Then they ate all they liked.

"This is rather childish," I said. "You just going to ignore me?"

Arnold opened his eyes and couldn't enjoy his food so well after that. He chawed what was in his mouth faster than he liked and stroked his belly like he was saying sorry to it. When he was done he said, "We just don't want your company, I guess. I thought we already made that plain."

The shame as I drew my pistol made me stagger a step to the side. It appeared I now had so little charm, personality, or wit that I had taken to using a Colt at every turn to get what I wanted. I was breathing fast like I wanted more than my fair share of air as well as everything else, and I imagined Cordelia saying, "Is that all you know how to do?" Before she could roll her eyes at me like she wished I had more imagination, I raised my shooter and held it to my head. "I shot her by mistake," I said. "I shot at her feet. It was a dreadful thing to do, but nobody loved her more than I did. I traveled the earth looking for her."

Maybe to rile me, Cordelia put the knife in her mouth and pressed the butter off it, pulling it between her lips. "When I think how far you trailed her before you nailed her, it gives me the creeps."

"I can't live with myself. I won't last three days in that damned wilderness."

"You could ask to join some other outfit."

"They don't know me," I said.

"More chance they'll take you along."

The leaves of the quaking aspen shuddered and turned white. "You're laughing at me."

Arnold had a way of looking at you like he wanted to study your shoes. "I don't like to be bullied."

"I don't want anything from you," I lied. "I want to get out of my mind." The nose of my Colt was pressing the bone of my temple, hard, like someone else was holding it. "I'm scared to be alone with it." I remembered, from the last time I got my gun off, the pleasure it gives. The explosion blows away all your cares, and for a few precious moments your mind is perfectly vacant. I was digging the gun into my skull and squirming away from it at the same time. "I don't know who's using it."

"I'm sorry," he said. "I don't know how to help you."

I believe I aimed to miss, but I had to wave the piece about airily before I fired, as if I didn't care. The speed of the bullet made my scalp draw back. I felt the heat of it as it flew over, like a finger tracing its passage on my hair. The certainty of what it would have done to my brain was very clear; and when I thought how tantalizing a prospect that had seemed, I lost all the strength in my legs and dropped to my knees.

It was like that coffin Duffield told me about, the one they resurrected and opened and let fall onto the stone floor; soon as I hit the ground I turned to dust. All that was left of me was a small number of atoms, pin-bright and tiny, but I heard the emigrants in camp leave off what they were doing for just the length of time it took to judge that the bullet had gone free to the sky, taking nothing with it, and at that moment a voice annihilated me with its presence. *Someone who supposes there is nothing wrong with him*, the voice said, *has a disease no doctor can cure.*

It was only when I came to myself a little that I found I was unharmed, and it struck me that the revelation I'd been given concerned Mama. There was no cure for her. That was why I had never been able to help her, and being told that in no uncertain terms made me feel a good deal less alone. You know when you go into a library and you notice how much silence it contains—it's stored to the ceiling with it—and you breathe easier and deeper, knowing there's more than enough for everyone? That was the feeling I had. I sat back on my hunkers and looked up at Cordelia and Arnold, like I'd gotten outside of my mind at last.

She handed him the loaf, came up to me, took the pistol from my hand, and whacked me across the ear. "That's for what you did to me at Bear River." She tossed the shooter to one side before she was tempted to use it.

"What I did to you?"

"You left me there on my own. I cried and screamed fit to be tied. I tore my clothes like a girl at a revival. Three men had to take and duck me in the river before I quieted down." For the first time I noticed she was wearing a dress she'd borrowed from some girl who was neat and pretty and shorter in the arms than she was. "You know why I kept on screaming? I was ashamed. I knew when I stopped I'd be obliged to explain the facts of the matter. Why it looked like I'd stood back and done nothing to prevent a murder, and how come I didn't appear to have any other friends in the whole world besides a girl like you."

She stood there and waited to see what I had to say for myself. That borrowed dress gave her the looks of an overly large charity-school girl. I'd abandoned a fifteen-year-old girl where anything might have happened to her. What could I say? My ear started a slow trickle of blood. All around was the stir of wagons, the air full of the dirt they raised as they pulled out. Arnold was holding the bacon sandwich down by his side. He didn't want to draw attention to it, but time was getting along. Already the bacon was cold; the bread would soon be dirty as a white boy's neck.

"I'm sorry," I said. "I don't know what I'm doing wrong, besides everything." I found myself thinking about the time I fucked Pontius. "I lost my conscience somewhere."

"Ness tried to be your conscience. Not that you listened to her much. You didn't listen to anyone. You had eyes like a piece of taxidermy when you were gonged. I suppose you paid Ness some attention, if it was only lying to her and hiding from her. Then she took the stage home at Jacobsville, and you were on your own after that." She said it like she was nothing, or that's how I'd treated her anyway. She was teetering on crying and the red-scratched whites of her eyes dared me to say any different.

"Well," I said, "I'm looking for a conscience again. You'd be a good one."

I think I meant it. But I wasn't used to saying anything sincere; it struck me as false. In my mind I heard someone guffaw.

It was too rich for Arnold. "We'd better get under way," he said and steered off. He hoisted his cold spoiled sandwich at a small dog yonder. It yelped and ran away as though it was a rock. Cordelia had folded her arms like it wasn't going to be as easy as all that to get around her. Then in her fast unfriendly manner she punched out, "She wasn't much of a ma but I guess you must be lost without her."

"I miss her like sin."

"Nothing you can do about that."

"She's dead and she's not dead. I won't hear from her again."

Arnold was hitching up the mules, looking at me like I was in the way.

"We have a lot in common, you and me," I said. "Remember the night you cut your wrist when Mrs. Bird threatened to put you out on the street? That's how desperate I was ten minutes ago with a pistol to my brains." I stopped because Cordelia was staring at me hard; she didn't like to be reminded.

Arnold was heading toward us. Quickly I said, "Won't you have me along?"

He started to fill in the fire pit and Cordelia went to wash plates and think it over. I was at the mercy of an orphan girl I'd abandoned, who now had a perfect opportunity to pay me back in kind. My heart was like a tin cup in the hands of a crazy infant, being banged on a table. As well as everything else, I was curious about her. What would it be like if she got attached to you, I wondered. I watched her struggle with herself horribly; it was like seeing what I'd put her through the day I shot my mother. Finally it was over. She came back to where I was, beside the buried fire, bleak and composed. But then our eyes met and burned up. I was thinking about the girl who cut her wrist, and she knew I was; our faces were uneasy mirrors, and I waited to see how she would get shut of me, if she would have any style about her.

"I hope I don't regret it," she said.

"I can come?"

"I'd like to be friends, if you think we can." It was ferocious, the way she said it.

"I'd like that," I said carefully.

She made a mouth like I was awfully slow. "Yes," she said, driving at me, "but do you think we can?"

"Yes," I said. "I do."

"I'll talk to Arnold." She stood taller, a fifteen-year-old boss.

In a small voice I said, "Can I have some bread and butter?"

"In a minute." She got something out of her pocket and handed it to me. "Here."

It had evidently been in the river with her. Some of the address was perfect but a corner had slid off and disappeared in a blue rain. It was stiff at the hinges when you opened it and the pages were as loud as a large church Bible. It was the letter from Ness I got at Salt Lake City. "There's nothing about me in it anyway," Cordelia said. "I don't know why I kept it." It was a letter between two people she knew, that's why she'd kept it. It was all the history she had.

I lowered my eyes. "That was kind of you," I said, as if she'd kept it safe on purpose to give it to me. Then I looked up. "I can't thank you enough for everything." It was the best I could do right then. It wasn't much. It didn't sound good but I believed every word of it.

This time when I read the letter, Ness didn't seem cold at all. More than anything she seemed terrified for me, knowing how blind I was and the direction I was going in. It was like she was shouting at me to turn back before it was too late. It made me shiver. But she told me her news and where to find her, and there was enough about her adventures to make me want to hurry home. I squeezed all the meaning out of the ink that I could, and gorged myself on some bread Arnold gave me. Then we gathered up and rolled out.

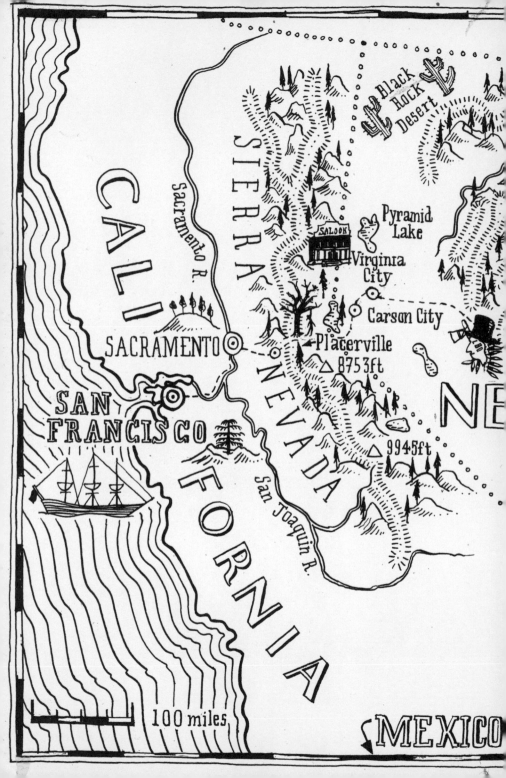